The Viewpoint Murders

Callum Dalziel

Published by Callum Dalziel, 2023.

Scott's Law
The Viewpoint Murders

A DI Ron Scott Novel

Dedicated to my wife, Joyce, with all my love.

Chapter One

THE PHONE CALL CAME at three o'clock in the morning. It was a gruff voice that answered.

"Scott."

"Sorry to wake you, boss, but we've got another one."

"Another body?"

"Yep, definite homicide... either same perp, or a damned good copycat."

"Right! Where are you?"

"I'm at the scene now, boss. You'll know Tower Hill?"

"Well, I should. It's nearly in my backyard."

"That's the locus."

"Okay. I'm on my way, Pamela."

Detective Inspector Ron Scott ended the phone call between him and his Detective Sergeant, Pamela Cameron. After he had a quick wash, got dressed, and grabbed his ready bag, he was at the scene ten minutes later.

Tower Hill in Gourock was only about five minutes from his home on Ashton Road as the crow flies. But cars aren't crows. He had to wind his way up to Victoria Road, then double-back somewhat to Tower Drive, and then to McPherson Drive, where a turnoff led to a single-track paved road that climbed up to Tower Hill Park.

It was a popular Gourock viewpoint, roughly half-an-acre in size and nearly three hundred feet above sea level. On its flat top, there was a paved car parking area, a cairn, a memorial plaque, and a twenty-foot-high crenellated stone tower dating back to the 1800s.

When Scott arrived at the scene, there were four cars already parked in a row at one side of the parking area: a liveried patrol car with its light bar flashing neon blue; DS Cameron's red VW Beetle; Professor Hamish McLeod's silver Peugeot 106, and a Toyota Camry.

The professor was wearing a protective 'bunny suit', hood up and masked, and he had blue forensic booties on his feet. Scott opened the boot of his BMW and soon had donned the same style outfit.

Scott approached the professor, who was viewing the body by flashlight. He was crouching and had his back to Scott as the DI came up behind him.

"Well, well, Ronnie, here at last!" Professor Hamish McLeod didn't look up from the body.

"How'd you know it was me, you old scarecrow?" said Scott.

"Oh, the smell of stale whisky, extra-strong mints, and an overdose of that overpowering aftershave you use to try to hide the aroma of acetone. That's what did it."

"I'll have you know that I haven't had a..." Scott began to remonstrate.

"Only kidding, laddie! When your constables say, 'Here's the boss' and try to look busy, when they've just been standing around like stookies and kicking their heels since I arrived... well, it doesn't take Sherlock Holmes."

Scott glared at the two constables.

"Get this bloody scene taped off... wide perimeter... jump to it!" he ordered.

They jumped to it!

"Sorry, boss. My fault," said DS Cameron sheepishly. "SOCO are on their way. ETA five minutes. I should have secured the scene. I'm still in a bit of a daze from being woken from a sound sleep."

"Well, Cameron," said Scott, "you just go over to my car, open the boot, and you'll find a half-gallon plastic container filled with ice-cold water. Take that container and pour the lot over your dizzy head, okay?"

Pamela's jaw dropped, and she crossed her arms over her chest indignantly, her head cocked to the side, her eyebrows raised.

Scott realised that she might be taking him seriously. "Don't be daft, lass. I was joking... you know? That infamous 'Scott's humour.' But there's no nine-to-five in CID. Don't forget that."

"Oh! Right, boss! Humour... got it! So, if I were to tell you to 'go and bile yer heid'... would that be classed as humour?"

Pamela Cameron had only been DS under Scott's command for six months. She was still trying to figure out this enigmatic, mercurial man who could be spouting dry humour one minute, then issuing acerbic reprimands the next. She had come from a small country station in the Borders town of Peebles, where the pace had been much slower than her new posting to Greenock, the next-door town to Gourock.

Scott replied, "Depending on circumstances, it could be seen as cheeky; or as outright insub..."

"*Ahem!* While you two play Jokers Wild," interrupted the professor, "is anyone interested in our *corpus delicti?*"

"Sorry, Hamish. What have we got?" asked the DI, keeping his distance from the body so as not to contaminate the scene.

"Preliminary, of course... as always, at this early stage. What we have here is a dead body."

He paused for effect.

"Sorry, I always enjoy the looks on your faces when I say that, *ha-ha*. We scientists can do graveyard humour just as well as you coppers.

"Our victim is a teenaged female. Her age, I would estimate to be between fourteen and sixteen years. She is small in stature. She has short dyed-blonde hair with dark roots. There are obvious signs of strangulation... a deep ligature mark around the neck made with a thin cord that cut deeply into the flesh. She was stabbed with a smallish sharp instrument, maybe a penknife... looks like about... erm... fifteen to twenty times in the breast and abdomen area. The punctures were made through her clothing. The number will become clearer at the autopsy. And her eye colour is... indeterminate..."

"Indeterminate?" asked Scott with raised eyebrows, although he suspected and feared what was coming. "You have a flashlight, Hamish, right?"

"Indeterminate," continued the professor, "in that she doesn't have any eyes. They have been carefully removed, just like the last victim. I hate to use the clichéd 'with surgical precision,' but we'll be more certain after the full examination has been completed. Oh, and the stabbing was carried out post mortem. Hence the absence of blood."

"That was a nice little postscript, Hamish, as though it were a minor detail. So, she was stabbed after she'd been dead for... how long?"

"Time? Time is always a bugger. Hard to tell. More details maybe after the PM. But the stabbing was possibly some time after the strangulation. The wounds are not the result of a frenzied, slasher-type attack. They're not in any pattern, but the punctures were deliberately and calmly executed. I'm speculating, but I think the stab wounds were an afterthought. Like he was playing with the corpse. Similar to sticking pins in a voodoo doll. There were no such wounds on victim number one. If he is escalating, it's a strange way to go about it. It's baffling, to be frank. But my name's not 'Frank,' and my 'ology' begins with 'path.' You'd need to talk to someone whose 'ology' begins with 'psych' regarding post-mortem mutilation."

Scott looked at his DS. "So, that's why you said on the phone 'another one'... because of the missing eyes?"

"Or a copycat, boss."

"Nah. Unlikely to be a copycat. Unless it was someone who knew about the eyeball removal. That's a detail that we have not released. So, we may have a murderous, psychotic 'eyeball-collector' on our hands?"

"Aye, sir," replied Pamela, without a hint of irony.

"And now using a life-sized actual human 'voodoo doll.' For what purpose?"

"Presumably to send a message to us or the next victim," Pamela replied.

"Hmm. Very cultish. Or feigned to look cultish."

"So, you believe the perp is going to kill again?" asked Pamela.

"Unless we put a stop to this spree. Who found her?"

Pamela pointed to the two figures sitting in the Toyota.

"Arthur Watt and his son, James. They're having a cup of Bovril from their flask. I could fair have used a cup, but they didn't offer."

"And they were up here on Tower Hill at three in the morning for what, exactly?"

"Star gazing. They are amateur astronomers."

"They told you that?"

"Yes. They've got all the gear: binoculars, star charts, and a star-finder, the kind that you manipulate two plastic disks to set the date and time, and it shows the starscape as it is right there and then."

"Is that what's called an astrolabe?"

"No, boss, that's a different instrument. What they have is called a Planisphere. Theirs is a Phillip's one, 'as recommended by Mark Thompson, TV Astronomer on the BBC's *Stargazing Live.*'"

"You had a *really good* look at it, then."

"Couldn't resist. I asked if I might take a look. And I noticed they also have a Philip's Moon Map. As good as it gets for studying craters, etc."

"No telescope?" asked Scott.

"One on the rear seat. A Celestron. An expensive motorised one, as far as I can make out. But for what they were going to study tonight... the Moon, they said... they knew that binoculars would be the best choice. That's true. I used to do a bit of stargazing myself."

Scott was going to say something about 'head in the clouds' or 'pure lunacy' but thought the better of it. Teasing was one thing: it revealed the sensitivity quotient of the officers he oversaw. A thick skin was necessary for this job. So far, DS Cameron had proved herself to be attentive, dedicated, and full of curiosity. Curiosity was a detective's chief asset, and he already had high hopes for his new DS, although he wouldn't tell *her* that.

Pamela was about five-four, very slim, had shoulder-length auburn hair that she usually wore in a ponytail, and she had, Scott had to admit, a not-unattractive face and figure.

"The light pollution here in Gourock makes conditions difficult for astronomy. Mr Watt told me they would usually drive to Corlick Hill in the Clyde Muirshiel Park. But tonight, with the clear sky, conditions here are adequate."

She outlined to Scott what else the two finders had told her during her interview.

"I can understand how they might at first have thought it was a shop dummy. Do they have a flashlight?" asked Scott.

"They have a red light so as not to spoil their night vision. But I think they have an ordinary flashlight, too."

"Hmm. The red light makes their story even more plausible?"

"It shows that they know what they're doing. Probably regular watchers of *The Sky at Night* and, I would think, the new one I mentioned previously, *Stargazing Live,* which is sadly missing the inimitable, but now, unfortunately, late, Sir Patrick Moore."

"Ah. Here comes SOCO now," said Scott.

The Scenes of Crime van trundled up the single-track incline to the locus.

The driver reverse-parked into a space on the opposite side to the other vehicles, allowing the van's headlights to illuminate the scene until proper lighting was put in place. A team of officers, all in protective forensic clothing, hoods up and masked, exited the van and gathered in a semi-circle around one figure who was issuing instructions. Then, the officer instructing the group broke off and headed over to where the body was as the others set about their work.

Nisha Chandara, head Scenes of Crime officer, addressed the professor first.

"How the hell do you always get to the scene before us, Hamish?"

"I speed," came the reply.

"We'll pretend we didn't hear that," said Scott, winking at Pamela. "Good, though, that you have already shed some light on the subject, Nisha," he added, cupping a hand over his eyes to partially shield them from the headlights.

"Hello, Pam. And Detective Inspector Scott," said Nisha. "Do you think we could get one of your flashy flashing motors to block off the entrance down there? And get the guys over there to turn off their flashy flashers while my team gets to work. I understand the necessity in certain circumstances, but I often wonder how you guys can concentrate on anything at a crime scene with those blue neons flashing. Enough to give anyone a headache, I think. I can imagine a young bobby, when asked what colour of shirt the witness had on, answering, 'It was white, then blue, then white, then blue... it kept changing, Your Honour.'"

Scott nodded to Pamela, both of them laughing at Nisha's joke.

"On it, boss," she said.

Nisha continued, "No more admittance, Ronnie—especially the press at this early stage."

"Of course. The access road will be blocked off right away. As for our worthy members of the fourth estate, the blue flashing lights seem to attract the press like flies to... well, you know what. Even at this ungodly hour, I know some insomniacal 'concerned' citizen," Scott used his fingers to make air quotes, "will have already phoned the *Telegraph* office."

The *Greenock Telegraph and Shipping Gazette,* to give the newspaper its full title, was widely read in the area and had recently gone digital with a website to supplement its print copy.

"Is 'insomniacal' a proper adjective?" asked Nisha, raising an eyebrow.

"It is now," said Scott confidently. "As for voyeurs, usually, with a crime scene not as isolated as this one, we would not discourage rubberneckers, as long as they stay behind the cordon. It's not unknown, as in the old adage, for a criminal to return to the crime scene. And we always keep an eye on the overly curious... the ones that are always asking us how we are getting on with our inquiries. That bastard who murdered the two ten-year-old girls in Soham is a prime example."

"Terrible case that!" said Nisha. "But some brilliant detective work, I think you'll agree."

"Yes. His frequent TV appearances and his demeanour made him a definite POI."

"Got a prelim assessment on our victim here, Hamish?" asked Nisha, glad to change the subject away from Soham.

The professor rhymed off what he had told Scott a few minutes earlier.

"Anyone touch the body?" asked Nisha.

Scott replied, "From DS Cameron's preliminary report to me a few minutes ago, the seventeen-year-old son was first to spot the body when he took a wander to relieve himself. He told Pamela that he thought at first that it was a partially dressed discarded shop dummy, a mannequin. He called over his dad, who immediately dialled 999. According to them, neither of the two touched the body."

"I can see from here," said Nisha, shining a torch directly on the victim's face, since the headlights were casting shadows, "that her eyes have been excised just like the last victim."

"Yes, we should be able to tell exactly from our examination under proper lighting, but if like the last one it will be a precise enucleation."

Nisha looked over her shoulder and shouted, "Good job, team! Get the tent up as soon as possible, please."

The SOCO team had laid down a broad pathway of interlinked metal footplates leading from their van to the body.

Scott had witnessed the procedures often... all too often, he mused, and yet he never failed to be amazed at the painstaking efficiency of a SOCO team at work.

Next, they would erect a blue forensics tent and install temporary lighting inside and floodlights outside, all powered by a generator running at the back of the van.

Video and photographs from all angles would be taken with the body in situ. Then, when Nisha was satisfied, the body would be placed on a portable pull-up table, not unlike an X-hinged gurney but slightly bigger and made of aluminium. Nisha and Hamish would then perform a closer visual analysis, video running all the time, two expert photographers flashing away. Meanwhile, the rest of the team would begin a fingertip grid-search of the entire area, looking for any clues, and bagging and tagging everything they found that might have evidentiary value.

That search would go on into the daylight hours and continue until Nisha was satisfied.

Scott had a quick talk with the finders, Mr Watt, and his son. The boy seemed to have been deeply affected, still shaking and snivelling despite the car being warm, and the hot Bovril. The beefy aroma reached Scott's nostrils.

Funny, thought Scott, *that a drink he'd normally turn his nose up at could seem like nectar on a chilly night, or at a football match with a greasy Scotch pie.*

The dad seemed quite calm and collected. "I think you can take your son home now, Mr Watt. I'll need both of you to attend the station tomorrow. At your convenience, of course. We'll need a written and signed statement from each of you. Just a formality."

"Certainly, Inspector," said Watt. Engine already running, he turned on his headlights, ready to drive off.

A man of few words, thought Scott.

"I'll have the patrol car see you safely off the hill. Not a great deal of room to manoeuvre, now."

Watt gave a thumbs up.

Arthur Watt was a well-built man in his fifties and appeared very tall, judging by how far his car seat was pushed back in the driving position. He was bald on top, with snowy white hair around his ears and at the back of his head, and he was clean-shaven with a ruddy face.

His son was tall like his dad and of slim build. He had thick black curly hair that was stacked on the crown but shaved around his ears in the modern 'pudding bowl' hipster style. His eyes were red from crying, his face chalk white. He looked much younger than his seventeen years. Scott's first impression was that this was a lad who led a sheltered life—going star gazing with his dad at three in the morning? He should have been out clubbing, chasing the talent with his mates. Yet sadly, the DI reflected, the COVID-19 crisis had drastically altered the lifestyles of this generation of teens.

"Hell of a shock for the boy," said Pamela as the Camry drove off.

"No doubt about it," replied Scott. "You can understand how he thought it was a mannequin that had been dumped. It's certainly a novelty for a body to be found by amateur astronomers instead of the usual 'someone-walking-their-dog.' Are you sure their reason for being here was legitimate?"

"I've been checking that further, boss. That star finder they were using is pretty darned good. But as the saying goes, 'there's an app for that'. According to the Time and Date app's 'Tonight's Sky', this is an excellent time for Moon viewing at this location." She pointed. "The Moon is almost full in the south-south-west."

"Jesus, Cameron, I can see that's the Moon," said Scott.

"Well, sir, that would be reason enough to be observing using only binoculars. The craters are clearly visible. I have a map somewhere at home that shows the Apollo landing sites. I can remember from that map that Apollo 11 landed on the Sea of Tranquillity. That's about three-quarters of the way down on the big dark shadow on the right of the Moon as we view it. Such a romantic name for such a barren place. *Mare Tranquillitatis.*

"There's also the bright star Procyon in Canis Minor and the constellations Gemini, Orion, and Taurus in full view." The newly erected bright floodlights were making it difficult to make out the stars, so she showed him on her iPad.

"Right, I got you. Orion's 'the Hunter' with the 'belt' of three stars, right?"

"Yes. And if you look closely below the belt, you can just make out the Orion Nebula on the app. With binoculars, it would be quite visible in the sky if we didn't have the glare of the lights."

"Okay, Pamela, thank you for your expertise. Seriously. You know, I might just come up here with a pair of binoculars tomorrow night. Fascinating view. I've been here in daylight, but never at night."

"If you do, tomorrow night, then you might bump into me, boss. Some planets will be visible. But of particular interest to you, it says here: *Uranus: view after sunset, bring binoculars, and a mirror.*"

Scott thought for a minute about why he'd need a mirror. Then he got the joke. "Good one, Pamela. Uranus... mirror. I get it. Good to see you're learning, *ha-ha!*"

Fickle as the Scottish weather can be, this was the proverbial 'calm before the storm.'

In the morning, a fierce storm moved in from the Irish Sea, bringing torrential rain and gale-force winds reaching up to 90 mph.

Chapter Two

GREENOCK POLICE STATION, Major Incident Room, 8 a.m. on the morning of the find at Tower Hill.

EVERYONE ENTERING Greenock police station had to submit to having their temperature checked, a high fever being one of the first signs of infection by the COVID-19 virus.

All had to wear FFP2 masks that, unfortunately, didn't protect one from catching the virus but went some way to prevent the risk of contamination to others.

All had to sign a sworn statement that they had not been in contact with someone who was in isolation because of viral symptoms or on medical advice.

Social distancing was implemented where practicable.

All officers and staff had been double vaccinated, and all had received the booster after the Omicron variant had taken hold.

It was ironic that, before this pandemic, people would have been seen as being suspicious if they were wearing a face mask. But now, after COVID, people were looked upon as suspicious, or as selfish dissenters, if they were *not* wearing a mask. There were even masks and scarves that looked like something Billy the Kid would have worn.

So, everyone in the Serious Incident Room sat six feet apart, and all had been certified as having been vaccinated.

DI Scott and DS Cameron were standing at either side of a big whiteboard, and beside that was a large-screen TV. The rest of the team were seated, quiet on the whole, because of the masks. There was none of the noisy banter that would normally be going on before a briefing started.

"Right, folks!" said Scott. "Let's have your attention.

"As you can see, we've added some details about this second murder to our info board and the presentation screen. We can't say for sure that we're in Rice Krispies land, but it looks like we may have a serial killer on our hands."

There was some muted laughter and groans from the team at the play on words.

"For that to be the case, we officially would need another murder with the same MO. But we do not want *any more murders*. This spree... if it is a spree... must be nipped in the bud, and quickly. Now, I'll hand you over to DS Cameron, who will bring us all up to date." Scott moved aside then took a chair in the front row, pulling up his mask.

"Thank you, sir.

"So... to the first victim." Pamela pointed the beam of her laser pen at a photo on the screen. "We covered most of these details at the first briefing; but this is a catch-me-up for those who have just been added to the team, and a refresher for the others.

"Sylvia Smith, age sixteen, had been in and out of foster homes and care units since her single mother gave up on the girl's delinquent behaviour when Sylvia was only twelve years of age. Yes, I said twelve! By age thirteen, she was absconding and mixing with teenage gangs, drug users, and older men who were using her as a sex toy. A bottle of *vino colapso* and, sadly, Sylvia was anybody's. She quickly moved from alcohol to drugs... any drugs she could get her hands on, her habit financed by housebreaking, regular shoplifting, muggings, and prostitution. This was Sylvia's life. But who are we to judge, right? A life is a life, and I hope that the old judgmental ways are well and truly a relic of the past.

"Her body was found in the car park at the Free French Memorial at Lyle Hill by a young couple, who said they were parked there for the view... at two in the morning in the pissing rain, if we are to believe their story."

The Lyle Hill car park was well known as a winching spot, a lovers' lane without the lane.

"Her body was not posed," Pam continued, "it had been dumped roughly by someone who didn't want to stick around. The results of the post-mortem tell us that the murder, by strangulation, took place elsewhere, at least six hours before. But what caught all our eyes... was that the lassie didn't have any! Eyes, that is."

There were muffled moans and uneasy shuffling as Pam pressed the remote control and brought up the next photo, a facial closeup.

Dark humour was a defence mechanism often employed by emergency services personnel to help them cope with the gruesome scenes that they often had to attend.

"This is our victim, a photo taken at the beginning of the post-mortem. It's difficult to look at, but the pathologist assures us that the eyes were removed 'with surgical precision.'

"Sylvia's last meal was a donner kebab, washed down with about a half a bottle of vodka and orange. At least the donner gave us something to look into. Indian takeaways."

DS Cameron took a sip of water from a bottle.

"We'd been canvassing the areas where Sylvia hung out. And, of course, special attention was given to kebab shops. CCTV footage collected from the Bombay Takeaway on the high street, showed that she bought her last meal there. She was then picked up on a security camera as she ate her kebab on the steps of the *Telegraph* office. After she'd littered, by chucking the wrapping paper at the office doors, she headed toward Clarence Street in the direction of the Ocean Terminal. No more footage after that. No sightings either. Was she picked up by a car? Was she dragged into a car? Or did she circle around to a squat?

"Although the body was found six days ago, we still don't know where she was staying, squatting, dossing, whatever, before her murder. Wherever that was, it may well have been the murder scene. So, I want you to concentrate mainly on that task. Where was Sylvia when she was murdered? Six days is a long time for absolutely nothing but a body to turn up. You lot need to get your fingers out! The lassie was petite: she wasn't bloody invisible.

"If her feral mates are hiding something... up the pressure. Someone must know where she was kipping. Check any known squats and drug dens... again. And check once more to see if any of the staff at our local caravan sites and holiday parks have any updated info. She sometimes broke into unoccupied mobile homes for a stay-over until she was discovered and chucked out. Let's just say the caravans needed some cleaning after her little sojourns. When the site owners put in a complaint, she'd drop off the radar.

"If she got arrested, you know the drill. She would get charged, then fail to appear in court, disappearing into her underworld again. Even a night or two in the cells was no deterrent. She got a bed and a couple of half-decent meals. All she missed were her regular fixes. The methadone she was given by the force medical examiner, the FME, kept her from crashing, but her tolerance levels were so high that all it did was keep her stable.

"So, that's priority number one. Find Sylvia's last hangout.

"Any questions before I move on to our most recent victim?"

There was some shuffling, nods of agreement, clicking of iPhone keys from those taking notes, but no questions.

"Okay," said Pam. "Victim number two."

She clicked to the next photo.

"This is Joan Walker. To be brief, the description of Sylvia applies equally to Joan. They might have been clones of one another. Same age, similar looks, even down to the bad dye-job... except that Joan came from a middle-class home with two respectable parents."

There was some shuffling and unrest at the 'clone' remark. Everyone in the room was aware that this was an indication that they might indeed have a serial killer on their patch.

"She was once a prefect at Gourock High, getting good grades, until she fell in with Johnny McInnes, a toe rag I'm sure you are all familiar with. She 'fell in love,'" the DS used air quotes, "and from there, her life went swiftly down the drain. Her parents were exasperated and hoped that this might be just a phase that Joan was going through. Then, she went to school one morning, her schoolbag nearly bursting with what were supposed to be books. Joan never returned home. Her mother noticed that some of her daughter's clothes were missing, along with money, about fifty quid, from the 'emergency biscuit tin' that was kept in a kitchen cupboard. I'd have had that locked away, but maybe that's just me."

There was some muted laughter and nods of agreement.

"She was a MISPER for a while until she was spotted hanging out with the lowlifes. The parents and social services tried their best, but by that time, she was too far gone. To them, she was a completely different lassie. 'A lost soul', her mother had put it. And, of course, McInnes had dropped her like a hot potato and moved on to his next young target to corrupt.

"Her body was dumped up on Tower Hill. The body was *meant* to be found. There are plenty of trees, bushes, and rough ground at the edges of the hill where the killer could have hidden the body. But it was dumped in the car park, in plain sight. Almost the same MO as with Sylvia. But there was something else apart from the empty eye sockets. She had been strangled, no doubt about that. 'Asphyxiation by strangulation' *was* the proximal cause of death. But she had also been stabbed multiple times post-mortem. What does that show? Anyone?"

There was a pause, and then PC Alex Alexander, known by the nickname 'Double Alex', pulled down his mask for a moment and piped up, "That the murderer watched Hitchcock's *Psycho* recently."

A bit of laughter from the team, and then DS Cameron said, "Do you know Constable Alex, you might be right. But, no offence intended, you're showing your age a bit there. *Psycho* has long been outranked in the slasher genre by movies like *Saw* and *Hotel*. However, I will give you half a mark in that the stabbing points to the killer possibly becoming more vicious. Both strangulations were carried out from behind. Not extremely unusual. But maybe the perp can't look his victim straight in the eyes, leading to...?" She looked around the room, eyebrows raised, eyes wide, questioning.

"The removal of the eyes," said DS Sandra Hamilton from her seat in the front row.

"Correct! Thank you, Sandra," said Pamela. "Some cultists have a superstition that the retinas of a dead person's eyes retain an image of the last thing they saw. There's an excellent movie on the subject, *Four Flies On Grey Velvet,* starring the late Oliver Reed. Nutter and alcoholic he might have been, but he was a damned good actor. Mind you; we're not psychologists. We'll leave that to the profilers at Police HQ, Tulliallan. But it's something to keep in mind. Our perp may be an introvert, shy and inconspicuous, maybe a bit of a loner. It's a stereotype, but sometimes stereotypes fit."

"Like the Norman Bates guy in *Psycho*. A weirdo and a loner. So, I wisnae wrang efter all," said Double Alex, to a mocking light round of applause from the others.

DS Hamilton said, "We're assuming the perp is a 'he', if we're thinking about *Psycho* types, but it could have been a woman, right?"

Pamela replied, "That is a real possibility. There have indeed been female serial killers. So, let's not rule that out. But the profilers are pointing to a male perpetrator in this case. The ligature was thin but strong, like garden twine or something very similar. Another possibility mentioned by the forensics team was an extending dog leash. They are working on an accurate ID of the material. Anyway, the strangulations almost decapitated the victims.

"Considerable strength was used and, unlike in the movies, *Alex*, strangulation till death can take as long as five to ten minutes of consistent pulling power. The victim will have passed out before that, but when the neck muscles are constricted, they push back. Our pathologist could explain it better, but that's what I took away from his explanation. However, don't rule out a possible female perp. Some of us lassies have considerable strength. But for the sake of convenience, we'll use 'he' until something comes up that shows otherwise."

There was a loud creak from the entrance door, and everyone who was seated turned their heads.

"As you were, as you were, people!" The sonorous voice was that of Chief Superintendent Sam Miller. "Need to get some WD 40 on these hinges so I can sneak in without causing a kerfuffle, *ha-ha*. I'll just take a wee seat at the back here, and please carry on with the briefing, DS Cameron."

Miller was a tall man, over six feet, in his mid-fifties, well-built, with a full head of grey hair, cut flat-top style. He was weather beaten from his recreational pursuits, yachting and golfing, and had a patrician bearing that made him stand out in any crowd.

The PCs on the back seats shuffled uneasily as the big man took a seat six feet away from them in the back row.

Still too close for comfort.

"Just pretend I'm not here, lads and lassies," said Miller, pulling up his mask.

"Thank you, sir," said DS Cameron. "I'm just finishing up on victim number two."

The Chief Super nodded.

"Now, to our strategy, team," continued Pamela. "In case we missed anything, there will be a thorough review of all the CCTV footage that has been gathered so far. DS Hamilton and I will be on that, aided by our very capable civilian analysts. Few folk on the street know that about twenty per cent of municipal CCTVs are not working or not being monitored. Budgets, you know! But you can be sure our criminal fraternity do. We now rely more on cams at private premises.

"DCs and PCs... I want you out there, on the streets. We need more intel on these two girls. Get to your snitches and narks. Shake them up! Plods to be on high alert... anything from the grapevine.

"While we have the resources, I want plain-clothed bobbies in unmarked cars at designated winching spots... twenty-four-hour surveillance... night shifts by younger PCs, a male and female in each car. No *actual* winching, of course."

There were laughs all around, and a few muted boos from some of the younger males... and, from the tone, at least one female.

"Information from SOCO and the lab points to our perp being forensics aware. The lab teams are just now getting around to working on the forensic analyses of everything that was collected from the crime scenes. They've found nothing so far that might help to ID our guy. Anything more the boffins find, you'll be notified immediately. But they are not hopeful, and they're playing catch-up because of staff shortages caused by this COVID nightmare."

She checked her notes.

"We need info from GPs about anyone with a missing eye. Opticians, too. An 'eye collector' may have only one eye, or an eye disability of some sort, and is therefore obsessed with eyeballs. That may sound crazy, but whoever is doing this probably *is* crazy. Check on taxidermists, although I believe they are few and far between these days."

She heard Alexander trying to whisper to a colleague but failing to modulate his voice because of the mask.

"Something you'd like to share with the rest of the class?" asked Pamela.

"Er... no... erm... aye! It was aboot them taxidermists. I was just saying that somebody must hae told them to 'get stuffed.'"

Hilarity took over the room, and even Pamela had to stifle a laugh.

"Good one, constable. I thought you were going to say that when it comes to taxi-dermists we've got plenty... what with ABC Taxis, and Inverclyde Taxis!"

There were playfully derisive groans for the length Pam had stretched to pull that one out.

"Okay." She clapped her hands twice, loudly. "Back to business." She wasn't too worried about the wee jovialities, however, since she had noticed that the Chief Super's big shoulders had been rising and falling vigorously as, presumably, he had been guffawing from behind his mask. Members of the public would probably be horrified at the jocularity, given the circumstances. But, as with graveyard humour, this was a coping mechanism well-recommended by psychologists. Even hardened police officers can only take continued states of extreme tension for so long without a break.

"Utilise the internet. Social media. Our civilian analysts are on that, but the more 'eyes-on', the merrier. Even the supposedly impecunious druggies have cellphones, nicked, of course, that they use for their shady deals and meet-ups. You might hit it lucky with an unintended or seemingly unrelated post. I'm sure you all remember the recent case where two constables were talking to a guy on the street when the idiot's phone rang with the 'novelty' ringtone... "Hello, this is your drug dealer." That led to a large drugs bust at his home and the recovery of seven grand in cash. Not the brightest bulb, that one. Indeed, I think the filament of his bulb was completely burned out."

Everyone *did* remember. That wasn't a made-up story: it was true!

"And a warning... everyone... I don't want to see any reports about the missing eyes. If one of you leaks, I'll find out who it was, and your career is over. Got it?"

Nods and murmurs of assent from the team.

"And PC Alexander, you can look up 'impecunious' later. Right! Any more questions?" asked Pamela, scanning the room.

DC Michelle Chen, a third-generation Chinese Scots officer in her early twenties, asked, "Have the psychologists at Tulliallan worked up a new profile, considering the additional factor of the stabbing of victim two?"

"They're working on it. When we get a new profile, you'll soon know about it," replied Pamela. "Keep checking in to the secure shared inbox via your cellphones; if you all remember your passcodes, that is. Anything new will be posted there, FYI."

"This eyeball thing," said DS Sandra Hamilton. "It might not be a fetish, but more like a signature. Like the 'Bind, Torture, Kill', BTK killer in the USA, or the Zodiac Killer?"

"Absolutely," said Pamela. "That's a distinct possibility."

"So, we might expect more eyeless bodies?" asked Sandra.

"We need to catch the bastard before he kills again. That's the bottom line," said Pamela resolutely.

Sandra said, "Nobody could miss your earlier reference to clones. The two girls could have passed for twin sisters. If he is going to kill again, can we assume that young girls matching his 'type' are more vulnerable?"

"We're working with a sample of only two murder victims. For all we know, the next target could be a more heavily built girl with long black hair. It may be a colour or shape of the eye that attracts our killer. So, best make no assumptions," said Pamela.

"If I may?" asked the Chief Superintendent, raising his hand like a schoolboy.

"Please, sir, go ahead," said Pamela.

"You said that our lab people think the killer is 'forensics aware'. I realise that there is a plethora of information to be had from films, TV crime shows, novels etc. on forensics. I've been led to believe that every contact must leave some evidence, even if only trace evidence. Now, our killer is not likely to be wearing full protective clothing... gloves, definitely... but not an obvious full forensic suit like SOCO wear. Unless one of our patrol cars were to stop Professor McLeod sleep-driving in the early hours, *ha-ha!*"

The Chief Super showed that he could make a 'funny', too. And it was well-received.

"Have you thought about looking at the less obvious kinds of disposable clothing that workers sometimes wear: painter decorators, or mechanics, for example? Those that wouldn't stand out like a sore thumb when suited up."

"That's a brilliant point, sir," said Pamela. "That will be included in our investigation notes ASAP."

"Aye, ye see. That's why the Chief Super gets paid the big bucks," exclaimed PC Alexander.

"I certainly wish that were the case in terms of my remuneration, Alexander. But I accept the compliment if that's what it was," said Miller.

"Oh, aye, sir. Compliment it was. Painter decorators, sir. I'll be watching oot for them fly buggers. Got my living room done recently... cost a bloody fortune!"

There was an outbreak of unrestrained laughter.

"Thank you, Alex. We can always rely on your astute observations and insights," said Pamela.

PC Alexander nodded vigorously at this perceived sign of approval.

Pamela looked over and gave a nod to DI Scott, who was repressing a laugh at Alex's comment.

Scott took up a position beside Pamela. "Thank you, DS Cameron. Now, if there are no more questions...?" He paused, looking around the room. "Well then. Briefing is over. Get out there, team, and catch this killer before we get a victim number three."

Scott pulled up his mask. The DI wore his sandy red hair in an uneven and untidy boyish fringe that he would never fail to ruffle, even after combing. He ran his fingers through it now, a sure sign that the briefing was indeed over. At five feet eleven, Scott was an imposing figure. His skin was post-holiday tanned, and his most noticeable feature—now hidden by his mask—was a rather manly dimpled chin that would have made Robert Mitchum jealous. Athletic in build, but in no way muscle-bound, he looked good for his forty-three years.

Pamela was already adding to the whiteboard:

DISPOSABLE WORK WEAR:

Workers wearing disposable protective clothing, for example, painter decorators, or mechanics. Maybe semiconductor workers. Lab staff, even doctors, nurses, and hospital workers cannot be ruled out. All could be garbed in seemingly inconspicuous ways to avoid forensic transfers yet be unlikely to draw the attention of the public or police. Who pays attention to a house painter walking the aisles of Homebase while still in his whites? Disposable clothing probably burned after the crime. Any suspicious fires? Use your imaginations! BOLO.

After most of the team had dispersed, Chief Superintendent Miller had been having a short confab with Double Alex. Scott thought he heard the words 'in the old days.' On his way out Alexander shoogled the door so that it squeaked and creaked a couple of times. He shook his head and tutted, but took no steps to remedy the situation. Everyone had their jobs to do, and this was not his. Break the lines of demarcation, and next you could be cleaning the toilets!

Miller strode to the front of the room to join Pamela and Ron.

"Good job, Scott and Cameron," he said, reading what was on the whiteboard and no doubt pleased to see that his contribution had already been added.

"So, what brings you to Greenock, sir?" asked Scott.

"Truth to tell," began Miller, "I'm getting bad vibes about this case. Call it policeman's intuition, if you will. But when the eyeball information hits the press—and it will, despite all your efforts—we are likely to have a public panic on our hands. There will be comparisons to perps from Peter Manuel to Bible John to Peter Tobin."

"I agree, sir. Two teen murders are bad enough. The removal of the victims' eyes would be ripe for sensationalism. I can just see the headlines: 'Eyeless In Greenock'. 'Police Blind To Serial Killer In Our Midst'. 'Freak Murdering For Eyeballs In Inverclyde.'"

"Exactly. You know the press all too well, Ron. Just tell me there have been no cockups so far. You know… something like the blanket in the Jeanie Boyle case," said Miller.

"Nothing that I'm aware of," said Scott. "The Boyle case is one that our trainee officers invariably study at Tulliallan as an example of what *not* to do at a crime scene. After all, that case has gone down as one of Police Scotland's longest unsolved crimes—until John Lafferty was finally convicted."

The teenager, Jeannie Boyle, had been murdered only yards from her home as she was returning from a dance at a social club in Greenock. A policeman had covered her body with an ordinary blanket from the back of his car, thus contaminating the crime scene.

"I suppose, back in 1986, it wouldn't have been unusual for a copper to place a blanket over a body for the sake of decency. We've learned a lot about crime scene contamination since then."

"I bloody well hope so," said Miller. Then he tapped his finger on the whiteboard. "This Johnny McInnes scrote. Been put through the wringer, has he?"

"Absolutely, sir," said DS Cameron. "He's come within a hair's breadth of grooming charges. But he has a knack for picking vulnerable girls who look younger but are over sixteen. Any even younger fans of his, he waits until they're past the age of consent. Sicko, no doubt, but he knows the law."

"He actually has fans?" the Chief Super asked with furrowed brows.

"He's a drummer in a rock band, sir. There is a propensity for teenage girls to be attracted to the 'bad boys.' Seriously, sir. I went out with one when I was in my senior year of high school. Powerful motorcycle, black leathers, able to grow a beard, pot smoker."

"And that was just DS Cameron," said Scott, trying to inject a bit of humour. Nobody laughed.

Pamela continued, "It's that teenage girls seem to grow up faster than their male peers. More so in recent years. I blame bovine growth hormone, but that's beside the point. They outgrow their own age group and are attracted by older lads. They're looking for excitement and thrills."

"Mm-hmm, I understand. In fact, I understand all too well," said Miller, frowning.

The Chief Super's daughter had 'gone through a bad stage' as people put it in those days and got herself 'in with the wrong crowd.' Now she was a respected cardiac surgeon at the prestigious Royal Jubilee Hospital in Clydebank.

"Okay, you two," said Miller. "I see the case is in excellent hands. The round-the-clock surveillance is a splendid idea, but I can only allocate such intensive resources for a limited time. Be aware of that. Oh, and keep an eye on that Constable Alexander. He may be 'old school' but he seems to be sharp as a knife."

Scott and Cameron looked at each other, trying not to laugh.

"Yes, Chief," said Scott, "a credit to the force is Double Alex." He revealed not a hint of sarcasm in his voice.

"I'll be off then," said the Chief Superintendent, and he turned, walked to the back of the room, and exited through the squeaky door. A moment later, he popped his head back in.

Scott pre-empted him.

"Aye, sir! WD 40. I've got some in the car. I'll even do it myself."

The Chief gave a thumbs up and squeaked away.

"The hell I will," whispered Scott to Cameron. "I like squeaky doors for catching out sneaky bandits."

"Yeah, that was a surprise visit. But at least he seemed satisfied with our progress."

"Don't let him kid you, Pamela. When the inevitable leak to the press happens, and the shit hits the fan, the Chief will be sure he's standing behind said fan. And he'll be all over us like white on rice."

"Uh, kind of mixed your metaphors there, boss. But I get you."

"Notice he got a wee jab in about resources."

"Aye, boss, I did. Budgets always come first to the higher-ups. I suppose I'll be in charge of monitoring the surveillance overtime?"

"Afraid so," said Scott. "If a child were involved, they'd probably forego overtime claims. That's an unwritten rule. But over-sixteens, and druggies, no chance!"

"Och well, just another weight added to the Sisyphean boulder."

"Ah! Sisyphus, the poor sod whom the Greek god Zeus punished for cheating death twice, by forcing him to roll an immense boulder up a hill only for it to roll down every time it crested the top, whereupon he had to start over. For eternity. And that's a long, long time. Lucky for you, I'm well enough educated to understand your classical reference. Double Alex would think you were talking about STDs, *ha-ha*."

"One thing about Alex Alexander, from what I've read about him. He's never been ambitious. Enjoys being a copper and knows his limits. You have to admire that."

"True. And he gives us all a good laugh at times. Black humour, his specialty. C'mon and I'll buy you a coffee."

"From the crap coffee machine?"

"Nah, I'll treat you to a 'Costa Fortune'. You deserve it. I was glad you did the briefing. I could feel one of my migraines coming on. Got that aura warning, and I slipped two magic yellow pills down my throat when everyone was distracted, so I'm fine now."

"The magic pills are legal, right?"

"Of course! Migraleve. Fix me up every time, but I need a minute or two for them to kick in."

"I didn't know you got migraines. You should have told me, so I'm ready to give you a break anytime."

"Oh, they are few and far between. I know what triggers to avoid. In my case, it's fresh cream, coffee, and certain cheeses. So, no need to worry. Don't want my driver's license suspended by the DVLA, now, do we?"

"Ouch, never thought of that. Your wee secret's safe with me, boss."

"Thanks. Now let's get out of here."

"Squeaky door?"

"Squeaky door!"

Chapter Three

"IT DOESN'T SEEM FAIR," said DS Cameron, sipping her latte macchiato and eyeing the caramel shortcake on the plate in front of her. "I've got the expensive stuff, and you get a glass of iced water. If you're a bit short, boss, I'll pay the bill... or we could share the cost."

"Not at all, Pam," said Scott. "I promised you a fancy coffee, and it's my treat. I don't want to take a chance after that migraine. Coffee can be a trigger. And water is actually helpful sometimes. For rehydration, you know? Plus, the water's nearly as expensive as the coffee."

"Well, I don't feel so guilty now," said Pam, taking a bite out of her caramel shortcake. "Mmm, this is pure luxury. Wait, that doesn't sound right. I don't mean I'm happy it's costing you more. I meant—"

"A treat's, a treat," said her DI.

Scott seemed distracted, looking something up on his iPad. He found what he was searching for.

"Thought so," he said.

"What?"

"I thought it was weird that the Chief Super was harking back to the Jeannie Boyle case. I wasn't even in the force then. But I had to look it up."

"And...?"

"Guess the name of the young PC who covered the body with a blanket from the back of his car and contaminated the crime scene?"

Pamela thought for a minute. "Not Double Alex, surely?"

"Nope. It was none other than PC Samuel Miller."

"The Chief Super?"

Scott looked deflated. "Damn. I suspect that mistake must have haunted him all his life, and still does."

"If nothing else, lessons were learned, and procedures were overhauled," said Pamela, using the passive tense so popular with officialdom. "That's what they told us in training."

"Hard for a young copper, though."

Scott's iPad chimed the 'Big Ben' chimes, drawing annoyed looks from those around.

"Sorry!" he said in a loud voice... probably only making things worse.

"Always forget to turn the sound down," he whispered to Pam. "It's an email from Pauline."

"There's always Airplane mode," said Pamela.

"I never figured out how that works."

"How is Pauline doing? Not the holiday she was expecting, poor lass."

Pauline was Scott's daughter. She and a fellow nurse had gone on holiday to Scott's timeshare villa in La Palma, in the Canary Isles. The two had only been there three days when a series of earthquakes triggered a volcanic eruption in the Cumbre Vieja area, on the western side of the island, where their villa was. They decided to stay on and volunteered to help wherever possible. Along with around seven-thousand others, they had been evacuated to the unaffected eastern side of the island. So, the two girls were now staying with a local couple, friends of the DI.

Scott had befriended Pepe Cuevas and his wife, Marianna, when they met at a local wine tasting on his very first visit to the island. Pepe was actually 'Capitan Cuevas' of the Guardia Civil, and the two coppers soon got talking about all matters police... the differences and similarities regarding Scottish and Spanish policing. It helped that Pepe spoke perfect English. Scott's Spanish was sketchy, although he had been trying to learn the language with the help of an app on his iPad.

The Canary Islands are territorially Spanish, although geographically, they are situated off the western coast of North Africa. Tenerife is the most popular of the islands with British tourists, but Scott and his daughter had been drawn to the smaller island of La Palma because, as Pauline put it, it was 'less touristy.'

"Oh, I'd better look. Do you mind?" asked Scott.

"Not at all," replied Pamela. "I've been following the volcano news on that YouTube feed you told me about."

"Yes. AfarTV. I look in when I can. It is distressing yet strangely addictive... the raw power of nature, the destruction, and then the terraforming when the lava reaches the sea. And the resilience of the people of La Palma is nothing less than heroic."

He opened the email. "Do you want me to read it to you?"

"Yes, please," replied Pamela, "you can leave out any personal stuff."

"Hah! Personal? Pauline doesn't *do* personal." He read:

"'*Hola buenos dias, Ronnie.*'

"Ronnie? Not Dad?"

"She stopped calling me 'Dad' when she was eleven, after the, erm..."

"D-I-V-O-R-C-E," whispered Pam, mimicking Tammy Wynette. "It's okay... you can say the word. It isn't a curse word, you know."

If only you knew, thought Scott.

He continued to read:

"'You probably know as much about the volcano as I do. On this side of the island, things are relatively normal, considering. We watch YouTube and listen to local news stations to get most of our info. Nobody who's not an official can get into the exclusion zone, although Pepe has been there, him being Guardia. He was suited up like a black and yellow bumblebee, breathing apparatus and all, to take air samples.

'The seven-thousand have been put up in hotels or in the houses of friends and family. Thankfully, most of the tourists have buggered off by boat or plane to Tenerife, then onto flights home. That left us a bit of room to breathe.

'Talking about breathing; that's the major worry here on the east coast. SO2 in the air. We're all masked up when we go out, but I don't detect the rotten-egg smell of sulphur on this side... so far, anyway. No doubt it'll waft over here depending on the wind.

'It was horrible that our villa was entirely engulfed by lava. I spent a night in tears. Then I realised that our loss seems minor when you see the devastation caused to other homes, 656, at the last estimate, the banana plantations, the businesses, the power plants, the churches, and cemeteries... I could go on, but I'm sure you've seen it all on YouTube.

'Anyway, me and Sophie volunteered to help. So, as fully trained and registered nurses, they've got us... wait for it... working at the animal shelter. No kidding! Dogs, cats, pigs, and goats... oh, and a rooster that crows his head off at all hours whenever it pleases him. It's a myth that roosters only crow in the morning. Either that or this one has gone bonkers with the upset. Tempted to wring its bloody... No, I won't go there, *ha-ha*. *Primum non nocere,* right? "First, do no harm." Even with troublesome cocks! LOL. Earthquakes continue to shake us up. When we get an above-magnitude-three, we really shake, rattle and roll. Marianna has lost a few plates and ornaments. But under mag three, you just feel trembly.

'Hope you are doing okay. Heard about the murders. You catch the SOB, Ronnie!

'Pepe and Marianna send their love. If you get a chance, Skype me tonight. I should be at Pepe's at eight and showered by half-past. No, make that nine. Boy, do those animals stink!

'Luckily, we're in the same time zone: no adding or subtracting to do with the time, lol.

'Love, Pauline xxx.

'PS: Tell Pamela I was asking for her. I bet you're reading this to her, *ha-ha*!'"

Scott didn't read out the next bit that said, 'You two shacking up yet?' [Two emojis: a bed and a red heart]

Pamela said, "Tell her I send my best wishes to her and to all those in La Palma." She took another sip of her piping-hot coffee.

Scott opened a reply text, typed a few lines, and pressed send.

"Is that it? I know brevity is the soul of wit, but..."

"I'll be in touch with her on Skype later; we'll catch up then, and I'll pass on your message," said Scott.

"Probably the wrong time to ask. But was your timeshare villa insured?"

Just then, Pamela's cellphone chirruped.

A second later, Scott's mobile ringtone began 'Scotland the Brave.' There were disapproving frowns and tuts from staff and customers alike.

As they each made to answer their devices, they already knew. Something had happened. Something big!

Chapter Four

"IT TOOK THEM HOW LONG to phone it in?" DI Scott asked.

"They say about an hour," replied DS Alison Weir, a short, heavily built, blonde-haired DS who was acting as FLO, Family Liaison Officer. "I think it might have been longer."

"So, a four-year-old boy goes missing from his granny's back garden, and we don't get a phone call until well after the golden hour is up?"

Scott was referring to the period after a reported crime, when evidence may be abundant and undisturbed, and memories are fresh.

Alison had joined Scott and DS Cameron in the DI's BMW that was parked at the back gate of Number 5, Beggie Road in Greenock. The house was situated on the far southwest outskirts of the town, and stood high on a hill, 350 feet above, and a mile away from, the town centre.

"The granny says it went down like this, boss. The boy had been bought a new pair of top boots. So, he convinces granny to let him go out in the garden to try out his new yellow boots, his raincoat, and rain hat, which, as described, sounds like a plastic sou'wester, red in colour.

"Apparently, the boy loved water, and he wanted to splash about a bit in puddles. Not unusual for a four-year-old. Granny gets him into his rain togs and tells him he can go out for five minutes, but no longer, or he'll catch a cold. She can see him from the kitchen window.

"She turns and walks to the work surface opposite the window, fetches the kettle, goes back to the sink to fill it... and looking out, she can't see Danny. Sorry, boss, the boy's name is Danny, Daniel Docherty.

"He has a habit of playing hide and seek. His usual hiding place is behind the garden hut. In their game, granny must put on a show of looking for him, then feign surprise when he pops out with a 'boo'. But since it's raining, she just goes to the back door and shouts on him.

"When there's no reply, she grabs an umbrella, sticks her feet in her own wellies, and heads out to the garden, no doubt not in the best of moods, especially since, according to her, the first thing that happens is that her umbrella blows inside out.

"But Danny is nowhere to be seen. She goes to the gate. This side of the garden has access to Beggie Road as you can see... and she looks up and down the road, calling his name. No sign of him!

"Now, the other side of the garden is fenced off from a strip of overgrown wasteland that leads to the burn. That's the Beggie burn, sir. You can hear it from here. It's fair flowing because of the heavy rain."

"Don't tell me...?"

"What, sir?"

"There is a gap in the fence, isn't there?"

"Well, yes, but how did you...?"

"Call it intuition!" said Scott with a frown. "Still doesn't explain the long wait to phone us."

"The granny says she panicked and called her daughter-in-law, Danny's mother, who called the father, who was at a friend's house. Then, when they all got here, the dad and his mate went scrambling through the brush, over to the burn that had now burst its banks. There is a path of sorts made by folk taking a shortcut from the top of the hill; self-proclaimed ramblers who had made the gap in the fence. Those who knew about it would take this 'shortcut' and push their way through the foliage, before sneaking through Hilda's garden and on to Beggie Road to make their way down to the town. If Hilda saw them, they'd get a bawling-out. But she'd not yet got round to having the fence fixed."

Pamela asked, "How high up are we here?"

"Must be over 300 feet," said Scott. "I'll check it out on an OS map later."

Alison continued, "Anyway, knowing the boy's attraction to water, and fearing the worst, as soon as he got back to the house, drenched, the dad called 999."

"Hmm, sounds plausible." Scott was rubbing his chin. "Ramblers love to cite that there are 'no trespass laws in Scotland,' conveniently missing out the part about private property."

"What resources do we have here now?" asked DS Cameron.

"The first search team arrived twenty minutes after the alert. Now there are specialist police and fire rescue teams scouring the area and methodically following the burn downhill. Apparently, even as well-trained as they are, the searchers wearing waders and using search poles are finding it hard to keep their feet in the fast-flowing water. They've had to rope up for safety, I'm told. Their vehicles have gathered at the cul-de-sac, up there." She pointed to an array of blue and amber neons that would have annoyed Nisha Chandara to no end. "A dozen uniforms are canvassing the houses."

"Give us a quick rundown on the state of the family before we go in," said Scott.

A quick rundown, it was. "Mother and granny in tears; father and pal fuming!" said Alison.

"Fuming? Why? Distressed, I understand. But angry... at whom... the granny?"

"At us, sir," said Alison. "They say we were slow to respond, and there hasn't been an Amber Alert put out."

"Good lord!" said Scott. "'Amber Alert.' Really? People have been watching too many cops shows from the States. We've even got youngsters dialling 911 now, for emergency services!"

"The family has no cause for complaint, in this case, boss. There was an immediate response from the emergency operator, and the call matched the 'high risk' criteria," confirmed Alison. "So, a 'Missing

Persons Command and Control Incident Centre' was set up immediately, and then you were called. The uniforms that are now canvassing door-to-door searched the premises, including the garden and the garden shed. The incident room folk have already put out the alert notifications via Facebook, Twitter, TikTok, and Instagram: Newspapers, radio stations, and TV have all been informed. The Chief Constable intends to have a formal press briefing at three. We got a good portrait photo of the boy from the mother, and I sent that to the incident room from my iPhone. The parents and gran have still to be formally interviewed."

"I suppose we'd better face the storm, then," said Scott.

All three got out, and Scott made his way over the sodden garden to find the gap in the fence. He was wearing a tan Burberry raincoat, but now wished he'd worn something with a hood.

Just then, a police helicopter flew overhead.

"The chopper has just arrived!" shouted Alison, pointing to the black helicopter with a yellow roof and POLICE in large yellow letters on the sides, as if she thought nobody else had noticed it.

The storm seemed to be getting worse by the minute, and Scott wondered if the helicopter was arriving, or actually turning and heading back to base.

Police Scotland had suffered three tragic police helicopter crashes. The first, in 1990, had been weather-related, the helicopter having been caught in a snowstorm. Sadly, a police sergeant was killed. A crash-landing into a field in Ayrshire in 2002 fortunately resulted in no fatalities. The chopper was a complete write-off, though. The latest one, in 2013, where the helicopter had crash-landed on the roof of *The Clutha* pub in Glasgow, caused ten fatalities and many serious injuries. The cause was found to have been 'fuel starvation.'

The back door of the house was thrown open violently, and a stockily built man, about five-nine, head shaven, boxer's nose, and stubbly chin, came running out into the garden. He looked up at the passing helicopter. He was already soaked to the skin.

"About fuckin' time!" he bawled at the sky, waving a fist in the air.

He turned to DS Weir.

"Where the hell did that come frae? Eberdeen?" he shouted angrily.

"Not Aberdeen. Glasgow Heliport is where the helicopter is based," said Scott as he approached. "Sometimes Cumbernauld airport."

"And who the fuck are you?" asked the man aggressively.

DI Scott pulled out his warrant card. "I'm Detective Inspector Scott, and this is Detective Sergeant Cameron. Now... *Who the fuck are you?*" Scott had got right up in the man's face.

The man backed off two paces.

"I'm... I'm Danny's faither," he pronounced 'father' in the vernacular.

"Mr Thomas Docherty," chimed in Alison, "the missing boy's father."

"I... I'm sorry," said Docherty, "I thought ye were frae the press. That raincoat, ye know? A cannae staun them press vultures. But I didnae think we'd be getting a visit frae Lieutenant Columbo."

Scott ignored the comment. Alison and Sandra looked at each other, with a silent, shared 'WTF' look.

Glaring at Docherty, Scott said, "In this extreme weather, the searchers are putting their lives at risk fulfilling their duties. And we will be glad of the press to get the word out, Mr Docherty. But my officers will keep them back for now. There will be a briefing in due time." If there was one thing Scott hated more than anything, it was a bully-boy; and Docherty struck him as just the type.

"Well, shake the rain aff, an' ye better come in," said Docherty, opening the back door that led straight into the kitchen and walking ahead of everyone, not holding open the door that was on a spring closer.

Obviously, he was not a 'ladies first' kind of guy, thought Pamela.

Scott did the honours.

The kitchen was small and neat and tidy. No dirty dishes in the sink, and work surfaces were clear of clutter. Immediately, after going through the far door, another door to the right took them into the living room.

Scott's hackles were up right away. There was a fog of cigarette smoke, and he noticed that the granny and the mother were both puffing away. A couple of ashtrays were full to overflowing.

He had been at the forefront of anti-smoking campaigns since his mother had died from lung cancer. Most smokers now, even at home, went outside to smoke. Yet, given the atrocious weather and the nervous tension, he thought he could understand the situation. He had never been a smoker, but from his mother's experience, he knew how addictive the habit was. Seeing patients, bald from chemo, in their dressing gowns, and smoking outside the door of a chemotherapy treatment centre was gut-wrenching.

Tommy was drying his head and face with a towel.

The women were red eyed from crying. The pal, a diminutive and plump wee ball of dough with a dyed-black comb-over, looked like he'd definitely been through the brambles. Dishevelled and dirty, he was trying to assemble a roll-up and failing miserably; his hands were shaking so much.

"Here... take one of mine, Matt," said the granny, throwing a Silk Cut to him. As he tried to light it with matches, they kept breaking.

"Damn it!" He spat the words out.

"Lighter," Gran threw him a disposable Bic, and he finally managed to spark up, drawing a massive inhalation, and after holding it in his lungs, he let out the smoke with a satisfied gasp.

"This is Detective... shit, I forgot yer name, sorry!" said Docherty, seemingly impervious to the smog.

Scott repeated his previous introduction, and he and Pamela held up their warrant cards for a few seconds, as was the norm. Scott often thought that warrant cards could easily be 'Space Ranger' badges from a toy shop. Nobody ever asked for a closer look.

"I'm terribly sorry about..." he began.

"Never mind yer sorries, mister," said the mother in an angry voice. "When are yees gonnie find ma boy? He cannae be far away. He's only four!"

She was a gaunt-looking woman with middle-parted, long, dyed jet-black hair, that had a white streak at the front on either side.

She burst into tears, her head and shoulders rocking up and down like a rabbi at the Wailing Wall.

The granny, sitting beside the distraught mum on the couch, tried to put her arm around her daughter-in-law to comfort her. To everyone's surprise, the mother, Jenny was her name, shrugged off the embrace and jumped up, wagging an accusing finger at the gran and screaming, "Don't you touch me, you stupid old bitch. It's all your fault. You were supposed to be watching him!"

DS Weir stepped between the two immediately, pushing Jenny back, little by little, the officer's arms out to the side, about waist height, as she had been taught in de-escalation tactical training.

'Scotland the Brave' broke the tension. Everyone but Pamela and Alison looked askance at Scott as if the ringtone was somehow inappropriate in these circumstances. Scott didn't notice and wouldn't have cared, anyway. He answered his mobile.

"Okay!" was all he said in reply to the call.

He looked at Thomas with what he thought was a sympathetic expression on his face, although he barely could disguise his dislike for the man, and said, "You'll need to come with me."

Thomas jumped up. "They've found something?"

"They want you to identify, erm... some articles, was all they said," Scott answered, trying to be diplomatic and failing miserably.

"I'll come as weel," said Matt Ross, the comb-over pal.

Female wailing increased in volume, and, as the three men left, Alison said, "You know what? I think I'll make us wimmin a wee cup of tea."

DS Cameron said, "That's a good idea, Alison."

The granny, suddenly much calmer, as if she could turn off the waterworks at the drop of a hat, said, "Aye, hen. And if you look in the cupboard above the kettle, there's a wee half-bottle of Martell brandy. I keep it... only fur medicinal purposes, you know? A wee splash in the cups would be jist the thing."

For some reason, this set off Jenny, who had plonked herself down on the chair Matt had vacated, to bawling even louder.

"You and your fucking brandy. You better no hae been..."

She didn't finish the sentence, but her eyes drew daggers at Hilda.

"Won't be a tick," said Alison, discretely motioning to Pamela to keep an eye on the two volatile women.

While in the kitchen, DS Weir made notes of how long it took her to go from the window to the kettle and back to the window and the sink. To be thorough, she timed how long it took for the kettle to boil and how long to make the tea, although granny hadn't said she had got around to that. Alison snapped photos on her iPhone from all angles, and some looking out to the garden through the window. She noticed a lady's umbrella, fully intact, propped up beside the back door. Teas all ready on a tray, she opened the cupboard door to find the brandy. She noted that it wasn't a half-bottle of Martell; it was a full-sized bottle that was three-quarters empty. Alison made a note to find out about Hilda's drinking habits. She took a snapshot of the bottle on her phone, then poured a wee drop into two cups and returned to the living room.

"Tea's up!" said Alison with a big smile.

———— ◉ ————

"WE FOUND ONE SNAGGED on a branch on the far bank of the burn, quite a way down. The other was even further down, caught up in weeds where there was a rocky hump." The search team supervisor, Keith Penny, mud splashed almost up to the chest of his waders, was holding up two large, see-through plastic evidence bags. In each was a small yellow top boot. He had to shout to be heard over the roar of the torrent. Beggie burn, as it was now, looked more like a small river. 'Burn' didn't seem adequate for the speed and depth of the water. In this storm, it looked and sounded more like rapids.

Tommy Docherty slid down onto his knees on the muddy bank and buried his face in his hands. He let out one anguished cry, then, looking up, he shouted, "They're his. Them's Danny's wellies."

"You are certain?" asked DS Scott, at once realising how stupid the question was.

"Jesus. Aye. How many kids' yellow wellies are there likely to be in the burn? I'm sure, but ye kin check. I folded doon the tops, and I wrote his name on the inside with one of they indelible pens. 'D. Doc' I wrote."

The officer holding the bags nodded to Scott. The ink surely had been indelible.

"It's weird that his wee boots widda came off. How could that be? Nae sign of his red hat?"

"The search goes on, Mr Docherty," said the second-in-command team leader, Grant Wylie. "We don't give up until..." His voice trailed off.

"Until yees find a body, right?" said Docherty.

"Until we find your boy," chimed in DS Scott. "This is still a missing person's case. You need to keep your hopes up, man. Just think! Danny could have thrown his wellies into the burn... like wee boats, you know? Until we learn otherwise, we're searching for Danny alive. There's a lot of ground to be covered. And a good bit of daylight left before nightfall."

In fact, 'daylight' didn't describe the murky, half-light of Greenock at this time of year, in this wild storm, with rain pouring down and the sky completely overcast.

Scott knew he was clutching at straws with the 'wee boats' story.

But Thomas seemed to perk up a bit.

"Aye, ye'r right, Inspector! Gies one of they poles. And you take one as well, Matt. If we cannae help, we should nae hinder."

Scott put his hand out to stop the officer who was swithering about handing over search poles to civilians. "Erm, I understand your wish to help," he said to Docherty and his pal, "but I need you to come back to the house. I need formal statements from all involved... for the record, you understand?"

Docherty blew up again, "Whit? D'ye think we had anything tae dae wi' ma wee boy's going missing? Are ye aff yer heid? I loved that lad mair than life itsel'!"

Scott made a mental note of the use of the past tense, 'loved'.

"It's standard operating procedure, Mr Docherty. We have a set of strict rules that must be adhered to; otherwise, we'd be seen to be negligent. Nobody likes paperwork and officialdom, but..."

"Officialdom, my arse!" shouted Tommy, "are ye gonnae be interrogating my wife noo as well? Ye saw the state she is in?"

"Interviews will be conducted by professionals trained to be respectful and discreet. All we need is that your initial statements are on the record as soon as possible. The mind can play funny tricks after a trauma like you all have been through. The sooner we have your recall, the better."

"Recall, ma arse," said Docherty. (*His arse seemed to concern him any time he got angry,* thought Scott). "You no think I... ony of us won't hae this morning doon like it wis tattooed on oor fuckin' arms?"

"No matter. It must be done. So, if you will follow me back to Beggie Road, the sooner it's over, the better."

Matt looked even more apprehensive and agitated than Thomas, Scott noticed. And he wondered why.

Scott knew that while they had been away from the granny's house, officers would have collected and taken into evidence all mobile phones, computers, laptops, iPads, and the like, along with any written notebooks, notes, sticky notes, or diaries that they deemed relevant. Furthermore, after the interviews at Beggie Road, they would accompany the Docherty couple and Matt to their homes to do the same. He surmised that Thomas's figurative arse was going to be like a well-spanked bottom by the time they were through.

DS Weir designated Thomas as the SPOC, the single point of contact within the family. This move, at least, satisfied his vanity.

The interviews were conducted by two experienced detective constables. It is a misconception fuelled by crime novels, TV shows, and movies that senior officers regularly conduct interviews. There are exceptions to the rules, but, in general, DCs make the best interviewers, as higher ranks are deemed too expensive a resource for such a role. And it builds confidence as the junior officers gain experience and hone their detective skills.

Chapter Five

JOHNNY MCINNES, SOMETIME drummer with the indie rock band *The Flack:* most-time tearaway and wise guy, was sitting on a beaten-up couch in a squat in a bottom flat of a deserted tenement in Grant Street, Greenock. The fug of cannabis smoke did not mask the overpowering stench of piss and shit. It just blended into a sickly mix... the unmistakable aroma of the typical squat or drug den.

"What the flack's goin' on?" he asked the others. The 'flack' was his occasional substitute for the more common vulgarity. Apparently, his band took on the name when a God-fearing club owner who eschewed swear words, on hearing them play for the first time, had shouted, 'What the flack is that racket?'

The others were six in number: two guys and four girls. They were lazing about on various manky mattresses, cushions, and blankets laid on the floor, and they were all high. The place was littered with empty cheap-wine bottles, empty beer and cider cans, overflowing makeshift ashtrays, and drug paraphernalia of every variety.

"Whit d'ya mean, Johnny man, man? We're hivvin a wee party courtesy of Big Malky. He's got a special on some crack, man. BOGOF. Malky's the Man, man!"

This came from the 'wee man, man,' Terry Duffy, a pint-sized, but thoroughly nasty piece of work who seemed to be compelled to add 'man' to his every utterance.

"No' the stuff, ya wee shite. The polis, and the murder of they two wee skanks. Double Alex and his girlfriend Tam Dempster dragged me into a close aroon the corner; an' they two wankers threatened a good kicking. Ah swore I had nuthin' to tell them. So, I just got heid butted instead of the kicking. Look at my bloody nose!"

His nose was indeed bloody, and he was trying to stop the flow with a now blood-soaked cloth of dubious origin.

"Is it broke, like, man? I think a broke schnozzle gies a man a hard man look, man." said Terry.

"Fuckin' better no' be. Spoil ma good looks, an' I'll sue the bastards!"

"Well, you'll no' be wanting to huff a line with that nose, drummer man, man," said Terry, laughing.

In a flash, McInnes was off the couch and kicked Terry full in the face with the sole of his boot. The wee man fell back, knocking aside a shaving mirror that had been razor-prepped with some lines of crack cocaine.

"Awe, fir fuck's sake, man. It wis on'y a joke."

"Joke's on you then. How many lines you lose?"

"I had fou..., erm, eight lined up," Terry sniffled and lied.

Johnny pulled out two ten quid notes and dropped them on the blanket. "Their ye go! Mair than enough com pen, eh, you lying wee cunt. But, mind, if you hear anything aboot they murders, you come tae me. Information is power. And power would dae your flacked-up head in. Ye widnae know whit to dae with it. Ye come to me, and I'll see you right. Got it?"

"Aye. Got it. Ta, drummer man, man." Then, when Johnny had left, muttering about 'that bloody stink hole,' Terry looked around at the others who were in various states of intoxicated obliviousness, and who probably hadn't even noticed the altercation.

"Anybody got a wee brush and dustpan?" he asked.

———●———

BIG MALKY, MALCOLM Boone, was indeed having a sale. He'd just received a delivery of a kilo of crack cocaine from his mule. So, he was busy overseeing the bagging and selling as fast as his top dealers could turn up at his 'bando', the abandoned house he was currently using, his gaff. Two skanky-looking girls were doing the weighing and bagging. Both had East European accents when they spoke with the few English phrases they knew. Both looked scared to death; both were crack heads.

Malky was set to make about twenty grand on an outlay of twelve. But Malky wasn't as happy as he should have been. The local 'polis,' as Scots tended to call the police, had identified two murdered girls. And Malky knew that both had been users. A trail of deals could eventually lead back to him, and that fact made him very uncomfortable.

So, Boone was being ultra-cautious. He was using a tactic that was popular with spies... drop sites. His five lieutenants: Alistair 'Mack the knife' McIntosh, Lee 'Tiny' Yang, Raymond, 'Raymie' Smythe, Douglas 'Duggie' Fyfe, and Gordon 'Gordo' Bryce, would watch the top dealers leave the baggies at prearranged drop sites.

Then, they would keep their eyes peeled from a distance while the next dealer in the chain picked up the drugs and left the requisite amount of cash in sealed bags. Sites were code named, and moved as often as four times a day.

After checking for police, another guy, or often a girl, would pick up the cash and take it by a roundabout route to Big Malky, who gave them their cut in cash or in dope. It was the job of the lieutenants to provide extra 'supervision' when required and to see that none of the gear went astray. The temptations were high. It was convoluted, but everyone involved knew their place in the pecking order. And, most importantly, it worked... with additional help from a few bent coppers, that is.

Communication was over burner phones or else phones that had been stolen. There were plenty to be had. And God help anyone who welched on a deal. Punishments were severe: from beatings, to slashings, to kneecapping, to being 'disappeared.' And everybody knew what being 'disappeared' meant. Mostly, the lower-level dealers were from the underclass, the detritus of society. No one would miss them, no one would talk, and bodies would never be found. The middle-class sellers and users were a different ballgame. From clerks to CEOs, the fear of exposure or withdrawal of supply was usually enough to keep them in line.

Malky ran his operations like military exercises. He was, in fact, ex-army: SAS, no less. And he proudly showed off the 'Who Dares Wins' winged-dagger tattoo on his upper right arm. Malky had the tattoo inked only after he had left the service. If captured, no soldier wanted to be identified as SAS.

Idiots who had never served, and didn't know the strict Hereford rules, sometimes wore such tattoos as 'stolen valour' tats, but at their peril. For the genuine SAS had a rule that if they came across such cretins, they would take them to 'an informal reunion', where after a toast to the Queen, a toast to the Regiment, a toast to 'absent friends', a toast to... on and on... the imposter would invariably fall into a drunken sleep and wake up to find that he'd had his bogus tattoo forcibly removed, along with a chunk of upper arm flesh.

A squaddie boasting to a lassie about being in the SAS was one thing. But to sport that tattoo without earning it... that was sacrilege.

Malky used to say that he only felt he was near to death once in his life, and that wasn't in Afghanistan or Iraq where he had served... it was at the hands of his trainers during the gruelling tests for entry into the Special Air Service.

He had almost died from hypothermia during the 'Fan Dance'.

Pen Y Fan, an 886-metre-high peak (almost 3,000 feet) in the Brecon Beacons, is the focus of the 'Fan Dance', an element of the fitness and navigation stage of SAS selection.

Part of a twenty-four-kilometre TAB (Tactical Advance to Battle), candidates must march over Pen Y Fan twice while carrying only a forty-pound bergen, rifle, and water. It was only by sheer force of will that he had fought the hypothermia (by going body-to-body with a wayward sheep) and pulled through. The sheep story provided a source of much ribbing back at base, where he had been covered with a space blanket and properly revived by a slow intake of hot drinks.

He had learned a lot during his army years; most important to him now was the ability to organise. A strict hierarchy was enforced, and everyone in his team knew where they stood. The Italian Mafia was an equally influential model, and 'to swim with the fishes' was not a benign or jocular threat in his organisation.

Before getting involved in organised crime, Malky had a clean, quite exemplary record. He played, or at least banged, the big drum in the Boys' Brigade band, was captain of his house in high school and had earned the Duke of Edinburgh award for orienteering. He had gone straight into the army on leaving school as a sixth-former at eighteen and had quickly earned enough merit to apply for special service.

But, on leaving the army, like many other veterans, he missed the regimen and felt that he didn't fit in to civvy society. His fierce temper had earned him a sentence of a year and six months in HMP Greenock brought up on assault charges. He was out in six months for good behaviour. From then, it was 'downhill.' Although the 'Big Man' Malky would say it was, in fact, the opposite. As far as he was concerned, he had gone up in the world.

In his alter ego, he lived in a posh house in Bearsden and drove a Mercedes-Benz SL sports car. His legitimate business was as a 'Security Consultant.' That is, he ran a team of bouncers and enforcers for clubs, pubs, and music venues. His employees were mostly disgruntled ex-vets like himself. To the police, Malky, the drug dealer, was a mirage, a chimera. The 'street' Malky was unobtrusive, shabbily dressed, always masked for COVID and for transport, no posh car. He used taxis. In fact, he actually *owned* the taxi business, although nobody knew that except for his shell, his proxy owner. He kept out of trouble and in the shadows of his actual business as a major drug dealer. His lieutenants and soldiers knew little about his semi-respectable side, and any who did knew they had better keep schtum! There were rumours he was financed by the Russian mafia. But, in Scotland, anything dodgy was attributed to the Russian mafia!

When 'Tiny' Yang, a massively built thug of Chinese descent, spotted Johnny McInnes walking towards the flat, he alerted Malky. Wonderful thing, new technology. You could set up a wireless CCTV in ten minutes or less and remove it in five. The small remote-controlled surveillance camera was mounted by heavy-duty Velcro at the entrance to the close and monitored on an iPad dedicated to that purpose.

"Go see to him!" was all Malky had to say.

Tiny pulled on a cagoule, sprinted out with unexpected liveliness for such a big lad, and confronted Johnny well before the entrance to the close.

Johnny froze when he saw Tiny. The drummer was soaked to the skin, but he really wanted to find out about the BOGOF. However, Tiny wasn't looking very welcoming.

"Yer looking for where?" Tiny bawled so that anyone nearby could hear, even though Johnny hadn't said a word.

"I'm, err, I was jist..." mumbled Johnny, hanky still held to his nose.

Tiny shouted as if to a deaf person, "Oh, the bookies! You're on the wrang street, mate. The bookies is that-a-way. Ye understand, right?" Tiny was pointing his beefy finger in the direction away from the gaff.

Johnny understood. Big Malky didn't want to see him, BOGOF or no BOGOF. More like 'bugger off!' And that's what he did. He pulled a scrunched-up plastic carrier bag from his pocket, fashioned it in the shape of a hat, and put it on his already soaked head, making him look even more like an eejit as he walked away.

Chapter Six

———◦———

PRESS BRIEFING AT GREENOCK Police Station public relations room. 3 p.m.

THE BRIEFING was chaired by acting Chief Constable Sally Macfarlane, in all her uniformed finery. She was known by her underlings as 'wee 'f'' in Macfarlane'. As opposed to someone who was a 'big 'F' in MacFarlane'—a very Scottish 'in' joke regarding the capital versus lower-case letter after the 'Mac', both of which were legitimate variants, and the contraction 'effin'. Sally was also known to be a 'nippy sweetie'... a woman not to be messed around. Tall and painfully thin looking, she was in her late forties. She had very angular facial features and wore little, if any, makeup, although it was clear that her thin eyebrows were pencilled on. Her hair was grey, and she had dyed it 'silver fox' and wore it in a very short, boyish style with a thinning fringe. Her skin was so white as to look almost translucent. Some would say that her dark eyes could laser cut you like a knife.

"Right! If you could all quieten down, please," the Chief tapped a glass of water that was on the table in front of her with a pen. The room came to order. She removed her FFP2 mask and spoke into the bendy microphone. There was a squeal of feedback from the speakers. She switched the button off and glowered at the officer in charge of the sound system. After an adjustment, the sound guy, looking chastened, gave a thumbs up from the back of the hall where the mixing-desk was.

Microphone turned on again, the Chief began:

"It is my unpleasant duty to report that we have a missing child on our beat."

The press pool shuffled and mumbled.

"The missing boy is four-year-old Daniel, known as Danny, Docherty of Number 5, Beggie Road. He was reported missing at around ten o'clock this morning.

"What we've been told is that the lad was staying with his grandmother, Hilda Docherty, at the above-mentioned address, and he had been playing in her garden, after he had nagged granny to let him try out his new yellow wellington boots in the rain. The boy, we were told, loved water, and splashing in puddles, like many children of his age. He was in full sight of grandma until she turned round to fetch the kettle to fill it in order to make a cup of tea. That must have been a matter of moments. But when Mrs Docherty again looked out to the garden, Danny was nowhere to be seen.

"Now, I must emphasise that, at this time, there are no suspicious circumstances regarding Danny's disappearance. Being such astute journalists, I'm sure that you've seen the police helicopter covering the area around Beggie Road and the Beggie burn."

There was a bit of chatter when the burn was mentioned.

"We have every reason to believe that Danny will be found... maybe soaked and the worse for wear, but found, nonetheless. So, I ask you all to utilise your outlets, TV, newspaper, social media... including you bloggers of the fifth estate who sneaked in at the back... to use your extensive access to the public of Greenock and Inverclyde and get the word out. The helpline number is up in big numerals behind me for you to copy down."

"Now... any questions?"

It seemed like every hand in the room went up, like a classroom of primary-school kids who had just been asked an easy question from the teacher.

The Chief pointed to a reporter in the front row. "*Greenock Telegraph*. Rhona. Since you're our local, you go first."

"Thank you, Chief Constable," Rhona Munro began, with an unexpectedly loud voice for such a petite girl. "We at the *Tele* got word of the police helicopter flying low over the Beggie burn area. But when we got to Beggie Road, it was cordoned off with police tape, and officers refused us, and other press, entry. Can you tell us why?"

The Chief guessed where this line of questioning might be going. For, after an injudicious comment by Donald Trump about 'No-Go-Zones' in the UK, the subject of any kind of exclusion zone was a hot potato in the news currently.

The Chief cleared her throat. "Quite simply, Rhona, we have cordoned off the area because, although not a crime scene, we have declared it an exclusion zone. This is to allow the search and rescue teams to muster, and to keep the family from being door stepped... the latter at the request of the family, I might add."

"So, essentially, you *have* declared a 'No-Go-Zone' here in Inverclyde?"

"Call it what you will, Rhona. 'A rose by any other name...' But there's a four-year-old boy gone missing. For one thing, our officers are canvassing households on the road. For another, the search teams are in clearly group-labelled hi-viz, easy to see each other and to recognise who's who. And they don't want to end up having to rescue civilians who, albeit with good intentions, blunder into the search area. With Beggie burn in spate and overflowing its banks, this is treacherous ground.

"And I reiterate, the family wants privacy. We need them not to be distracted in case they remember something heretofore forgotten. When they are ready to speak to the press, you'll be the first to know."

A voice from the back, a local blogger, shouted, "There are nae trespass laws in Scotland."

"You are quite correct, erm...?"

"Tam White, *Inside Inverclyde* blog."

"You are quite correct, Mr White. But... if anyone breaks the cordon or is found with their muddy hiking boots disrupting the search, my officers will arrest them for disturbing the peace."

"Disturbing the peace?" asked Tam. "How do ye work that one oot?"

"Disturbing the peace... which they surely will be doing with an arm twisted round their back up to their shoulder blades."

There was a lot of groaning and unrest among the press corps.

Standing at the back of the room was Inverclyde councillor, Reg Blaney. He turned to his PR woman and whispered, "I can't believe she just said that!" Then he coughed loudly and shot his hand in the air.

"Ah, Councillor Blaney. I'm so glad you could join us," said the Chief Constable. Sally had just been provocative... because she bloody well could!

"Thank you, ma'am," said Blaney, an ex-cop. Old habits die hard. "I would like to say that as councillor for this area, this ward, I totally agree with your reasonable precautions, and I'm sure that my colleagues on Inverclyde council would be unanimous in their approval." He was stretching it a bit here, but he went on. "Often, I have hiked up around the Beggie hill and burn. The views over the Clyde are spectacular, especially on a good day."

The blogger, Tam, asserted, "Well, ye cannae be up there often if you're needing a good day here in Greenock."

Laughter all round.

Blaney said angrily, "Now, that's just the kind of false weather talk I hate to hear. We, in Greenock, now welcome many large cruise ships to our port, as you well know. And if you take the time to look at the weather statistics, we come off well, as it happens."

"Against where?" asked Tam, "Siberia?"

The room now filled with uproarious laughter.

"Okay, Tam. We all like our little jokes about the weather here.

"We all know the one that goes: 'If you don't like the weather in Greenock, just wait an hour.' But the answer I'd give is that we stack up well against other European ports of call."

"Aye, maybe for a few days in the summer," said Tam. "And you kin count oot the times when the Gourock or Cowal Highland Games are on. It's guaranteed tae be pouring doon then."

"Good weather for much longer than a few days, Tam, and you know it. But summer is long gone, and with this current big storm only beginning, the area being searched is, as the Chief Constable put it, treacherous. The meteorologists are calling it an extra-tropical cyclone. And in the towns, we've got trees down, branches blocking roads, severe flooding, and some power outages. *I hope you are reporting on these conditions in your, erm, blog!*"

Tam knew that he was, unfairly, he thought, nicknamed 'Tam the Bam' (for bampot—idiot), so he decided, against his natural inclinations, to agree with the councillor for a change, rather than being his usual bolshie self.

"Aye, yer right there, cooncillor. Trees doon and everything... Two folks killed, I heard."

Another blogger, Pat Traynor of *Oor Toon, Greenock* spoke up, "Naebody was killed here, Tam. That was in Northern Ireland. Or was it Yorkshire? A tree fell on a car and killed the driver and passenger. But this is one of the worst storms to hit us since the hurricane in... Darn it... I can't remember the date. 1968, maybe? Anyway, I was in Boglestone Primary. We got a week off because the school had to be checked for damage. I remember that the roof blew off the Knights of Saint Columbus social club on Southfield Avenue and landed in somebody's front garden a quarter of a mile doon the road."

"I think you're showing yer age there, pal. If ye were in primary school, ye must hae been 'held back' a few years... like eight years, maybe!" said Tam, unable to resist the chance to aim a barb at a rival blogger.

"Okay, okay! Enough, you two. Please remember why we're here," bellowed Chief Macfarlane, tapping the water glass as before. Then, to councillor Blaney, in a more subdued tone, "Thank you councillor for your support. Now, who do we have? Ah, *STV News...* Moira...?"

"For the record, Chief Constable, of the officers flanking you on the podium, who is in charge of the missing person inquiry?"

The Chief introduced DI Scott as the Senior Investigating Officer, and DS Cameron as his second-in-command. FLO, DS Alison Weir was identified. Then she pointed out Keith Penny, who was in charge of the search teams, and his number two, Grant Wylie.

With the controversial issue of a 'No-Go-Zone' seemingly over and done with, the rest of the conference went as first briefings usually did.

"Will the family be appearing to make an appeal?"

"Possibly. But they are very distressed just now and want to keep their privacy for the time being. However, the family has given out a written statement that will be read out by DS Weir after you have finished with your questions."

This was a clever ploy by the Chief. She knew that they'd all be champing at the bit to hear the statement.

"Could this be a kidnapping?"

"We have ruled nothing out, but we are still at the early stages of our inquiries, and speculation is not encouraged. I ask you all to remember that when you do your reports."

In fact, those on the sex offenders' register were being interviewed as was routine when a child went missing; but Sally didn't want to stir the pot or have vigilantes on the rampage.

"How long did it take for the police to respond?"

"We responded immediately on receiving the 999 call. Protocols for 'Missing Persons—High Risk' were put in action straight away."

"We've heard the police helicopter. Are there dog teams involved in the search?"

"K9 units have been deployed. The search dogs are being directed by expert handlers not only to follow the burn down to the town, but also to search gardens, sheds, and outhouses of residencies they pass."

This was a 'wee white lie' from the Chief. Because of cutbacks, there remained only one dog handler with his German shepherd in Greenock. He was already on the search. However, he was waiting for K9 teams from other divisions to join him. Sally reckoned that they'd be on the job before anyone would notice her fib.

"If Danny isn't found soon, will you be asking for volunteers from the public?"

"For the reasons I stated earlier, the search is being carried out by experienced professionals. What we would ask of the public in the vicinity is that they check their gardens and outhouses. And, of course, that they report any possible sightings to our hotline."

The Chief announced that DS Alison Weir would read out a brief statement from the family.

Alison stood and read from a sheet of paper.

"We, Danny's parents, wish to thank everyone who is helping to find our wee boy. The family has been devastated by his disappearance. Nothing can describe the feelings we are experiencing. If anyone knows of his whereabouts, please, please get in touch with the police, or even the newspapers. Your anonymity will be respected. But just now we ask the press and media for privacy until we can face the cameras with dignity and express our feelings properly. We fully expect that Danny will be found safe and well, and we ask for your prayers toward that end."

The family had probably had help from Alison in drafting the statement. She sat back down.

Chief Macfarlane said, "Thank you DS Weir. And, to the press, I must point out that although Alison is the FLO and is in close contact with the family, she will not be answering questions at this time."

Since this press briefing was being held for a specific reason, Sally would have shut down any off-topic questions right away. Nevertheless, she was relieved that there had been no one pushing their luck—no mention of 'eyeballs', or the murders.

She closed with another request to get the information out to the public, and to let the reporters know that a photograph of Danny was posted on the Police Scotland social media pages, along with a description of what he was wearing when he went missing. And, finally, that physical copies of the MISSING posters were available for those who wanted them, asking them to distribute as many as they could to the public that they might be displayed as widely as possible.

Most took a handful of the posters. Tam waited, and took what was left, saying that he would glue them up to lampposts and have proprietors stick them in shop windows. No doubt, he was trying to polish his reputation. But he'd need a lot of elbow grease!

Sally was also pleased that no one had mentioned the fact that she was *acting* Chief Constable. They all would have been aware that the suspended chief constable Stanley McBride was on 'indefinite leave' while an inquiry was being conducted by another force regarding some shenanigans concerning drug money, and his suspected involvement with drugs kingpins.

He had been placed on what was euphemistically called 'gardening duties' on April 1st, 2021. The date was probably intentional. An anniversary of sorts…

Whether the advent date was by design or by accident, Police Scotland, as an entity, came into being on April 1st, 2013: April Fools' Day!

The previous eight regional police forces in Scotland, as well as the specialist services of the Scottish Police Services Authority, including the Scottish Crime and Drug Enforcement Agency, were merged on this auspicious date. The merger made Police Scotland the second largest police force in the United Kingdom (after the Metropolitan

Police Service) in terms of officer numbers, and by far the largest
territorial police force in terms of its geographic area of responsibility.

Before the merger, Greenock police station was the headquarters
of K Division of Strathclyde Police. And after the merger, it,
unsurprisingly, became the headquarters of K Division, Renfrewshire
and Inverclyde. Officer numbers were usually in the region of
six-hundred and fifty.

———— ◉ ————

HAVING BEEN SPARED any serious grilling from the press because
of Sally's clever handling of the briefing, Scott and Cameron headed
straight for the murder inquiry incident room to catch up with
anything new that might have come in.

As soon as the news broke, there were already a good number of
tips about Danny that had been phoned in or had been sent to the
Police Scotland social media sites, even though these sites had a caveat
posted clearly saying that they were not to be used for such purposes.
Civilian staff were manning the phones and sifting out the wheat from
the chaff.

Most folk were unaware that Police Scotland comprised close to
twenty percent civilian staff, all vital cogs in the machine.

Unlike the Danny line, the murder hotline wasn't exactly being
inundated with calls and information, considering how long it had
been since the first murder. The announcement of a second victim
would surely bring more tips.

Karen Hamilton (no relation to Sandra the DS) had her
wheelchair pulled up tight against her workstation. Karen suffered
from the rare condition arthrogryposis multiplex congenita, often
referred to as AMC, and was one of the most valued members of the
team. Her condition was no great hindrance to her ability to do the
job, and she utilised specially designed technical aids to assist. Most

important was a sophisticated speech-to-text application. She was on the line when the officers arrived.

When she had finished, she swivelled round and turned off the mic.

"Another crank call," she said, shaking her head in disbelief. "What on earth possesses these people? I can often tell right away by slurred speech that I've got a drunk on the line. Of course, that doesn't rule them out... Dutch courage and all that. Then we have the false confessions." She picked up a pile of printed hard copy.

It was rather paradoxical that computerisation was brought in partly to save on paper, but most of the reports had to be printed out for legal reasons, anyway.

"They usually get some stuff right... info that's been in the papers or online... but when it comes to details that only we know, they fall down. And all the while, I need to be discreet and ultra-cautious not to give anything away."

"Oh, I know," said Scott. "A PhD, and a published peer-reviewed paper on criminology, stands you in good stead, Karen. Not to mention you're a devious lady... in a good way, of course."

Karen laughed. "My deviousness was built up working here with you coppers."

Scott smiled and said, "So, Ms Devious, what have you got for us?"

Karen had three small piles of paper stacked neatly on her desk 'In-Trays.' One about an inch high, was labelled 'Improbable'; a middle-size pile, labelled 'Possible'; and a third tiny pile labelled 'Actionable' held only ten sheets.

"'Improbables' went to PCs. And you never know what they might turn up. Serendipity and all that. I have allocated the 'Possibles' to DCs Morris and Chen. You will want the 'Actionable.' She turned on her mic and issued a 'PRINT—FROM—TO' command, and a laser printer whirred into action. Karen retrieved the copies and handed them, still warm from the printing to Scott. Then she did the same for DS Cameron.

"Does that machine make toast?" quipped Pamela.

"*Ha ha!* It gets hot enough; after thirty pages it starts to smoke," said Karen. "Hold on. Another call," she said, then into the microphone on her headset, "Greenock Police station. How can I help you?"

Scott gave Karen a thumbs up, and he and Pamela took their papers to Scott's office for a thorough review.

The questions Karen would ask to assess the veracity of callers were simple 'trip-em-ups':

"What were the girls wearing?" That hadn't been released.

"When you raped her, did you know that her screams were heard by a neighbour?" Neither victim had been raped.

"Where did you kill her?" The girls had not been murdered at the deposit sites.

"How much blood was there?" No blood in either case. The first had not been stabbed; the second had been stabbed post-mortem.

"Did you close their eyes, or leave them open?" This was the kicker, of course. Some said the eyes were staring, others that they were closed, and others still, that they had closed the victim's eyes.

With these and other pertinent questions, Karen could weed out the false confessors, although a record still had to be kept... just in case.

———— ◉ ————

THE GROUND SEARCH WAS called off at four-thirty in the evening as darkness fell and the storm, after a brief lull, descended on Greenock with renewed ferocity, making it impossible for the searchers to continue. Nothing further had been found. No tracks, no snagged or discarded clothing... no body. The Police launch, *Semper Vigilo*, and the Clyde Pilot cutter, *The Cloch*, had been sweeping the coast around where the Beggie burn entered the river. Their powerful searchlights had found nothing so far. They, too, returned to base when it got to where the skippers and crews could hardly see their hands in front of their faces.

Chapter Seven

SCOTT WAS WONDERING if the missing boy might be in any way connected to the murdered girls. The girls had both been discovered at elevated viewpoints, and Beggie hill was another high viewpoint overlooking the Firth of Clyde. It was a popular site for photographers, and also for ramblers. Bikers used it too; both mountain bikers and scramblers who had created an unofficial bike track that led to the town.

However, a murdered four-year-old would be a completely different MO.

Serial killers invariably kept to a pattern. The only reason for such a diversion would be if the killer had some kind of grudge against the Dochertys and either the kidnapping or the murder of Danny was for revenge.

When interviewed, they had been asked the standard question: 'Do you know of anyone who might have wanted to hurt the boy, or anyone who might have a grudge against you?' The answers had been in the negative.

Another line of enquiry was to look into people on the sex register. That was standard procedure when a child went missing. So far, everyone who had been interviewed had provided an alibi for their whereabouts. These types tended to keep verifiable accounts of their movements, knowing that they would be interviewed any time such a crime occurred.

None of the family had criminal records, although granny Hilda had been cautioned once some years previous for public intoxication.

Matt Ross had no record. He had once been a POI in a robbery case, but nothing had been proven. Tommy had a totally clean sheet.

Scott's team was investigating conceivable motive for harm being done to Danny. Until something was found, anything was possible. But nothing stood out until—

———◉———

SHARON LINTON, ONE of the IT analysts, had called DS Hamilton to have a look at something she had discovered on the web, not about the murders, but about Jenny Docherty. Sharon, known as 'the quiet one', was a rather podgy woman in her forties whose long, black, corkscrew hair with broken ends did not suit her age at all. As a civilian analyst, she was tasked with combing through everything IT: web searches, social media, phone logs, and anything else retrievable online regarding persons of interest, POIs.

There was an advantage to having civilian intelligence analysts. Unlike their police counterparts, who can be too focused on facts and evidence, the civilians were more comfortable formulating hypothesis... or as some officers regarded it... 'making wild guesses.' Not feeling constrained by evidential principles, they could come up with off-the-wall suggestions that often proved to be right.

"You got time to look at a couple of Facebook videos?" asked Sharon, pointing to the monitor on her desk.

"As long as it's not cats, or what somebody had for dinner, or 'baby's first potty experience,'" said Sandra with a shrug.

"No, it's from Danny's mother's Facebook. Three weird selfie videos posted on the week before he disappeared."

"Okay," said Sandra, drawing up a chair beside Sharon. "*Roll the tape,* as they say."

In the first video, Jenny Docherty is made up like the late Amy Winehouse, with heavy black eyeliner, turned up cat-like at the outer lashes. Her hair was piled up in an untidy beehive, and her lips were ruby-red.

It's a face and half-body shot, and Jenny is holding a teddy bear... it looked like a Paddington, but the iconic Paddington hat had been removed, and black hair made from thick black knitting wool was crudely added. The bear was wearing yellow wellingtons.

Suddenly, Jenny produced what looked like a long hatpin, and began ferociously stabbing the bear, while making disturbing, aggressive sounds and sometimes even growling.

When she finished, she held the tattered bear up to the camera and used a mime to a clip from the film *Cool Hand Luke,* where the prison captain is berating Paul Newman, as Luke, with:

'What we've got here... is a failure to communicate.'

At that, she stabbed the bear in the eye, leaving the hat pin sticking out. The miming was spot-on and must have been well-rehearsed.

"I've checked the actual clip, and the captain says this to Luke, after he has beaten him across the face with a heavy baton and knocked him into a ditch. It's a very violent and memorable scene, the captain having the most obnoxious voice, and a face only a mother could love," said Sharon.

"Jeez," said Sandra. "That's not the Jenny we've been used to seeing, crying and hysterical over her missing son."

"Hysterical, maybe, but not in the same way."

Sharon played the clip a couple of more times, and the rage and violence were apparent.

"The boots on the bear," said Sandra. "Danny was wearing yellow wellies... that can't be just a coincidence."

"And the black hair."

"Yep. And the black hair," repeated Sandra, looking horrified.

"But there's more," said Sharon, moving on to the next clip. "It's another lip-sync. It seems these kinds of clips are quite popular with social media trendies. I've even seen one of the 'Cellblock Tango' from

Chicago, the full song, mimed by a twelve-year-old girl, the acting perfect, with not a mime out of place. That was chilling coming from such a pretty, innocent face."

Sharon pressed play.

Jenny was made up like the Wicked Witch from *The Wizard of Oz*, green-faced, red-eyed, and quite scary looking. Danny was on her lap dressed as Harry Potter, waving a magic wand, oblivious to his mother's words. For what Jenny was mouthing was not the expected '... and your little dog, too,' quote that has frightened the bejesus out of generations of kids. No, the words were from a gruff male voice, saying: *'And this is the reason I'll be sent to prison.'*

It was a very short clip, but why, the two viewers were asking themselves? Why? And the voice sounded almost demonic. Was the implication that Jenny felt that she would be going to prison because of something to do with Danny?

Next, Sharon played the last clip she had collected from Jenny's Facebook 'acting'. It was just her, no makeup except for the heavy eyeliner, a bit more subdued, and it was a facial close-up. The song she was miming should have been 'Do You Want To Build A Snowman,' from the film *Frozen*. But instead, it was a parody version, *'Will You Help Me Hide A Body?'*

Sharon said, "When I looked that up, the parody clip even has a warning that it is *Dark Wit!*"

"No kidding," said Sandra. "That's from bloody Creepsville!"

"Actually, as I said, it's a parody from *Frozen*," said Sharon, quite seriously.

"I know that!" said Sandra, rolling her eyes. "But Creepsville is my private nightmare place, where everybody's a creep."

"Like the staff canteen?" asked Sharon. The injection of humour didn't take their minds off what they were both thinking. To them... Jenny was now a serious person of interest.

SOCIAL MEDIA WAS ON FIRE. Two teen murders and a missing four-year-old had spiked the public interest, and awareness of the cases was spreading. Social media platforms were humming with rumours, false information, and downright libel. What a handy way to point fingers at an enemy while shielded by perceived anonymity!

For the murders, there was the 'Inverclyde Ripper' meme. For the missing boy, the 'Paedo ring' meme, or 'the parents did it.' Blogs and comments were full of malice, especially toward Danny's mother, Jenny, after someone had written that she had been named as a suspect by the police. One commenter 'revealed' that Jenny was a swinger who was 'into witchcraft.' The swinger part, as it turned out, was true.

The Docherty's sex parties were being compared to *Eyes Wide Shut* and *Rosemary's Baby*. Even *The Omen* had been mentioned, and the reputations of Greenock and Gourock were being sullied by those who had never even been there, with wild talk about *The Wicker Man*, as though the towns were somewhere in the wilds of Scotland.

Someone had reported on the story of an ancient coven that had been linked to the Granny Kempock Stone in Gourock, and the stone's connection to a 'witch', Marie Lamont. She, along with a group of other 'crones' had been burned to death in 1662. Legend had it that the Kempock Stone marked the site where there had been an altar to Baal in Druid times.

Some folks were blaming the Freemasons. The Kempock Stone has Mason's marks carved on it, although stone masons usually only left these marks on their building work, not on rough stone.

Rumours spread that there were Satanic rituals being performed by secret covens in places like the 'mysterious' ancient tower on Tower Hill, or on Craigs Top, another viewpoint overlooking the Firth of Clyde. It has a triangulation pillar that some were saying was being used as a sacrificial altar. In fact, trig pillars are nothing more than concrete pillars, about four feet tall, which were used by the Ordnance Survey to determine the exact shape of the country. And the Tower on Tower

Hill was not 'mysterious'. Its provenance was known. It was built as a study and lookout point. An entry in the OS Name Books of c.1856 says 'the tower was built by the late General Darroch, from which the view obtained of the firth and surrounding scenery is very extensive.'

The ubiquitous Russian mafia were suspects, although no one seemed to know why.

The fictitious 'Great Reset' came into play by those credulous souls who believed that intentional depopulation was being carried out by 'the elites.'

Alien abduction was a favourite theory.

The Traveller community was not left out. After it was discovered that there had been an altercation between an incensed councillor over rubbish being left behind, the Travellers who encamped at Newark Castle for a period every year, were being blamed.

After all, as one non-politically correct bigot had written, 'Gypoes, Tinkies, and Pikies are notorious for kidnapping Townie babies.'

Those of a Nazi bent spouted Nazi propaganda and had managed to re-kindle the odious 'Jewish Blood Libel' accusations.

Other theories were that rogue paedophile Catholic priests were murdering kids to cover up for the Masons (or was it the Jesuits?), secretly holding positions of superior power in the Vatican.

And it just went on and on. Venomous conspiracy theories aimed at just about any group or institution one could think of.

Chapter Eight

GIVEN THE DISCOVERY of the Facebook videos, DS Sandra Hamilton was thoroughly reviewing the statements that had been given by the family and Matt Ross. She was at home in her flat on Brisbane Street, Greenock, with her colleague, DC Michelle Chen. They were both kneeling on the living-room floor of Sandra's apartment. There were papers in wee piles all around them, photocopies of the statements. Sandra thought they could manoeuvre the documents better here than on a cramped table at the station. The two were officially both off duty, but a missing child case usually got special attention, *sans* overtime. It was a tradition.

"The more I read, the fishier it looks," said Sandra. A brunette with a tangle of curls, brown eyes, a nose that turned up at the end just the right amount, and very full lips, Sandra had that most coveted hourglass figure that has been admired since the days of Marilyn Monroe. She was anything but skinny.

Michelle was short and slender, had striking oriental looks, with large almond eyes, and a snub nose. She wore her straight and coal black hair in a 'policewoman's ponytail,' a style that could be tucked up for the wearing of the iconic police bowler. On the beat, it was short hair, or a ponytail. She had chosen the latter. And although now CID, she'd kept the style.

Like many immigrant families, her parents had worked hard, putting in long hours running a chain of Chinese restaurants, but they wanted their daughter to 'do better' than them. She had a Bachelor's degree in sociology and joined the police force after a roommate from college had been raped. Her roommate had committed suicide after a disastrous trial where she had been portrayed as 'easy going, and sexually promiscuous' by a despicable defence lawyer. Only 'doing his job,' of course.

Michelle was also the liaison officer for the extensive and rather parochial Chinese community in Inverclyde.

"Aye," said Michelle, shuffling some papers that were laid on the surrounding carpet. "The timeline doesn't add up, for starters."

"Yep," said Sandra. "And far from being grieving innocents, on closer inspection, each one of them comes across as suspicious. Who do you want to look at first?"

"The granny, Hilda?"

"Agreed," said Sandra. "I believe it's with her that the timeline begins to be manipulated. The whole 'Danny-in-the-garden-with-her-making-tea' scenario is crap. I don't think she saw Danny go out that morning at all. I think that she woke early with a hangover, took some painkillers, washed them down with a 'hair of the dog' then fell sound asleep on a chair in the living room. That is when Danny woke up and went it alone to try out his new rainwear."

Michelle said, "We know that the three-quarter-empty bottle of Martell wasn't kept purely for 'medicinal purposes'; Alison, the FLO, drew our attention to that. We have conformation from neighbours that Hilda is an alcoholic. She is known to be belligerent and often at odds with her neighbours over petty issues. As one neighbour put it, 'Hilda could cause a row in an empty hoose.'

"She even spent a night in the cells once for public intoxication. And, from that report, it seems that Hilda was not a 'happy drunk'. She was lucky not to be charged with more serious offences, including an assault on a police officer. But she went from drunken hellcat at night, to little old granny when she sobered up in the morning, and they let her off with a caution."

"She's got a temper on her alright. One neighbour says that about a month ago, there was some kind of altercation about wheelie bins.

There had been a mixup, and Hilda got the neighbour's bin by mistake. Shouldn't really have mattered, but the neighbour paid for that bin-washing service and wanted her squeaky-clean bin back. There was a row in the street, and Hilda ended up rolling the clean bin at the neighbour, full speed ahead, colliding with her and nearly knocking her off her feet. That incident, technically assault with battery, was never reported to the police, but apparently there have been others. For example, another neighbour was burning garden rubbish, and Hilda had a washing out to dry. Tempers flared then, with Hilda being the more aggressive of the two, throwing a bucket of water on the fire when she had no right to have invaded the neighbour's garden in the first place. Of course, these 'neighbourly' reports are anecdotal and subject to bias, but Hilda is certainly no innocent old gran."

"Talking of wheelie bins," said Michelle, "that shed in the garden was found to have ten bin bags filled with empty booze bottles. Brandy, vodka, whisky, wine... even the old Buckie, Buckfast. Hilda was not a choosey drinker."

"Ha, if my granny wanted to describe somebody like that, she'd say that they would 'drink it through a pishy cloot' where alcohol was involved."

"Huh?" said Michelle, eyebrows raised.

"It means she would drink alcohol through a piss-soaked cloth."

"Well now. That's a saying I must have missed while growing up," said Michelle. "And I kinda think I'm glad I did! *Ha-ha!*"

"Gross, isn't it? My gran was a mill worker at the Gourock Ropeworks, which, curiously, was actually in Port Glasgow. The mill lassies apparently put the 'un' in 'uncouth.'" explained Sandra. "New girls went through an initiation, where they had to pee in a bucket in front of the others.

"Then there was the 'long stand' where they were sent to the office and told to ask for a 'long stand.' The newcomer would think she was being sent for a coat stand or similar. Of course, it was only after she had been standing there for about an hour, nobody answering her repeated questions, that the lassies in the office would let the dupe in on the joke. They had indeed given her *a long stand.*"

"That's actually quite funny," said Michelle.

"And another thing. Because of the noise of the looms, they had a secret sign language to communicate with each other. Male supervisors knew that something was going on behind their backs but were always too slow to turn and catch the clearly sexual innuendo of 'thumb and forefinger held with an inch between them', or the 'hands wide apart separated by about a foot.' Some of us lassies still use those two nowadays, don't we? But here I am rabbiting on about my granny. Let's get back to the granny in question, Hilda Docherty."

"I wonder what she was collecting empty booze bottles for?"

"From what I found out, there's a business that collects empty bottles. You had to have saved a load of them, and then a van comes and collects them, like every two months or something. You get a stamp to stick in your 'savings book,' and there's a catalogue with a load of useless shit you can choose from when you get enough stamps. Kinda like the old cigarette coupon thing. My gran was into that. She got me a 'silver' bracelet that turned my wrist blue."

"Your granny must have been quite a woman."

"Oh, she was. Hardy Scots Irish stock. She smoked like a lum, unfiltered Woodbines, drank like a fish, was always on a 'see food' diet... and would you believe it, she lived to the ripe old age of ninety-two, active until her very last days."

"Incredible!"

"There was a running joke in the family that she was buried in a lead-lined coffin with a lock on it: not to keep grave robbers out, but to keep granny in, *ha ha!*"

"Right, who is next?" asked Sandra, picking up another report. "Mother! Jenny of the dubious Facebook posts."

"Oh my, "said Michelle. "Now, those are creepy as hell."

They were referring to the three homemade selfie videos that Jenny Docherty had posted online, about a week before Danny went missing.

"We have seen those videos played over and over... and that's the conclusion of everyone who has viewed them. Creepy as hell. Nothing she said in her interview raised any red flags. But to be rid of her boy in order to have sex parties, not just that once, but to be rid of this 'nuisance' for ever? It's a horrid thought. Would a mother do such a thing? The answer is yes, it has been done. I'm a fan of True Crime stories on YouTube and in podcasts. And the Casey Anthony case in the States has so many similarities that it's uncanny. In that case the motive was a bit different. A new boyfriend who hates kids. What to do? Maybe the kid must be out of the picture! But the boy disappearing from under the grandmother's nose is the same."

"Oh, I know that case from Court TV. Let's hope the outcome isn't the same, with a skeletonised body of the kid being found months later."

"We're a right pair of true crime buffs, then. As if we don't get enough on the job. But, hey... it's all experience, right?"

"Hah. Going by the comments on some threads you read, there are plenty of folk watching YouTube while they're supposed to be working. I don't think we'd get away with that."

"I don't know about that. As long as it is work related. Remember Pamela saying, 'utilise the internet.'"

"True." Then, out of the blue, Michelle asked, "What time is it?"

"Half nine."

"I'm hungry, are you?"

"I'll rustle up some cheese on toast, or scrambled egg. That's about as far as my culinary skills go."

"Nah, how about getting a takeaway delivered?"

"Okay."

"Fancy a Chinky?" asked Michelle with a cheeky laugh.

"That's racist language," said Sandra, feigning outrage.

"Ah, but it's like the 'N' word in the States. Only the niggers can use it!"

"You are incorrigible."

"We Chinese are often accused of being 'inscrutable,' but I've never found out if that's meant to be a slur or a compliment. I'll take 'incorrigible' any day. And I'll look it up in the dictionary later, so it had best be a compliment. Right, a Chinky it is. What do you fancy?"

After clearing away the food containers, the two officers returned to the analysis of granny, Hilda Docherty, forgetting that they were supposed to have moved on to Jenny.

Michelle asked Sandra, "So, what would we have for motive for her to lie?"

"She was afraid of being charged with neglect and child endangerment. Serious offences. That's why she made out that Danny was in her sight, except for a minute when she went to fetch the kettle," said Sandra.

"You reckon then that Hilda woke for a second time, still in a bit of an alcohol and painkiller haze, only to find that Danny was gone?"

"And it was only then that she phoned Jenny, when she should have called 999 straight away."

"And the salient fact here is that Danny could have taken off, or been taken, much earlier than we were led to believe."

"Exactly," said Sandra. "We know that he loved water. We know that he could hear the roar of the rushing water from the Beggie burn. We know that he wanted to try out his new yellow wellies. It got light at around eight, and he set off on his adventure like Dick Whittington."

"Definitely a plausible scenario. Plus, she'd desperately want to hide the fact that she was a 'morning drunk.'"

They both took a minute to make some notes.

"Next?" asked Michelle.

"The dad, Thomas. Tough looking character with a foul temper, and a dislike for the police. The story is that when Jenny got the call from Hilda, she called him, Thomas, then went to Matt's house where Thomas was... doing what? I don't see any reference to anyone having asked what he was doing there."

Michelle said, "Right. That stood out to me. Did he know that Matt was Hilda's booze supplier du jour and was there to buy?"

"And if he knew about Hilda's drink problem, why trust her with the care of Danny?"

"Their story is that Danny was to stay overnight with Hilda, because Thomas and Jenny were hosting 'a wee pairty fur adults only.'"

"They definitely were swingers, then? God, what a family," said Sandra, adding, "not that there's anything wrong with that," and offering Michelle a wink and a smile.

Michelle made a finger-down-the-throat gesture accompanied by a boaking sound. "As long as they're adults and consenting, I suppose. But you've got to admit, Sandra, erm, they're not exactly a good-looking pair."

"It's the kink, I suppose. Who knows what the guests looked like? *Eyes Wide Shut,* you know? Or maybe masks like the Venetian balls?"

"Uh, I had chicken balls with my sweet and sour. Noo, we're on to Venetian balls. Bag over the head, more like."

"Or keep the lights out. 'It's better in the dark,' as that Hamish Imlach song goes."

"Never heard of it. Anyway, this is becoming like an Agatha Christie where everyone has means, motive, and opportunity. Everyone involved is a suspect," said Michelle. "Which brings us to 'Mr Comb-over' then, wee Matt. You know he's been arrested, right?"

"Aye, it's nae wonder he looked like he was shitting his pants, as Alison, the FLO, described his demeanour in the granny's house that morning. When he was told that a police car had been stationed outside his house, and that a routine search would have to be made, he turned white as a ghost apparently," said Sandra. "And here we get to the great Martell robbery.

"Stacked at the back of his garage, behind a row of empty Amazon boxes, they found two dozen cases of the brandy... or is it cognac? Nae matter. The way he was escalating, he was well on his way to trying a Brink's Mat type bullion robbery."

"*Ha-ha*. That would be a Brink's 'Matt' robbery," said Michelle, using finger quotes around the 'Matt.'

"Funny one! But after him and a pal successfully hijacked a Morton's rolls van and realised that bread rolls have... surprise, surprise... a short sell-by date, they moved up a level to robbing a meat delivery van. Bringing home the bacon, you might say. Then, to their latest heist... a delivery van from a cash-and-carry delivering booze to local clubs and pubs. They went for the Martell because they thought it was the most expensive. Probably true."

"I remember the hilarity that the great Morton's rolls heist caused. We were all saying, 'the buggers will steal anything in Greenock, even yer morning roll's no' safe.'"

"Aye, and that's not to mention the seagulls."

"Right. They pests will grab a roll right out of your hand as you go to take a bite."

"I told you not to mention them," joked Michelle.

"Well, the seagulls of Greenock, Gourock, and Largs are so infamous that Alistair MacLean even wrote that book about them."

"Huh?"

"Aye. *Where Seagulls Dare!*"

"Ouch! What a rubbish joke! Seriously, though. Do you think Matt is connected to Danny's disappearance?" asked Sandra.

"Well, he's going to be given the third degree while he's in custody," said Michelle.

Chapter Nine

SMASH!

The battering ram, called 'The Enforcer' or 'The Big Red Key', was wielded by a burly officer and breached the door with one heavy blow.

"Police! This is a raid. We have a warrant. Stay where you are and do not move!" The order was repeated three times as six police officers pushed their way into the flat. Armed only with drawn batons, they threw open internal doors, repeating the warning at each.

The time was 05:50, and it was still dark on the Greenock high street. Conditions were ideal for a raid. Visibility was down to a few hundred feet as the high winds and torrential rain whipped down the street, the buildings on either side acting as a funnel. The street was empty of people and traffic, and the two police vans had arrived in stealth mode. The top-story residential flat that was being raided was above two shops... a barbershop and an estate agent. Officers quickly located light switches, and the rooms were illuminated. In a cramped bedroom, a woman let out a piercing scream to be answered by:

"Police! Stay where you are. We have a warrant to search these premises."

The woman who had screamed was sitting up in bed, a duvet pulled up to her neck to hide her nakedness. Beside her was a man, his hands clasped behind his head, leaning back against the headboard, smirking as though he hadn't a care in the world.

He looked to be in his early thirties. He was thin, but muscular with a defined 'six pack'. He had tousled black hair, cut 'short back and sides', and his arms and torso were covered with black-inked Celtic and Maori tattoos.

She was slim with long dishevelled blonde 'bedhead' hair. And it looked like she had gone to bed with her makeup on; her mascara was running.

"By the sound of it, I guess I'll be needing a new door. You gonna let us get dressed or are ye up fir a peep show?" he said, still grinning.

A robust policewoman said, "You can both get dressed in front of me and my partner. We don't want you hiding any evidence now, do we?"

"Aye, and whit are you, darlin'? You a carpet muncher, or are you straight an' want a look at my cock? It's getting hard already. Kinky, I am, aboot wimmin in uniform," he said, laughing now.

"Well, big boy, I've got just the thing, here on my utility belt that'll soon fix your problem." She patted her holstered taser. "It packs 50,000 volts. I'm sure it would soon de-bone your boner."

The female officer's partner, a lanky lad with a fresh face, said nothing, hoping that he looked intimidating. He didn't.

"Is that a threat?" asked the man with a cheeky grin.

"One wrong move from you, boyo, and it's a promise!" said the genuinely intimidating female, a heavily built sergeant who had worked in the prison service before joining the police. She was used to idiots with their false bravado. "You can turn your backs and I'll throw you some clothes. That's the best we can do."

"Oh, prefer the arse view. I get it."

"Don't push your luck. It's damned cold out there; but if you want to be marched out to the van butt naked, we can oblige."

The smartass complied with the dressing arrangements.

In the hallway, after the arrests had been made, Chief Inspector John Wallace was delighted with how the raid had gone down. He was wearing a stab vest, as were all his officers, and he sported a black waterproof jerkin with attached epaulettes, the three silver pips showing his rank. Unlike his officers, he didn't wear a hi-viz tabard. As he had surveyed the flat a few minutes ago, he had been amazed at just how much cannabis was being grown under hot-lamps and fed by a makeshift hydroponics system. And there was evidence of crystal meth being cooked; not to mention rolled up wads of cash tied with elastic bands that were stashed in all sorts of unlikely places.

"Good job, team!" he exclaimed. "This is a worthy bust. When we get a tally, this lot will probably amount to over ten grand. Plus, everything went over smoothly, with two apprehensions, and no injuries to officers or perps. Pub tonight... twenty-hundred-hours... first round is on me!"

There was an approving round of applause from his team... whether for the bust, or the impending booze-up, he wasn't sure.

Chapter Ten

AFTER HAVING BEEN SHOWN the strange video mimes created by Jenny Docherty, Scott assigned DS Hamilton and DS Weir to pay her a visit under the guise of a welfare check. They were to wait until they were sure that Thomas was out of the house, and Jenny was on her own.

Thomas left at nine in the morning. At half-past, Alison and Sandra were let in out of the storm by a dishevelled Jenny Docherty.

"I have nae had time to get myself ready," said Jenny. She was still in her jammies and had on a grubby pink-towelling dressing gown.

"Want me to make you a cuppa? Tea or coffee?" asked Alison.

"Oh, that would be great, hen. There's a jar of Nescafé in the cupboard. And that powdered milk stuff. Put two sweeteners in mine, would you?"

Alison went into the kitchen. Jenny was fumbling with a packet of cigarettes.

"I need ma nicotine fix," she said, then as an afterthought she asked, "Is that okay with you?"

Sandra said, "It's your house, Jenny. I've been on that nicotine chewing gum; trying to give up the ciggies. I think I could go a wee fly puff myself." She put her hand in her coat pocket to fish out her cigarettes.

"Here... take one of these," said Jenny, passing a packet of Silk Cut to Sandra while lighting up. She leaned across and lit Sandra's cigarette. They both took a long drag and exhaled with satisfaction.

"Ahh, that's better," said Sandra. "I don't know if I'll ever quit the habit."

Rapport building. That's what Sandra was doing. Putting Jenny at ease and gaining her confidence.

"I always say, 'I've stopped smoking... hundreds of times,'" said Jenny with a throaty laugh.

Alison came in with a tray on which there were three steaming mugs of coffee. She put it on the table, then dipped into her handbag and brought out a packet of custard creams. "Help yourself to a bickie, Jenny."

"Thanks," said Jenny, taking one. "Very thoughtful of you."

Alison went through her welfare-check spiel.

"Have you been able to sleep?"

"I got some sleeping pills from the doctor," said Jenny. "But I only used one. It left me groggy after I woke up. I don't want to be doped up. I want to be *compos mentis* in case... in case..."

It was clear to the two officers that the tears were real as Jenny cried. She wasn't putting it on. She was genuinely bawling her eyes out.

"We understand, Jenny," said Alison, passing Jenny a box of tissues that were on the coffee table. "You mustn't give up hope. The search teams are far from finished."

"But it was freezing out there last night," said Jenny.

"Look Jenny, Danny may not even be up on the hill. It's more likely that he followed the burn down, and saw the houses lit up and the streetlights as it got dark. He might have crawled into somebody's shed and fallen asleep. That's why we have officers doing door-to-doors. And an appeal has been put out for people to check their sheds and outhouses."

Jenny seemed to perk up a bit at this thought.

Then she asked, "But what about hypothermia?"

Sandra said, "The human body has amazing resilience. There's a mysterious reaction called the 'mammalian survival mechanism.' I'm not an expert, but as far as I know, in certain conditions of extreme cold, the body, especially that of a child, can go into a state of hibernation, or suspended animation to preserve life."

Sandra had only heard about this phenomenon from someone else. There was a case where an unwanted baby had been dumped in a snowdrift in freezing conditions off the side of a road. The baby was found, and the doctor that attended pronounced with absolute certainty that life was extinct. The baby was put in a body bag and taken to the morgue. However, the subsequent autopsy found that the baby had actually been alive, but in suspended animation, when it was put in the sealed-up bag. It had died from suffocation in the body bag. It was a perturbing case that had stuck in Sandra's memory since she had been told about it. But she sure as hell wasn't going to tell Jenny that story.

When Jenny had calmed down somewhat, and after some more mundane conversation, it was Alison who dropped the bombshell after encouraging Jenny to have another custard cream. That ploy was used to put the person being surreptitiously interrogated off their guard.

"Jenny, we don't want to upset you any more, but something has come up in our enquiries that I'd like you to explain. It's about some selfie videos you posted on your Facebook page about a week ago."

Jenny exploded.

"So, this is why you're here. Welfare check my aunt fanny!" She jumped up and pointed her finger at Alison.

"You... you're supposed to be a support officer, and all you are is a fucking spy. Your folk went through this house from top to bottom. They even inspected my underwear drawer. They made sure to tell me they'd found some sex toys. So what? I told them. Tommy and me are sexually experimental. We're swingers, yeah. But so what?"

"We're just trying to clear up, erm... an anomaly. Those mime-over selfies were strange, Jenny. People even posted comments about you being into witchcraft, you being a demon, even suggesting that Danny has been sacrificed by a coven you're a member of," said Alison.

Jenny was still shouting, "Did you even check the web for mime-along clips? It's a fucking hobby, you know... a challenge to get it spot on. There are probably hundreds or thousands of mimes the same as mine. Some are much more gory."

"People have hobbies like knitting, or jigsaw puzzles, or doing crosswords, Jenny," said Sandra. "These videos of yours seem to people to be sinister... considering what happened. You must see that yourself?"

"So, folk think I sacrificed my son to the devil. And you two believe that is even possible. Well, I'm done! Get the fuck out... the two of you!" shouted Jenny.

"We had to..." began Alison.

"Out! Out! Out!" screamed Jenny, pointing to the door. "And if you want any more from me, I'll want my solicitor present. Got it?"

The two detective sergeants 'got it' okay. They left without saying another word.

"And fuck your custard creams!" shouted Jenny, as the packet of biscuits hit the door as it closed behind them.

"So, that went well," said Sandra to Alison, who was driving the car back to the station.

"You know what, Sandra?" replied Alison. "In a way, it did go well. Look at how quickly the grieving mother could turn into a screaming banshee."

"Yeah. Quite a temper, huh? Do you think that temper could lead her to do something to Danny... maybe accidental, maybe deliberate? Was the wee boy cramping their lifestyle?"

"Hmm. I'm not sure, Sandra. But one thing I am sure of is that Mrs Jenny Docherty deserves more scrutiny."

"Agreed," said Sandra. "By the way, do you believe in witchcraft and witches?"

"Believe in them? I even know some... white witches, that is. Wiccans, they like to be called. I nearly joined a coven when I stayed on the Isle of Arran years ago. The ancient standing stones on Machrie Moor attract pagans on the four Celtic holy days."

"Nearly joined?"

"Ah, well, I decided it was too damned cauld in Scotland to go dancin' aboot in the scuddy at Hallowe'en."

They both laughed at the thought of it and made jokes about the state of tits and willies when exposed outside in the freezing cold.

———◉———

THE VOICE ON THE PHONE was that of a young girl, obviously Scottish, with a broad west-of-Scotland accent. In Glasgow and its surrounds, even the patois had a patois name: they called it 'the Patter.'

"Have ye got the dough?"

"I can't get the amount you want. The bank would flag that up. A person can't just go to a bank and withdraw ten-thousand pounds without being under scrutiny." The man's voice was polite, with a cultured Scots accent, and he sounded either angry or nervous.

"It's ten fuckin' grand, or nae deal. Ten grand, or I go to the polis."

"You'll need to give me another week. I'll try to liquidate some of my assets."

"Ye kin liquidise yer erse shite in a blender, for a' I care. You got one mair day. Then, nae mair stallin' or I'm going to report that I was raped."

The phone went dead.

The little bitch is giving me an ultimatum! he thought. The first two were easy. Dirty little junkie whores. What made them think a man like me, a decent man, an educated man, a professional man, would sink so low as to be wanting to have sex with them? An offer of twenty pounds for oral sex in the back of my car. That's all it took. Then... they were mine.

Chapter Eleven

INTERVIEW ROOM THREE, Greenock police station.

"THE TIME is 9 a.m. and I am Detective Constable John Hammerman, and with me is DC Richard Toomey. This interview is being conducted with the suspect, Mr Matthew Ross. Mr Ross has been advised of his rights and has not requested a solicitor so far. The interview is being recorded on video and audio. Will you state your full name for the record, please?"

"Matthew Ross."

"Your full name, please." He knew Matt's full name, but he just wanted to hear him say it.

"Matthew Algernon Ross."

"And please confirm for the record that you have been read your rights, and you have not requested that a solicitor be present to act on your behalf. And that you are aware that you may end this interview at any time and request counsel."

"Aye, that's right. An innocent man disnae need a brief," said Matt.

"Okay, thank you Mr Ross, now I'd..."

Matt interrupted, "Look, ye kin caw me Matt, an' stop fuckin' aboot wi the 'Mister' shite."

"Very well, Matt. And you can call me Detective Constable Hammerman, or sir... okay?"

Matt just shook his head at the officer. "Whatever, mate!"

"On the day your home was searched in connection with the missing boy Danny Docherty, you were present when our officers found a quantity of stolen brandy, correct?"

"Cognac," said Matt. "And I didnae know it wis nicked. I got it frae a pal that told me it had fell off the back of a lorry."

"Well, that phrase, in and of itself, implies 'stolen', does it not?"

"It implies 'fell off the back of a lorry', like maybe it went over a big bump, or took a corner too fast. That's all it implies."

"Come now, Mr... erm, Matt. You don't expect us to believe that the goods in question literally fell off a lorry. The phrase is a well-known euphemism for 'stolen', is it not?"

"I'd say it wis a roon aboot way of talking... a circumlocution. You numpties can look that one up later. But anyways, I'm no gonna admit I knew the gear was nicked. To me, it wis jist a bargain. I thought he'd maybe got it frae France at one of them Booze Cruises to Calais super-marts where booze is cheap. I didnae ask for details. You dinnae look a gift horse in the mouth, right?"

DC Toomey spoke up. "We have a witness, the driver of the van, who gave us a full description of one of the hijackers. That description matches you perfectly, Mr Ross. It seems that in the heat of the moment, even though you wore a hat that hid your, erm, distinctive hair, your 'Billy the Kid' mask slipped, and the driver got a good look at your face. He's willing to pick the perpetrator out of a line-up."

Hammerman added: "And don't forget, Matt, this is an armed robbery we're talking about. You and your mate, who has already confessed and named you as the planner and instigator, are facing twenty years in Barlinnie. You were both armed with baseball bats and knives. We have your fingerprints on the van door."

"That's no possible. I was wearing..." Matt stopped abruptly, realising his mistake.

"... Gloves. You were wearing gloves, Matt. And, clumsily, you managed to cut the finger of your gloved hand. That left more than enough blood for a DNA sample which is being tested at the lab as we speak. We're talking a hefty sentence here... not a rap on the knuckles. So, what have you got to say to that?"

"I want a solicitor," said Matt.

Chapter Twelve

MATT ROSS HAD BEEN moved to interview room number one, at Greenock police station, after having been given a toilet break, a cup of sweet, milky tea, and a bite to eat.

Albert Graham was the duty solicitor who attended when Matt had requested council. He was an overweight, unkempt man, with a head of black greasy hair, rheumy eyes, two double-chins, and he had a bit of toilet paper with a dot of blood stuck to his cheek where he'd cut himself shaving. He wore a shapeless grey suit, and the jacket's bump at the back collar showed that he slumped a lot.

The interviewing officers now were DI Scott and DS Sandra Hamilton. This was one of the serious occasions that warranted senior officers to be conducting the interview.

It amazed Scott that so many of the folk that he had arrested talked about summoning 'their' solicitor, when very few actually had a solicitor. Those that did, invariably referred to Beltrami, a famous but now deceased Glasgow defence lawyer who had a reputation for getting his clients off. The firm continued under the Beltrami name, Beltrami & Co, and criminals thought that the name, alone, would intimidate police and prosecutors.

Sandra's nose twitched.

Women have a significantly better sense of smell than men do, because they have so many more neurones in the olfactory bulbs in their brains.

Body odour. Aye, Matt was nervous, but her sniffer-dog nose traced the smell to the unkempt solicitor, Albert Graham. It was excessive, even though she was used to being in the company of sweaty and testosterone-fuelled male police officers. She shot him a quick look of disapproval but said nothing. The man was blissfully unaware that he stank to the high heavens.

Sandra began, "Previously, Mr Ross, you admitted to the theft of cases of cognac. Now that we've told you that your DNA has been collected from the crime scene, your partner in crime has confessed, and named you as the instigator, and the van driver has positively ID'd you: what do you have to say now?" asked Sandra in a monotone voice.

"You lot are allowed to lie in an interview. How dae I know you're no making shit up, like?" He looked at his lawyer, who just shook his head.

After a brief pause, Matt went on, "Okay. I'll cop to the robbery. But not to the 'armed' bit."

"You were in possession of a knife... a very illegal commando-style knife. We recovered that knife from your garage. You dropped it in an oil drum. But our ever-resourceful SOCOs fished it out. The oil did not destroy fingerprints and DNA. You committed armed robbery; you have been charged with armed robbery. Understand?" said DI Scott.

"Ye kin prove it in court! I'm no admitting to armed anything, understand?" said Matt defiantly.

Sandra leaned over and whispered in Scott's ear, "Cocky wee bastard, isn't he?"

"I'm sorry. I didn't hear that. Could you repeat what you said for the recording?" objected the smelly brief.

"Oh, I was just saying to the Inspector that the clock almost seems to be ticking faster," said Sandra. "It's a misperception brought about by the environment of a closed, rather claustrophobic interview room. I mean, you can almost *smell* the tension."

"Just so," said the solicitor, fully oblivious to the sarcasm. "But I would appreciate it if all comments were discernible."

"Well, discern this, Mr Graham. The stolen cognac has led us to a much more serious crime, and I'm moving on to question your client about that now," said the Inspector.

"What... what do you mean 'a more serious crime'?" blustered the solicitor, his face reddening.

"We'll come to that. If you'd care to follow along," said Scott.

The solicitor's face looked like it was about to explode, and Sandra had visions of Mr Creosote, the exploding fat man in a Monty Python sketch. "My objection goes to relevance, Inspector."

"Oh, it's relevant to the stolen cognac, as you will see," said Scott.

A shrug from the solicitor.

Matt was becoming fidgety. The custody sergeant had told Scott that, cocky as he pretended to be, every time he had opened the hatch and looked into Matt's cell, the prisoner had been wide awake, pacing, or banging his head on the thin blanket of his cell bed. The sergeant had been forced to intervene on more than one occasion, and he'd said that Matt was tearful and highly distraught. Of course, going down on an armed robbery charge could cause that type of behaviour. But Scott now knew it was more than that... much more.

Scott continued, "You were involved with the initial search for the missing boy, Danny Docherty, before the police were called. True?"

Matt's face was flushed. He looked at his solicitor for guidance.

"I object to the course this interview is taking. I cannot see how you can move from stolen cognac to a missing boy. There is no logical connection to be made. Your line of questioning is not relevant to the charges you are bringing against my client," said the solicitor.

"New facts have come to light, Mr Graham, and, as I said before, I can assure you that we will prove relevance as we outline the fresh charges," said Scott.

Graham harrumphed but indicated with a lazy hand signal for Scott to go on.

"Do you own a green parka, one from North Face... specifically of the design Men's Artic Parka?"

The blood drained from Matt's face.

"Erm... aye... that is, I used to," said Matt. "North Face, aye. Dunno aboot the other bit."

"An expensive piece of gear at what? About three-hundred quid. Or did that fall off the back of a lorry too? No matter, do you know where that parka is now?"

"I... I hung it up on a coat stand in a pub. Aye... noo I remember. Some bastard stole it." Matt's hands were visibly shaking. He put them down between his legs, clamping them tight.

"So, you didn't report the theft of such an expensive item? What would you say if I tell you that very parka was found under a pile of rocks and covered by bushes, tree limbs, and bracken at the top of Beggie Hill? What would you say if I told you that, wrapped in that parka, we recovered the body of Danny Docherty? What would you...?"

Matt broke down in hysterics and began banging his head on the table. "No, no, no... not wee Danny. He was ma pal. It cannae be..."

"Restrain him, constable," Scott signalled to the PC, who was standing guard inside the interview room door.

Matt was physically held back by his shoulders, but he continued to weep and bawl. His solicitor threw his own head back and stared at the ceiling, as if in realisation that this was going to be more than an armed robbery case.

"You may feign surprise, Mr Ross, but I put it to you that this information comes as no surprise. I put it to you that you were responsible for the boy's kidnapping and death. Read the caution, please, DS Hamilton," said Scott.

Sandra read the formal caution. It had been given to Matt when he was first arrested, and again before the interview. But it had to be given again with the fresh charges. No chances were to be taken.

"Matthew Algernon Ross, I am arresting you for the kidnapping and murder of four-year-old Daniel Docherty. You do not have to say anything, but it may harm your defence if you do not mention when questioned, something that you later rely on in Court. Anything you do say may be given in evidence."

"Do you understand the caution, Mr Ross?" asked Sandra.

No reply.

"Do you understand...?"

Matt murmured in a plaintive tone, face buried in his hands. Yet, all present heard him say, "Aye, I understand." Then louder, more tearful. "But it was an accident. It was a crazy, stupid accident!"

Scott gave Matt a moment to collect himself, then went on, "Two of the houses in Beggie Road have iRing cameras. One has CCTV that records onto a dedicated disk. So, we know that on the night before Danny's disappearance, your car was parked outside Mrs Hilda Docherty's house at 5, Beggie Road. How about you take it from there?"

"I advise my client to say nothing more," said Graham.

"You go fuck yerself'. You're dismissed... and go get yourself a shower. You are totally minging, man."

"I..." began Albert.

"Just go!" shouted Matt.

Scott, eyes wide and brow furrowed, just shrugged, looking directly at the brief.

The man now seemed more concerned about himself than about his client. He lifted an arm and sniffed an armpit. Then the other arm. Seemingly satisfied that he smelled of roses, he got up without uttering a word, and left the room. Discretely, Sandra took a small bottle of perfume from her pocket and spritzed the back of her wrists.

"Let the record show that Mr Ross has dismissed his solicitor. Do you wish to request another?" said Scott.

"No. I've got to get this off my chest."

"So, the night before, at Hilda Docherty's…" prompted Scott.

"I was delivering a bottle of Martell. We had an argument aboot the price. She's a stingy old witch. And she cannae stand me. She damned well hates me, but she still gets me to bring her booze. She laughs at my hair. Says why don't I be a man and get rid of the comb-over? She says she knows I'm a paedophile. That's just because I train an under-twelves five-a-side team. That's just no true, and you kin ask the boys.

"But the old bitch keeps on about it. She says to Danny, 'Don't you sit on his lap, Danny. And don't let him touch you. He's a bad, wicked man.'

"Danny knows that's no true. He was mair frightened of Hilda than he was of me. I cannae prove it. But I think she beat the wee guy… I saw her one time, giving him a hard slap on the leg. Left a red mark, that did."

Sandra said, "We'll make a note of that, Mr Ross."

"Like I said, there was a bit of an argument over the price, so I quoted her rock-bottom. She went to get the money. She keeps all her dough in a bag under the mattress in her bedroom. She thinks nobody knows that. So, Danny comes to me to show me his new top boots. He tells me his granny won't let him try them out… in a puddle, like.

"So, I thought. I know how I can teach the old bitch a lesson. Me and Danny hatched a plot, see. When he went to bed that night, he was to make sure he had his parka, a snorkel he called it, and wellies in his room. I told him I'd knock on the window, quiet like, early in the morning, and he was to unlatch it, and I'd sneak him out so he could splash about in the puddles.

"I knew he'd be chuffed to go with me to see the burn… you could already hear the roaring water from the back of the house. And it was still pouring doon with rain, so I reckoned it would be spectacular by the morning.

"I was only going to teach Hilda a lesson. I intended to let her get a panic on, then I'd return with the boy after a while.

"I'm surprised your ace coppers didn't notice that the bedroom sash window was unlatched. Because I only pulled it doon frae the ootside."

"Okay. Noted," said Scott, frowning and eliciting a nod from Sandra. "Go on, please... you hatched this plan with Danny. I assume you carried it out the next morning?"

"You know, the rain was that heavy, and the storm was getting worse. I nearly didn't go. But I didn't want to disappoint the wee fella. So, I thought I'd tap his window and tell him it was far too stormy for him to come out.

"I put on that green parka, pulled on waterproofs over my trousers, put on my hiking boots with gaiters and headed off. I didn't take my car. It's only a twenty-minute walk from my place to Hilda's.

"It was fair chucking it doon, and a strong wind had got up. I was soaked by the time I got to Beggie Road. I sneaked round to Danny's bedroom window, hoping he'd still be sleeping, and would have forgot aboot the plan. I gave the window a wee tap. It was slid open by Danny. He had only managed to push the window up about six inches, and foolishly, I pushed it open more to give him the bad news.

"There he was, all dressed for the weather, bright eyed and bushy tailed. I'd told him the night before to get well wrapped up. He'd certainly done that. He had on a woolly balaclava, and a hoodie with the hood up over that, and then his snorkel hood over that to top it all off. He had corduroys troosers tucked in his yellow wellies. And he was wearing woolly mittens. I turned round to point out to him how stormy it was, and before I knew it, he'd scrambled out and landed at my feet. Before I could grab him, he made a dash for the fence, beckoning me to follow. I pulled the window doon shut and ran after him."

"What time do you think this was?" asked Sandra.

"I know I'd planned to arrive at eight in the morning; so round about then... maybe a bit later... but nae mair than ten minutes."

Sandra gave Scott an 'I-told-you-so' look. The timeline, according to Hilda, was way off. Scott nodded his agreement.

"I caught up with him, just beyond the fence," continued Matt. "He held out his hand for me to take it, and I made the stupid decision to plod on to the burn. I was scared that if I tried to pull him back, he might go into hysterics and wake the whole neighbourhood."

He said this as though this was the only stupid decision in the whole crazy scheme.

"You know what it's like back there. A tangle of bushes, brambles, long grass, tree roots... the lot. I held tight onto his hand. He was getting more excited the nearer we got to the sound of the burn. He was actually pulling me along. Being small, it was easier for him to duck under the obstacles.

"I'll let him see the burn, then take him straight back," I thought.

"When we got to the burn, it was overflowing its banks. The water was gushing down the incline, brown and foaming, even carrying some fair-sized branches and all kinds of debris. We were standing well back from the bank, up on a wee knoll overlooking the torrent. I held Danny's hand firmly. He was jumping, literally, jumping with joy. Suddenly, he pulled his hand away from mine, leaving me holding a mitten. I was relieved that he bolted away from the burn and up the embankment a bit. My heart was pounding. He got himself up on an enormous boulder. He was doing a 'muscle man' kind of flexing of his arms. 'I'm the king of the castle' sort of thing.

"The boulder was wet and covered in moss. Before I could get to him, he slipped. He slipped onto his bum first, and I was going to laugh. But he kept going, and I saw his head hit the boulder hard. I ran to the spot.

"When I got to him, I pretty much knew he was dead. His eyes were rolled back in his head. I took my parka off and laid him on it. I tried CPR... for what seemed like ages. But there was no pulse at his wrist or at his neck. He was totally limp. No breath from his mouth, no heartbeat at his chest. I checked the back of his head. There was no blood—not even a bruise that I could see."

Sandra said, "The autopsy revealed that his skull was fractured. A comminuted fracture: bleeding was internal. That's what killed Danny."

Matt Ross stared at her. His eyes had a haunted look, and tears welled up again.

"Do you want to take a break, Mr Ross?" asked DI Scott. Sandra realised that Matt was staring past her, not at her, as if he was envisioning the scene by the burn.

"Wha... no, no..." said Matt with a start, like he'd just been woken from a nightmare.

"I, erm, I didn't know what to do. My mind was reeling, adrenaline pumping. If I take him back, I thought, I'll be accused of kidnapping him and bashing his head in. No one would believe my story.

"So, I took off his yellow boots, and put them into the burn... right at the edge, hoping they'd get caught on the bank further down. One did. The other kept going."

Scott asked, "What about his red sou'wester hat? What happened to that?"

"Hat? He wasn't wearing a hat," said Matt, looking confused.

The two detectives looked at one another. Sandra noted in her legal pad: 'No red sou'wester hat. Proof that Hilda Docherty was lying with her description of events that morning.'

"Sorry, go on please," she said.

"I wrapped Danny's body in my parka and hefted him on my shoulder. He was hardly any weight at all. I scrambled to the top of Beggie Hill. There was a kind of crevice. I laid him in there, and covered the body with stones, and then branches with a covering of ferns. There were plenty of broken branches, with the storm, like. I left him wrapped in my parka. I had a crazy thought that I didn't want... I didn't want him to be cold. I was out of my mind."

"Your ploy of sending the boots down the burn worked. It was a dog handler who thought that to be thorough, he'd search upstream. It was counterintuitive on his part. Nobody thought that a boy that age on his own, as was the belief at that time, would climb *up* the hill. He'd head downhill for the house lights that were in view in the distance downstream. Furthermore, because of the cold, wet parka, and since you had covered the body with freezing cold stones and wet branches and ferns, the helicopter FLIR didn't pick up a heat signature," said Scott.

"It wisnae a ploy. That's not why I did those things. I panicked. I wasn't thinking straight," Matt said.

"So, you were soaked, covered in mud..."

"I took the shortcut from the top of the hill... you know, the one that's been created by the scrambler bikes? It took me almost right to the back of my house.

"I hopped the fence and intended to have a shower. But my phone was ringing. Caller ID told me it was Tommy. Of course, I knew why he'd be calling, so I answered it. He told me Danny was missing, and he was on his way to pick me up to help look for the boy.

"I told Tommy I'd be in my garage, and I'd put on some cold-weather gear, and I'd help him. So, I ran round to the garage, quickly washed my hands and face in the sink there and pulled on a one-piece boiler suit over my wet, muddy clothes. An anorak over the boiler suit, and I discarded my boots, and had just put my feet into my wellingtons, when I heard Tommy's car horn out front. I should have confessed then and there. But, knowing Tommy, I thought he'd never believe the story. He might have beaten me to death. I needed time to think. So, I joined him, knowing full well that I could have taken him to the body. But I didn't.

"That's it. That's the whole story, so help me God. I kidnapped Danny, but I didn't murder him... well, I suppose I did, in a way... didn't

I?" He broke into loud sobbing, his shoulders heaving, tears pouring down his cheeks.

"That will be up to the procurator fiscal to decide," said Scott.

Danny cried out, "If we still had hanging in Scotland... I'd be glad of it. I'd be glad to be punished righteously. I deserve it. I deserve to be hung." He pounded his fists on the table, giving Ross and Cameron a bit of a start.

Sandra made a note. 'Matthew Ross... suicide watch!'

Chapter Thirteen

—◦—

THERE IS A SCOTS WORD, 'bealin'; it can mean hot and festering, angry, and sometimes boiling.

Well, today, Malky Boone was fair 'bealin'.

"Hae ye all seen this?" He was holding up his iPad, turned toward his cronies, that showed a résumé of the top story from the *Greenock Telegraph* website edition:

POLICE have smashed an £82k cannabis farm which was operating right in the middle of Greenock town centre.

Local officers pounced after they were tipped off about possible drug cultivation within a building on the high street.

"Noo, ye see that last bit? Ye see they words, 'after they were tipped off.' There's a fuckin' clype oot there, men. A stoolie, a snitch, a grass... ye understand?"

"Somebody grassed on the grass guy. That's bad, Malky. You get your shit frae him?" Gordon Bryce was the first to talk, while the others shook their heads, tutted, and jesused and fuck-saked.

"I dinna tell anybody where I get ma stuff, Gordo. Ye should fuckin' know that!"

"Aye, right big man. Sorry!" said Gordo.

"And... eighty-two fuckin' grand, my hairy Scot's arse. Lucky if it wis a tenth of that. Fuckin' polis. Crooks and liars, lads. Never forget that. The pork chops are a bunch of fuckin' crooks and liars."

The assembled lieutenants all nodded in agreement, Gordo giving a hand over bent elbow salute to "fuck the pigs!"

"But hear this!" Malky went on. "It's the principle of the thing. Okay, Joe Cunningham and that stupid bitch shacking up with him were askin' to get busted. Growin' their ain weed in the toon centre! And cookin' a bit of meth as weel. Fuckin' fruitcakes. But I hid to gie him credit for his brass baws. Joe thought that the polis would think nobody would be stupid enough to run drugs frae a flat right in the middle of the toon.

"And he was right, in a way. If he hidnae got grassed up, he'd probably still be supplying me... er, forget I said that... he'd probably still be in business."

The assembly chuckled at Malky's wee slip up. But they knew fine well that Josie Cunningham would not be operating on Malky's patch without the big man's imprimatur.

"So, as I say. It's the principle of the thing. Let this one go, and there'll be rats crawlin' oot of the widwark."

"Whit d'ye want us to dae, Malky?" said Tiny. "The usual... 'snitches get stitches?'"

"Depends on who it is, man," Malky said. "First thing you gotta dae is find oot who the snitch is, right? You get on to yer bendies. There's a monkey in it, for accurate ID."

'Bendies' was Malky's name for bent coppers. A monkey was five-hundred pounds, clean cash, no counterfeit notes.

Douglas 'Duggie, 'bananas' Fyfe put in, "I don't think this bust would have gone down if the Old Man was still in charge." He was talking about the suspended chief constable, Stanley McBride.

"Dinna be daft, Duggie. The high-ups only deal wi' other high-ups. That bawbag of a chief coonstable was supplementing his up-and-coming polis pension. He's been bent since he was a DI wi' the Met. They punted him up here to Scotland to get rid of him.

"I think he wis greasing a lot of palms. It'll maybe all come oot in the washing. But I doubt it. Too many big fish shitting their pants. It'll get closed doon. You wait and see. Like the Dunblane massacre. Sealed for a hunerd years 'in the public interest.' Public interest? Nae way. It's tae protect them that cannae be named. And don't ask. I said they cannae be named, okay?"

Nobody mentioned that fish shitting their pants was a rather strange metaphor.

Raymond Smythe, or Raymie to some, had said nothing so far at the meeting. A lanky lad with a dyed white-blond crew cut, he wore a large earring in his right ear, a simple gold ring, 'pirate style' he thought. Everyone in the area, all but the most sheltered and naïve, knew of Smythe's reputation.

He was quiet... or seemed to be. But then, many psychos are like that: he was also cruel, perverted, and pure bloody mental.

Typical of his psycho profile, he had tortured and killed animals since he was seven. At an even younger age, he would catch spiders, pull their legs off, then drop the body into a wee hole he'd carved out in the windowsill, just the right size to watch the legless creatures squirm.

At age ten, he had stolen a cigarette lighter. When left alone with his baby cousin, he'd burn the soles of the baby's feet, just enough to not leave a mark or blister. When the baby cried, nobody suspected Raymie's cruel involvement. And Raymie just loved that.

When Smythe was eleven, there lived in the area a man called Willie Gibbs. He was a simple man, a real gentle giant who bred budgies in his back garden sheds. He stood out, not just because of his size, but also because he was always seen wearing a deerstalker hat. The kids would say, 'Big Willie sleeps wi' his hat on, because it's pinned tae his heid wi' a six-inch nail through the top.'

One day, Willie had given Raymond a telling off when he had witnessed the boy kicking a malnourished and timid dog. Next morning, Willie found his budgies had been massacred, all with their necks twisted and broken. For the first time in his adult life, the big man had been reduced to tears. It had never dawned on him that the wee nyaff he'd reprimanded was the culprit. Never in his wildest dreams could Gibbs have imagined that a wee boy could be that cruel. But Raymond was all that, and more.

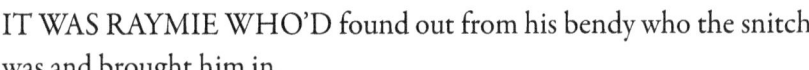

IT WAS RAYMIE WHO'D found out from his bendy who the snitch was and brought him in.

In the cellar of Malky's current temporary gaff, he and his five lieutenants were playing cards. Malky's centre of operations moved often, and fast. Bent coppers on his payroll would warn his team if the Drug Squad were getting interested. They always were paid by one of the lieutenants, and Malky stayed in the shadows, 'Mr Anonymous.'

He and his five goons travelled light, always ready to re-locate at the drop of a hat. The gear was invariably kept backpack ready. Malky may not have been a Boy Scout, but he liked their motto... 'Be Prepared.'

The only light-source in this cellar was a single bare bulb hanging from its cable. Very *Callan*-esque. In fact, when Malky looked in the mirror of a morning, he was the spitting image of Edward Woodward as he had looked in that MI5 assassin series, and in the movie, *The Wicker Man:* receding hair, intense eyes, sharp nose, chiselled jaw, and all. Although the 'receding hair' was now getting closer to 'balding.'

They were joking about the 'wee man, man', Terry, and Malky started the ball rolling with, "there's *The Wicker Man*, man."

"Well, ye got Dustin Hoffman, man," said Raymond.

"Aye, an' he was in *Marathon Man*, man," said Tiny.

"No to mention *Little Big Man*, man," added Mack Mackintosh, as the laughter grew.

"Whit aboot *The Rain Man*, man?" said Gordo.

Malky butted in with, "And *The Godfather*, man."

They all looked at each other. Then Tiny plucked up the courage to say, "Erm, Malky, nae offence... but *The Godfather* hisnae got 'man' in it, man!"

Malky's face took on a serious, murderous look. "I'm the fuckin' boss here, an' I make the fuckin' rules!"

There was silence and down-turned eyes. The threat of violence was palpable.

Then Malky broke into laughter. "Anyway, Marlon Brando was in *The Godfather,* and he was the High Heid Man, man! Right?"

The laughter was strained, but when Malky made a joke, it was safer to laugh. And nobody mentioned that *The Wicker Man* didn't fit with the Dustin Hoffman, man theme. Malky topped up their glasses from a bottle of Martell brandy. Martell seemed to be the 'in-drink' in Greenock at this time.

"Noo," said Malky, "is this Martell a cognac, or a brandy?"

There were no replies until Gordo asked, "Whit difference does it make... it's no near as good as a good bottle of Grouse, the Famous, eh?"

"The Famous Grouse, Gordo? Nae way! Your usual is the auld Eldorado... or Buckfast, *ha-ha!*" said Malky.

"Aye, well, ye know... when I kin afford a decent dram, I prefer a Grouse." said Gordo. "And there's nothing wrang with a bottle or six of Eldorado."

"You know what's so special aboot this Martell, Gordo?" asked Malky.

Gordo shook his head.

"It came to me free, son... an' I've got a dozen bottles. Well, minus this one."

"So, is it cognac or brandy?" asked Tiny, curious to know the answer.

"It says 'cognac' on the label... but gies a minute."

He picked up his iPad and did a Google search.

Then he read aloud in a mock-posh English accent.

"Cognac is not the same as brandy, but is a type of brandy and earns its name following very strict production methods. Cognac is an amber-coloured alcoholic drink, made in France, in the wine growing regions of Charente and Charente-Maritime surrounding the town of Cognac. It is made from distilling white wine to create eau-de-vie, ageing it in..." Etc.

Back to Malky-speak. "So, ye get the idea, right? Funny they named the toon after the drink, though. Noo, here's another wee tip for you bawbags. Google... is... your... best... friend!"

"An' here I thought it came frae Russia," said Gordo with a shake of his head.

"Google?" asked Malky, confused.

"Nah. Cognacs," said Gordo.

"That's Cossacks, no Cognacs, ye dumb ass!" said Malky, and the laughter started up again.

"Bloody hell. A Royal Flush!" Malky slapped his upturned cards on the table.

Unlike in the movies, the odds of getting that hand were actually astronomical.

It crossed a few minds that Malky's cognac talk might have been a distraction for him to perform a bit of sleight-of-hand with his cards. But nobody dared say so. They all threw their cards on the table. Except for Gordo.

"Shit, Malky... look what I got," he said, now slowly placing his cards on the table one at a time so everyone could see. An Ace of Spades, an Ace of Clubs, an Eight of Spades, and an Eight of Clubs with a Two of Spades kicker. It was the black aces and black eights that concerned him.

"The fucking 'Dead Man's hand!' You know... the hand held by Wild Bill Hitchcock when he was murdered. Shot in the back of the heid while sitting at the poker table," said Gordo with a worried look on his face. "Bad omen!"

"Dinnae worry aboot it, Gordo," said Malky. "You must have been playin' the wee man, man's cairds! And it's Hickok, no Hitchcock, you asshole. Where the hell did you go to school?"

"Oh, I was singled oot as being a somebody. I went to a special school," said Gordo, proudly.

"Figures," said Malky. "It's a wonder ye didnae go on to Oxford or Cambridge."

"Well, just shows whit you know. I did go to Cambridge. Tae visit ma granny when she was dying. She's deid, noo. Never left me a penny, mean old cunt."

Everybody groaned.

Including in a chair in the shadows, wee Terry; but that was a different kind of groan. His mouth had been duck-taped, and his arms and legs were tied to the chair.

"Talk of the devil," said Malky to the card players.

He got up and went over to Terry, ripping off the duct tape anything but gently. He open-hand-slapped Terry twice, and hard. With difficulty, because his mouth was so dry, Terry said, "I... I admit it. It was m... me. Ye don't have to torture me any mair. I admit it."

"Oh, that's good, sunshine," said Malky, "but this isn't torture to get ye to fess up. Although it's good to know that Raymie-boy's bendy cop earned his five-hunered quid. Naw, wee man... this is punishment. And since the rest of us have seen enough already to jist aboot make us puke, we're gonna leave you in Raymond's capable hands. Raymond enjoys his work; but he disnae like an audience. Cramps his style, like."

Terry begged, but Malky stuck the tape back over his mouth and beckoned to Raymond. "Up to you, Raymie. Make an example of the wee shite."

———⊙———

TERRY, THE WEE MAN, MAN, had been dumped at the side of Auchenbothie Road, a tarmacked single-track road, with passing places, that led from Upper Port Glasgow to the picturesque village of Kilmacolm.

As a farm tractor rolled toward him, Terry crawled out from the muddy ditch he was lying in and flagged down the driver. The farmer could hardly believe his eyes. Confronting him was a naked lad, with his hands over his genitals, who was covered from head to toe in mud and what might be dried blood. It looked like the boy could hardly keep on his feet, and he was visibly shivering.

The farmer stopped and helped the distressed youth into the tractor cab, allowing him to cover himself as best he could with a tartan rug that the farmer usually sat on for comfort when his haemorrhoids were playing up.

"For goodness' sake, son! What on earth has happened to you?" asked the farmer, a sturdy little man, called Donald Cannie. He had a rugged, weather-beaten face, was dressed in dungarees, with a well-worn Barbour over the top, and he wore a battered Harris Tweed bunnet on his head.

"I... I've been done in, mister," said Terry without his customary 'man'.

"Done in? I should say. You look like you've been run over by a combine-harvester."

At the farmhouse, Terry was soon seated in a chair in front of a roaring log fire. Still, he couldn't stop shivering. The stout farmer's-wife, Liz, brought in a large basin of hot water, and began to sponge the boy down. Terry flinched, hands over his genitals.

"Don't you worry aboot that, son. I've seen a lot of them things in the barnyard, and a sight bigger, too."

As she cleaned the wounds as best she could, she noticed that the boy was covered from head to toe in tiny cuts. And there were what looked like cigarette burns interspersed between many of the lacerations. She'd heard of the supposed torture, 'death by a thousand cuts'... but that, she thought, only happened in the likes of Sax Rhomer's *Fu Manchu* novels. They had become a particular favourite of hers since she had found them archived as audiobooks on the web. Liz had become a fan of 'Old Time Radio' shows as well, and would listen to 'The Shadow', 'Suspense', 'Lights Out', 'Dragnet' and the like, almost literally till the cows came home. Nostalgia was an escape from the drudgery of life on the farm, and, with her iPhone, Liz could listen with earphones even while working.

"We'll have to get him to a hospital," she said to her husband. "he's going in and out of shock. He needs professional care."

"Naw, missus!" Terry seemed to come to life at the mention of 'hospital.' "Nae hospital. Nae polis. Please! The gang that did this to me will get to me, even in the hospital. And the polis... the polis are in on it."

"He's delusional," said Donald, shaking his head.

"Naw! I'm no delusional, man. It's aboot drugs... big money. I clyped, and they warned me if I go to the authorities, their bent coppers will have me offed, man."

Liz had covered the boy with a clean, thick blanket, and he was holding on to it, fists clenched, like his life depended on it.

"Listen," said Terry, "I'll give ye a phone number, man. Ma maw's a nurse, genuine, state registered, right? She'll pick me up and fix me up good. Nae polis, right? Nae ambulance... okay, man?" He even added 'man' when he was addressing Liz. "An' tell her to bring me some claithes, man."

After feeding him two bowls of delicious homemade soup, Liz reluctantly did as the terrified boy had asked. His mother turned up, still dressed in her NHS-blue nurse's uniform, wearing a coat just slung over her shoulders. She was clearly upset, but seemed to know what Terry's injuries were all about. She got him dressed and thanked the farmers as she helped the boy to her car. Before getting in, Terry turned to Liz and shouted, "Missus! That soup, man. That was the best soup I've ever tasted." His mother waved goodbye, wondering what the heck was wrong with *her* soup.

She noticed that Liz, the 'tough' farmer's wife, was crying.

———◉———

THAT VERY NIGHT, HELPED by his mother, a skinny, bent-over, half-limping Terry, hoodie pulled up, and wearing a black COVID mask that went right up to his eyes, boarded the ferry at Ardrossan, bound for Brodick on the Isle of Arran. He was lucky to catch the last crossing. The ferry would remain docked at Brodick when it arrived, services cancelled because of the storm. Indeed, there had been an accident while docking at Brodick. 'While manoeuvring alongside, the vessel made light contact with the harbour wall, which resulted in minor cosmetic damage to the ship, with no injuries to people,' reported a spokesperson for the company. An understatement, if ever there was one. Terry had nearly been thrown over the railing as the ferry nearly tore away half the dock.

Arran, promoted to tourists as 'Scotland in miniature', was only a fifty-five-minute sail, around fourteen miles across the Firth of Clyde on the Caledonian MacBrayne ferry. The island would be quiet now, it being winter, with only residents and the hardiest of visitors present. The visitors at this time were usually climbers who hoped to get to the top of the island's highest peak, Goat Fell, especially should it be snow-capped. At 2,800 feet, it is one of four Corbetts on the island.

The Corbetts are the mountains in Scotland between 2,000 and 3,000 feet high, with at least 500 feet of descent on all sides. They are one climbing challenge down from the better known Munros, Scottish mountains over 3,000 feet, those that enthusiasts wish to 'bag.'

If not for travel restrictions, Terry would have been heading for his uncle's 'Scottish Pub' on the Costa del Sol in Spain. But Arran would have to do since he couldn't get out of the country. His sister, Andrea, had followed in her mother's footsteps and was a nurse living in the Arran town of Lamlash. Her flat overlooked the Holy Isle, in Lamlash bay, that was once a hermitage for the Celtic Christian saint, St. Molaise. It was now a Buddhist mindfulness retreat.

Andrea worked at the small, seventeen-bed, Arran War Memorial Hospital, and she would be able to change his dressings to avoid infection, and treat him professionally with salves at home.

Another plus was that Arran had an almost non-existent crime rate, and only two bobbies policed the island.

If Terry kept his head down in Lamlash, he'd likely soon heal, and survive to... well... to plot his revenge.

Chapter Fourteen

———◈———

PAUL WHEELER WAS OF medium height, had a medium build, and he was in his late thirties or early forties. It was hard to be sure because of his boyish, clean-shaven face. He could pass for an accountant, or a bank manager, or a civil servant. He parked his black Porsche 911 Speedster across the road from the pub in Gourock that he was interested in buying. It had once been a thriving, lively place, very popular with the locals. It had an upstairs lounge where a variety of local bands and single self-accompanying singers once had drawn the crowds on Tuesday nights and at the weekends. Thursday night was karaoke night.

But the trusted and successful landlord had succumbed to prostate cancer, and the temporary replacement was an arrogant sod who lost customers as fast as he could say 'you're banned, pal!' That's when he was there at all. The new guy took the term 'absentee landlord' to heart. So now the brewers were putting the pub up for sale at a knockdown price... in fact, they were nearly giving it away as long as the buyer contracted to sell their beer. Any port in a storm.

Paul made his way around to the passenger door and opened it. He helped his wife out of the low-riding sports car. As she swung around on the seat, her black leather skirt rode up, showing her shapely legs up to the crotch.

"Never fails to turn me on, that view," he said.

"Yeez, and if it ever does, will you trade me een for a new model like you do weeth your cars, Paul?" she said, as she stood and re-adjusted her skirt. It was on the very short side in mini skirt terms, so it took little adjusting. Her accent was decidedly Eastern European.

"You are my one and only Russian bride, Alexandria. Besides, I couldn't afford a trade-in; not with your pre-nup terms, anyway, my darling."

"You got bargain, *krasavchik*... hindesome man. A poor girl meyust have insurance, *da*? Looks don't leeast forever."

"You know damned well that I fell in love with you from the moment we met. And you were anything but poor. Your dad is a Mafia Don, for god's sake, and must be a million... if not billionaire. I'll never forget that time I was in St Petersburg to do as you say a 'leetle beezsness' with him. When I saw you, it was love at first sight."

"And me with you. But I know nothing about Mafia. My father eez beeznessman. Very good beeznessman... like you, yes? Eez this where we are going? This, erm, 'pub'?"

They crossed the street, and Paul eyed the outside condition of the premises. It needed a good coat of paint. Maybe three coats, he thought. And the sign had a letter missing, probably deliberately knocked off by some local wag, so it read 'The —hore Bar.'

"Well, I'll be renaming *The Shore Bar*... and 'hores' will not be welcome," said Paul. Alexandria laughed.

They entered through a door that looked like something out of Dracula's castle, complete with a brass lion's-head knocker. Inside, the patrons immediately went quiet, and all turned to look at the strangers.

One of those places, thought Paul. This was not an untypical reaction in a Scottish pub that the clientele regarded as their 'local'.

The decor was supposed to be 'Scottish baronial'. That meant lots of wood panelling, a stag's head above the bar, a targe with crossed claymores, tartan rugs hanging here and there, and a coat of arms with lion rampant and a... a rat! Was that supposed to be a rat? He couldn't be sure. The motto read 'Wha Daur Meddle Wi' Us'. Next to that was a framed portrait of Queen Elizabeth at her Coronation, the frame draped with a Glasgow Rangers scarf that somehow didn't look out of place among the other tat.

Sectarian bar, thought Paul. Again, this was not unusual in the area. Paul had once heard a story about a guy who walked into a rough, spit-and-sawdust pub in Glasgow. As he approached the bar, a bruiser of a man put his hand out to stop his progress. "Haud up! Are ye a Billy or a Tim?" the man asked aggressively.

"Oh, I'm an atheist," said the newcomer.

"So what? Are ye a Protestant atheist or a Catholic atheist?" returned the hard man without a glimmer of humour.

They sat at what could only be described as a wooden picnic table, the kind you see at a picnic spot, with a middle bench table and two attached struts on opposite sides to sit on. Alexandria decided not to try to get her long legs under the bench; so she sat on the edge of the 'seat', facing the bar, to the obvious approval of the customers who were either standing at the bar, or seated on swivel bar stools that were now swivelled away from the bar and facing the strangers. They were staring at the newcomers as if they were exotic animals in a zoo.

Obviously, never been taught that it is rude to stare, thought Paul. The barflies were the only customers in the place. A lanky, scruffy looking guy, on a bar stool, a woman on a bar stool with two men flanking her. Paul couldn't help but notice that the woman had one glass eye. But then, it was rude to stare. Two other middle-aged guys at the far end of the bar, sniggering and eyeing up Alexandria unabashedly.

"Your usual?" Paul asked his blonde, blue-eyed wife.

"Yeez. Geen and tonic... with ice and slice of lemon. I myust have ice and lemon." The Russian accent was clear when she emphasised the 'must.'

Ice, maybe, thought Paul, lemon, maybe not.

Paul made his way to the bar with a confident stride. He was dressed expensively in a calf-length black Crombie overcoat, over a Pierre Cardin suit. His shirt was pink; his silk tie was lemon yellow. His shoes were shiny black-leather Italian Valentino's. He wore his fair hair tightly swept back in a ponytail about six inches long. In this bar, Paul and his gorgeous wife might have come from another planet.

Paul noticed that the gantry was sparse, with many empty gantry brackets. A two-litre of The Famous Grouse whisky hung beside a two-litre of something called The Old Fox, presumably a cheaper brand of Scotch. The Famous Grouse label was stained and grotty looking and Paul suspected it had been decanted many times with The Old Fox. Two empty spaces, then a Smirnoff vodka beside a clone called Orloff, and a single bottle of Gordon's gin. On the shelf below were three bottles of Four Crown cheap wine and two of Emva Cream sherry, a sticky-looking Drambuie, a bottle of Bailey's Irish Cream, and, presumably for their colour rather than their popularity, a bottle of green Chartreuse liqueur that looked unopened stood beside a bottle of Blue Curaçao.

A handwritten sign above the gantry read bluntly: 'Nae Cheques, Nae Tick.'

The barman, a guy in his twenties, was standing at the far end of the bar, looking out through a dirty window on to the street, and pretending to be busy polishing a whisky glass.

"Ahem!" Paul cleared his throat loudly to get the barman's attention.

The barman wore his hair in hipster style, black, slicked back on top, and shaved to above the ears. He had a face full of acne and a dour look about him as he sauntered over to where Paul was waiting to order. There was no 'what can I get you, sir?' or any such. He just stared with a kind of vacant, questioning look that could be interpreted as anything from 'what the hell are you doing here?' to 'you want something?'

"Erm, a gin and tonic and a pint beer shandy, half and half," said Paul.

"A shandy?" asked the barman, a look of disbelief crossing his face.

"Aye, half and half, I'm driving."

"So, that your motor across the street?"

"Aye, that's mine."

"Must be great to hae money, eh?"

Paul didn't answer. He wanted to order drinks, not to be interrogated by a spotty-faced ignoramus.

The barman poured the half and half shandy.

"It's no' ony cheaper, ye know. Same price as a *real* pint."

The guy to Paul's right at the bar never turned but sat facing away from the bar, staring at Alexandria. Out of the corner of his mouth, he said, "There's a tradition in this pub that a stranger buys everybody a drink. To show they're friendly, you know?"

"There's nae such tradition," said the barman, snapping the lid off the tonic on the bottle opener, "Elkie tries that one on with aye body new that comes in here. Dinna listen to him."

Paul said, "Ice and lemon in the G&T, please."

Again, the barman looked peeved.

"Well, ice, I kin dae. But lemon, naw... unless ye want me to run roon tae the Co-Op to buy one lemon, fir one customer, fir one drink."

There was sniggering from the coterie of customers.

"Just ice will do," said Paul.

Paul paid for the drinks, and as he turned to walk to his table, Elkie's foot deliberately caught Paul's heel.

Paul tripped, just a little, but enough to spill a drop of his shandy.

Elkie said, "Here, will ye no watch where yer goin'? If you'd spilled that on my good jaiket, I'd hae ma solicitor on to you!" His 'good' jacket was a black and red plaid 'cowboy' jerkin type of thing with a faux sheepskin collar that was manky. Indeed, manky was the perfect word to describe Elkie from head to toe.

Paul regained his balance and stood still with his eyes closed, pondering. But when he looked at Alexandria, she was shaking her head vehemently and mouthing, 'No!'

Paul continued to the table without turning or uttering a word.

"Nasty leetle man," said Alexandria. She had managed by now to get one leg over the bench seat so that she was straddling it, showing more leg than Tina Turner in her best form.

"No lemon? Is no G&T without lemon. I drink this, we go, okay?"

"Well, there's no use asking for a look at the upstairs floor," said Paul, pointing to roped-off stairs. Strange to say, the barrier was rather elegant, two brass stands with a red rope and gold tassels. A plank of wood with 'Nae Entry' would have suited the ambiance better.

Paul downed half of his shandy, and Alexandria knocked back her sans-lemon gin and tonic in one gulp and banged the glass down on the table with a thump.

Watching Elkie slide off the bar stool, staring at Alexandria's legs while adjusting his crotch with vigour, like Michael Jackson with genital crabs, and slink into the toilet, Paul said, "Okay, Alex," handing her the car keys, "you go on. I'll be out in a minute." He often called her Alex for short. Indeed, the Porsche's number plate was 'ALEX 1'.

As she left, Paul headed through two sets of doors to the, to his surprise, reasonably clean toilet.

Elkie glanced back at him briefly.

"Er, haud on a minute, pal. I'm nearly done. I dinna want your kind gawking at my dick. How does a poofter like you get a wummin like that, anyways? She your beard?"

As Elkie pulled up his zip, the response from Paul was sudden, unexpected, and violent.

He caught Elkie by his greasy hair, pulled back his head, then smashed his face full force into the tiles above the urinal. There was no hesitation as he twisted the bloody-faced man around and, grabbing him by the collar and the seat of the pants, ran him straight into the mirror above the sink. The mirror cracked, blood trickling down the broken glass. Elkie slumped and cried out in pain. Then Paul, once again gripping Elkie's hair tightly, pulled him back a bit and smashed his face onto the edge of the porcelain wash-hand basin. There was a grinding noise of teeth breaking. But Paul wasn't done. He manoeuvred the groaning victim over to the electric hand dryer. Holding Elkie's face below the outlet, face up, Paul pushed the button.

The man's face was a bloody, burned mess, but he could still scream; and scream he did as the roasting hot air continued to blast him. Paul held him there until the cycle ended, then let the broken man drop to the floor.

"Have you ever heard of the Wheeler family from Glasgow?" asked Paul, running his blood-stained hands under the tap.

"Wha... wheel... er... Wheeler?" mumbled Elkie.

"Aye. Wheeler. Big crime family in Glasgow. Started with ice cream vans, then in no time at all they'd offed the kingpin and taken over Glasgow's underworld."

"Ah... Ah think so. Not... noto...!"

"Aye, notorious, you're dead right. Well, I'm *Paul* Wheeler, and you, sunshine, have just been dealt some Wheeler justice. Now, I must warn you..." Paul pulled something small and black from his inside jacket pocket.

"This here," he said, pointing the Beretta PX4 Storm Compact pistol at Elkie's head. "This isn't your Dirty Harry 44 Magnum. But this wee jobbie can put just as big of a hole in a cheeky cunt's head. Let's say, some squealer that went to the polis to say he'd been beaten up..."

"No... m... me, big man... nae polis... promise." said Elkie, spitting out a tooth in a gob of blood.

At that moment, the man who had been standing at the bar with the girl with the glass eye popped his head in the door.

"What the fuck is going on...?"

Paul immediately turned and pointed the pistol at him.

"It's just business, pal. Noo, you can fuck the fuck off if you know what's good for you. And nae cops or my folk will hunt you all doon, and everybody in that bar is dead. Got it?"

The man retreated, and, saying nothing to the barman, he and his pals, after a whispering confab, left the bar casually as if nothing was wrong.

Paul took two steps back and looked at himself in the broken mirror.

"Now, look what you've done to my tie, Elkie. It is Elkie, isn't it? Shouldn't be hard to trace you if needs be, huh?"

Paul took off his blood-spattered tie, bent down, and tied it around Elkie's neck... tight.

"A wee souvenir for you. If you can get that cleaned up, you can sell it and buy half-a-dozen of your 'good jaikits'. And, by the way, if your mammy never taught you that it's rude to stare at folk, I hope I have."

Elkie didn't hear him: he had passed out from shock.

Paul walked calmly out of the toilet and went straight up to the barman who was standing nonchalantly polishing what was probably the same glass.

Paul beckoned him to come closer.

"Listen, son," he said in a cold tone, "I'm going to be your boss soon. Now, given your attitude, I might not keep you on. But smarten up a bit, and I think everybody deserves a chance. Although, you definitely need to do something about that acne. But for now, there's a wee bit of cleaning up to be done in the toilet there."

Paul took out his wallet and slapped a fifty-pound note on the counter.

"Nae polis, now. You call the cops, and you'll end up like that piece of shite in the bog who's no longer being a smartass."

People who had dealings with Wheeler said that, despite first impressions, there was something about his eyes that gave away the potential for violence in him.

"Nae problem, er, boss," was all the barman said, as he pocketed the fifty quid.

After Paul had left, the bar was now empty, and the spotty barman went up close to the mirror that was behind the gantry. He pulled at a cheek and stretched it with his fingers. Then he proceeded to squeeze a couple of zits. His next customers would be blissfully unaware that, on the shelf directly below the barman's face, sat the ice bucket. The lid wasn't on it!

Alexandria was seated comfortably in the Porsche. Paul crossed the road casually, calm and relaxed, and got in the driver's side.

"You know," he said. "That's not really a bad wee pub. I think it has potential. Should I buy it?"

"You must remember zee lemons!" said Alexandria.

Then, she said, "What happened your nice coat? Eez all bloody. You need dry cleaners, no?"

Paul looked down at his pure-wool coat, got out of the car, removed the coat, and stuffed it in a street-bin. Back in the car, he said, "I'll buy a new one."

Chapter Fifteen

PCS MHAIRI HENDRY AND Tom Dempster were in plain clothes, in an unmarked Mondeo, parked under an overhanging tree at the edge of the car park at Lamont's pier in Port Glasgow. The pier was a disused and rickety wooden structure that jutted out into the Clyde. It had a 'DANGER — UNSAFE' sign at its roped-off entrance for good reason. To the left side of the pier, there was a slipway that was still used by small-boat owners. And nestling in the trees across from them was a small boatyard. About 800 feet behind where they'd parked, but hidden from them by the trees, stood Newark Castle.

Back in the days of sail, Port Glasgow had originally been called 'Newark'. Then, it became The Port of Glasgow, and soon after just Port Glasgow, the definite article soon being dropped.

In 1710, the town became the main customs port on the Clyde, trading in tobacco, cotton, timber, sugar, iron and hemp. It held this position until 1812.

Until a navigable channel was eventually dredged through previously impassable sand banks to allow ships to sail upriver to the city of Glasgow, they had deposited their cargoes at Gourock, Greenock, and here, at 'the wee Port.'

The lucrative goods of tobacco, rum and sugar from the Caribbean, and the other goods, were then transported to the city of Glasgow, and elsewhere, by other means. But the Caribbean trade in particular led to the existence of names like Jamaica Street, Antigua Street, Tobago Street, Virginia Street, and Sugarhouse Lane in the next-door town of Greenock.

One report read: 'In the eighteenth and nineteenth centuries, Greenock and nearby Port Glasgow were Scotland's gateway to a lucrative in-trade in sugar, tobacco, rum... and sometimes humans.'

That meant slaves. There was a passionate debate going on in Gourock regarding their coat of arms that depicted a slave coming off a three-masted ship. Some wanted it to be redesigned; others said it should stay as it was. It was their heritage, warts and all.

It was now a quarter after 3 a.m. and the two PCs had taken over from the previous team at midnight. This car park was well-known as another winching spot, but tonight, at this time, in this storm, theirs was the only car there.

It was a novelty for Tom to be in plainclothes, in a non-liveried car, and to have a pretty PC as his partner instead of his usual one... Double Alex!

Earlier, they'd seen one young couple park on the opposite side of the car park from them. They watched as the pair's car windows steamed up, followed by a bouncy-bouncy. That lasted all of five minutes.

Later, an older couple in a silver Mercedes had the steamed-up windows, but no bouncy-bouncy followed. The woman got out and half-ran to the bushes, presumably to relieve herself. She was soaking wet in seconds. In this storm, she might as well have stood beside the car and just 'let it go!'

None of this concerned Tom and Mhairi. They were there to watch for a body being dumped. And they were only one of six teams staking out different potential sites that had been picked out by the psychological analysis team at Tulliallan. It was a long shot, and, as DS Scott had foreseen, the original plan of round-the-clock surveillance had been curtailed to cover only the hours of darkness.

"Can we put the heater on again for a wee minute?" asked Mhairi, with an exaggerated shiver.

"Aye, well, the windows are steaming up, and we've not even got around to necking," said Tom, a genuinely 'tall, dark, and handsome,' specimen of a man. He turned on the engine.

"Feigned, Tom!" said Mhairi, "the boss said, 'feigned necking' if it looked like someone was watching us."

"Is there a difference?"

"You're damned right there is. As they say in America, you don't even get to first base!" She said this with a coy smile that kind of turned Tom on a bit.

Mhairi was a real stunner. Her mother was Italian, her father a Scot. She had the kind of figure most women would give their eye-teeth for, and men could not resist staring at, even if their wives gave them a wee dunt with their elbow. She had luscious black hair that reached to her shoulders. Her eyes had a striking natural violet hue. By the grace of God, or nature, her face was perfectly proportioned. Brow, eyes, nose, lips, and chin: she had the look of a young Elizabeth Taylor and wore makeup to intentionally copy that look, even though the style came from three generations before her time.

As a wee girl, she had seen *Black Beauty*, a favourite of her gran's, and, looking in the mirror, she could see how alike she was to Elizabeth. So, she decided to model herself on the famous actress. As her figure developed, she was blessed with a comparable shape, and had asked her gran where she could buy those 'pointy' bras. The comment had caused much hilarity among her female relatives. At fourteen, she had even fallen madly in love with Richard Burton!

Tonight, she had her hair tied up in bunches with red ribbons, to enhance her 'young teenager' look. And she had a pink sparkly hair grip holding back her fringe.

"I'll put the heater back off if you don't stop your teasing," said Tom.

"That's not teasing," said Mhairi, giving him a playful punch on the arm. "This is...!" And she leaned over and gave him a big smoochie kiss on the cheek. *Mwwwaa*!

"Shit, Mhairi. I'll be all lipstick. I'm a married man, don't forget. My wife'll murder me if..."

"Oh, don't worry Mr Married Man. My lipstick might look like the kind that would leave the telltale lipstick on your collar, but I can assure you it is waterproof, smudge-proof, kiss-proof, and wife-proof."

Tom had turned on the vanity light and angled the rear-view mirror to look at his cheek, while dabbing non-existent lipstick with a white handkerchief.

"I'll take your word for it."

Mhairi said, "This car is rocking alright. With the bloody wind. I hope we don't get a broken tree branch smashing through the window. No sane person would be out on a night like this!"

"Maybe a cuddle would help after all," said Tom, only half-joking. Then, seeing Mhairi's exasperated expression, he thought he'd try to cheer her up by showing off with a relevant stormy passage from Robert Burns' *Tam o' Shanter* that he had memorised in school for a recital competition.

Ahem:

"The wind blew as twad blawn its last;
The rattling showers rose on the blast;
The speedy gleams, the darkness swallowed;
Loud, deep and lang the thunder bellowed.
That night, a child might understand:
The Deil had business on his hand."

"What the hell was that?"

"Rabbie Burns," said Tom. "Our Scottish National Bard."

"Well, he should have been 'barred' long ago. Do you no' think I'm scared enough?"

At first, Mhairi thought Tom was still playing the fool when he shushed her, finger to his lips.

"Hold on! Quiet! We've got company." He quickly switched the interior light off and killed the Mondeo's engine.

A black Citroën LX van, rear windows fully blacked out, passed them going very slowly. Its front-side tinted windows were probably a legal shade during the day, but at night, you couldn't make out any of the occupants. It didn't pull into any of the parking bays; instead, it pulled up to the entrance to the pier, stopping just before the sign. Its lights were off before it even stopped. No sound from an engine now; it had been switched off too.

Then, Tom said to Mhairi, "Do you hear that?"

"Aye, another engine... a boat?"

A quick flash of headlights from the Citroën gave them a glimpse of an RIB, a Rigid Inflatable Boat, heading for the pier, bouncing madly on the waves. In a minute, the outboard motor was cut. Men with flashlights exited the van.

"What the devil is going on?" said Tom in a half-whisper.

Suddenly, his side window was rapped loudly. Having been concentrating on the pier, neither of the PCs had noticed the man approach their car from the side.

Tom rolled down his window, just about an inch. A head came into view as their visitor bent down to talk. He had an oilskin hood pulled over his head, and his face was fully masked by a black balaclava. Only his eyes were visible through the eyeholes.

"Noo, dinnae panic, young lovers." The voice was low and menacing, no matter the reassuring words. "I'll no' ask what you're daein' here at this time o' night, in the middle o' a fuckin' hurricane. You no' got anywhere else tae dae your winching? And macho man here looks a bit old for you, hen."

Mhairi said, "I'm over sixteen, mister."

"Anyway, this is a police operation. Highly classified, ye ken? You wee minkers need to start yer engine, and drive calmly oot of here, ken? An' ye never seen anything here... in fact, ye wir no' here at all, should anyone ask. Ye ken? I've got yer number plate written doon. Ye dinnae want us polis paying yer folks a visit in the middle of the night, noo, dae ye?"

Tom made a mental note of the Aberdonian accent.

Tom began, "But we're..."

Mhairi cut him off before he could say the word 'police', and in the most scared-wee-girlie voice she could muster said, "Aye, mister. We're oot of here! Get goin' Tom before we get into trouble." Her voice was louder, banging her fists on the dashboard, "C'mon! This guy is serious. Don't mess aboot. He says 'go'; you go."

Tom got the message. He had noticed something that the man had pointed to for a second to prove he was serious. And it wasn't ID.

Tom started the engine, rolled up his window and, as the black figure stood aside, he made a wee flourish of a skidding take off, throwing up a spray of water from behind his car, and turning with a squeal of the Mondeo's tyres onto the exit road.

He sped along Castle Road, past the castle, then pulled into the empty car park at Ferguson Marine, the only surviving shipyard in Port Glasgow. There was no night shift at the yard. Orders were down, and the yard was struggling. Mhairi had already called it in using her personal radio. Breathlessly, she'd given the station sergeant the code words and position of the incident. The code was 'Gold, SA, Tac'. That is: 'Major Incident... Silent Approach... Tactical Firearms Unit'. The sergeant didn't question her call. He knew this was for real, because no one would be careless with a Gold code.

"Okay," said Tom. It was he who had noticed that the man in black was wearing a side-arm. The man had pulled aside his coat to reveal a shoulder holster to emphasise that he wasn't kidding. Tom, who had recently been on a course about illegal firearms, had noticed the Smith and Wesson crest on the handle of the revolver. That brand was not issued to UK police, not even to special ops. And even special ops would have shown ID.

"I want you to stay here to guide them in. I'm going for a look-see. I think our guy's car is parked at the castle. I'll do a recce. Don't worry, and no arguing. Get my PR out."

She didn't argue. She opened the glove compartment and pulled out another police radio. He took it and pushed the tiny earphone into his ear. She put in her earphone, too.

They dialled up a one-to-one channel, not wanting any crosstalk from control.

"Good. You slide in here, and if anything goes down before Gold arrives, you beat it out of here immediately!" said Tom.

When Tom got out of the driver's door, Mhairi slid over behind the wheel. "Be careful," was all she said.

Tom was dressed all in black, as it happened. A black leather jerkin, black T-shirt with a polo neck, and black skinny jeans. That wasn't any tactical choice for plain clothes. It *was* his plain clothes; how he usually dressed in casual wear. He liked the 'man in black' look.

It was freezing cold, and the wind and rain were cutting. He kept to the shadows of the shipyard outhouses, slipped past the unmanned gatehouse, and then stayed in the tree line to the right of Castle Road.

He whispered into his radio. "Passing the castle car park. One car... probably our man on lookout. There's a treeless stretch coming up. About a couple of hundred feet. I'll crawl it."

Mhairi just whispered, "Okay," to let him know she could hear him.

Commando-crawling flat on the ground, using his arms and legs to push him along, he kept his head turned away from the parked car. Obviously, face blacking wasn't something a police officer kept handy on a normal stakeout. When he snatched a quick look, he saw that the rogue car was facing out toward him with its lights out. If anything would give him away, it would be his face. With that thought, he scraped up some mud and rubbed it on his hands and face. That might not last long in the rain, but it would be enough to get him into the thicket.

He was almost into the cover of the trees when the car's headlights came on full beam. There was a loud crack. For a second, he didn't feel it. Then a searing, red-hot pain shot through his left shoulder. He had never been shot, but he knew that was what had just happened.

Get to the trees, he thought. Get to the cover of the trees!

"Jesus, Tom! What's happening?" came Mhairi's voice in his ear, still a whisper. Sprinting for the copse, he said, all too calmly, "I think I've been shot, Mhairi. Get on to Gold. Tell them there is a wounded friendly in the cluster of trees just beyond the castle car park in the direction of the pier. Bad guy armed in the near vicinity. I'm going to hide. Over-and-out!"

He didn't want to become a target for the tactical firearms guys when they turned up. *Turned up, the sooner the better!*

Now, his concern was evasion. The shooter would not stay put. The shot would have warned the others at the pier. Either they would skedaddle, or one or more would come to see what was going on.

His left arm was useless, and he could feel the blood running down and dripping off his fingers, leaving a blood trail. He used his right hand to guide his left hand into his jacket pocket. For an agonising few seconds, he thought he was going to pass out from the pain. Crouching low, he made his way into what seemed like the middle of the thicket and slid down in the mud at the base of a tree.

Crack!

Oh shit, he thought. But it wasn't another shot. It was a branch cracking as it was stepped on. But it wasn't close... yet.

Then another crack, closer. Even over the noise of the wind howling through the trees, he heard it, and...

The man in black appeared from behind one of the trees to Tom's right. He was drookit, wearing a black oilskin coat, and his face was still covered by the ski mask.

"Noo, whit the fuck have we got here? The fuckin' SAS?" he asked belligerently, referring to Tom's muddy face, that was getting less muddy by the second.

Tom thought he'd try honesty, even though he knew this guy wasn't who he claimed to be.

"I'm police... like you!"

"That'll be right," said the man, his pistol pointing at Tom's face. "I got you now. You're the wincher frae the car park. I told you, sonny. We're special ops. I've got a license to kill!"

Mhairi had crept up on the man silently.

Thwack!

She had retrieved her extending baton from the boot of their car. The blow caught him hard on the wrist. The gun dropped out of his hand.

Thwack!

The man let out a howl. Another blow with all the strength she could muster, just above the elbow of his gun hand. Without hesitation, Mhairi bent and grabbed the weapon, rolling to her side on the muddy ground, and coming up with it pointed at the man.

She was like a cat when she moved, thought Tom.

The man shouted, "Fuck! You've broken my fucking arm, you wee bitch."

She tucked the gun into her waistband.

Thwack!

The man's left knee made a horrible cracking sound, and he crumpled and went down.

"And your fucking leg, I hope," said Mhairi, moving over to where Tom was sitting under the tree.

"I'll need to stop the bleeding," she said, looking at his arm.

"I'm okay," said Tom. "You keep an eye on him. Others might come... from the pier, you know?"

"You could bleed to death. You need a tourniquet."

As she bent to inspect his wound, another figure came, as if from nowhere, gun pointing at Mhairi.

"Shoot the fuckers, Paddy!" shouted the man on the ground.

Paddy took aim, then his gaze froze.

Before Mhairi even thought about taking the gun from her waistband, a loud, disembodied voice ordered, "Armed police! Drop your weapon! Friendlies... get flat on the ground!" Mhairi knew right away what was happening and dropped flat beside Tom.

The gunman made the mistake of not lowering his firearm.

Pop-pop, pop!

The second man didn't fall immediately, but his pistol lowered. He seemed to just stand as if frozen to the spot. Then he dropped to his knees. The top of his head had been blown off. He fell forward onto the ground with a splash, and there was no more movement from him.

The next order was clear and loud:

"Armed police. Get flat on the ground, arms outstretched above your head. Do not make another move, or I *will* shoot!" The armed officer was pointing his Heckler and Koch machine pistol at the injured man on the ground. The Aberdonian thrust one arm out above his head, waving a hand.

"I've... my arm's broke, ken? That wee cunt broke my arm... and my leg."

Another ARU guy appeared and pointed his rifle at Tom and Mhairi.

"We're... we are... blue team," said Tom weakly as he began to lose consciousness.

"We're fucking cops," shouted Mhairi, "and my partner's been shot. We need medical. Right fucking now!"

Whomp, whomp, whomp!

The police helicopter appeared from over the hill at the Clune Brae, the midnight sun spotlight piercing the murk, lighting up the area, blinking between the trees.

From a loud hailer on the chopper came:

"This is Commander Sykes. We're putting down in the Coronation Park, as close to you as possible. Muster there. Operation successful. Threats eliminated. All baddies in custody. Well done!"

An ambulance soon pulled up on Castle Road, blues flashing.

"You're going to be all right," whispered Mhairi into Tom's ear, rain and tears running down her face while she pressed hard on his wound to staunch the flow of blood, one bloody hand over the other. "You're going to be all right, Tom."

But he couldn't hear her.

Chapter Sixteen

———◉———

"YOU'RE GOING TO BE all right, Tom." The voice came out of a bright white light. It was the voice of an angel.

"Mhai..." he was about to say Mhairi's name, but no. As his vision cleared, he realised it was the other angel in his life, his wife, Mary. She was gently resting her surgically gloved hand on his hand that had a cannula inserted. Although she had a mask on, he'd recognise those green eyes and blonde hair anywhere.

"Whe... where am I?" he mumbled, mouth like the inside of a bus driver's glove.

"You're in hospital, Tom. You were shot, remember?"

"Sh... shot?"

"They say that Mhairi saved your life. I'll be forever thankful to her."

"I'm in Inverclyde?" he asked, referring to his local hospital.

"No, love. They flew you by helicopter to the Golden Jubilee in Clydebank. Hah! Trust you to get the posh place," she tried to laugh, but began to weep.

"Hey, hey! I'm not dying, am I?"

"No, silly," she dried her eyes with a tissue. "Remember that scar you had on your upper left arm from a vaccination? The one that never went away. Well, you're going to have a bigger one there. That's where the bullet entered. It cracked a bone and lodged there. They got it out. The doc is keeping it for you, for a souvenir. But you lost a lot of blood and, if not for Mhairi restricting the flow of blood as best she could, the surgeon said you might have died from shock."

"My arm? Yes. Remember now. It was on fire."

"They say that either you were lucky, or the gunman was too far away, or he was a terrible shot... he was probably aiming at your head."

"Did they get away... him and the ones at the pier? The RIB?"

Just then, there was a knock at the door of his private ward.

"Can I come in?" asked DI Scott, popping his head in.

"Of course, Ron. Come you on in," said Mary.

They had been given special permission from the surgeon to visit Tom, as long as they kept their masks on, and kept applying anti-bacterial hand gel any time they touched something.

"Did they get away?" Tom repeated.

"Well, hello to you, too, PC Dempster," said the DI, pulling up a chair and sitting on the opposite side of the bed from Mary, but a good four feet back. "No, they did not."

"Sorry, sir. Thanks for coming," said Tom.

Scott continued, "All but one was apprehended without a firefight. One dead, however, where you were, near the castle. Triple tap. Two in the chest, one in the head. Didn't know what hit him, the basta... erm, sorry, Mary."

Mary just shrugged.

"I've heard worse than that from the kids in my school. And I teach in a primary school!"

Scott laughed and then continued, "Two of them tried to escape in the RIB. They headed upriver. But *Semper Vigilo* confronted them from the Langbank side, while *The Cloch* had sped upriver from Greenock and cut them off. Armed sharpshooters were deployed on both boats. That wee pilot cutter can sure move. Twin Rolls-Royce engines, you know? Anyway, the tactical team on the police launch shot out the RIB's Mercury outboards, and the daft bastards jumped from the RIB and tried to swim for it. They were soon fished out. Some would say the good guys should have left them there. Five minutes, I think, before you freeze to death in the Clyde at this time of year. But then the good guys wouldn't be good guys anymore, right?"

Scott enjoyed knowing little details about boats like *The Cloch*. He had a small yacht moored at the Kip Marina in Inverkip. It was up on ramps for its winter overhaul, just now. But during the summer, he had been sailing with his boss, Sam Miller, on a beautiful craft that he knew he himself could never afford.

The cost of divorce is much more than the psychological pain. But it was his fault, and he'd live with it. What else was there to do? "Suck it up!" He hadn't realised he'd verbalised the end of the thought.

"Pardon?" said Mary. "Are you okay, Ron? You were in a wee world of your own for a minute there."

"I'm so sorry. I think the lack of sleep is getting to me."

"And Mhairi? Is she all right?" continued Tom, not having noticed Scott's wee fugue.

"She is 'shaken but not stirred', Mr Bond," joked Scott with an attempt at a Sean Connery accent. "Her ju-jitsu, alongside regular baton training, certainly paid off. The guy she tackled is in Inverclyde Royal. I've heard that he is dismayed that he was beaten up by a wet and muddy Elizabeth Taylor lookalike. Mhairi broke his wrist, his arm, and shattered his knee. Apparently, he might be walking with a limp for the rest of his natural. They'll be calling him 'Peg' in the high security prison he will almost certainly be sent to. Although a native of Aberdeen, he has PROVO connections going way back to the Troubles. A rabid sympathiser. A real bad player... or so I'm told. My only concern is that Special Branch has become involved. Officially, they won't even tell us the names of the couriers. Guns and cocaine, they say, but no mention of the value."

Tom said, "But I'm curious, boss. Where the heck did the RIB come from?"

"Kilcreggan!" said Scott.

"You're not going to tell me there's a major drug dealing operation going on across the river in sleepy wee Kilcreggan?" asked Tom.

Scott took out a notebook and thumbed through the pages until he found what he was looking for. "Now, you didn't hear this from me! I pumped a friend in the Drug Squad, and he outlined the probable route, for the cocaine at least.

"From Afghanistan to Rotterdam by private jet, flying 'with diplomatic immunity.' Airbus H145 helicopter from Rotterdam, skirting Penzance, then north to the east coast of the Irish Republic. There, probably at an isolated farmhouse, the major haul of drugs would be unloaded, leaving a smaller amount of cocaine on board. The helicopter takes on the weapons and a supply of fentanyl that was produced in an underground lab in Dublin, and then it flies the lot to a bay in the sparsely populated southeast of Kilcreggan. The cargo is transferred onto the RIB, which crosses the river to Lamont's Pier. Bingo! And the bad weather wasn't a hindrance. It was a bonus to them."

Tom said, "It seems your friend knows a heck of a lot about it. If they had an opo going on with this drop, they nearly got me killed. Your pal's name isn't Commander Sykes, by any chance?"

Scott just shrugged.

"If there was an operation going on, they wouldn't let a local station like Greenock know. Especially if they didn't know the exact destination of the drop. Operational security and all that stuff. They'd say that anyone could have been bought off or blackmailed. That includes Police, Air Traffic Control, Customs and Excise, and the Coastguard. These squad guys are clandestine and insular... a self-contained unit... and they're suspicious of everyone. They have to be! But the Eire drop was the primary target, and that operation has been closed down, from what I heard." Scott was being matter of fact, but clearly, he was angry.

"All that way and nothing is spotted by the authorities... no interventions, nothing seized en route?" Mary was dismayed by the failure of the 'war on drugs'. As a primary teacher, she knew that dealers even targeted primary school kids.

"There is so much money involved, Mary. People are bought off to turn a blind eye. Transponders... that's the signalling device that tells Air Traffic Control where a plane is... are turned off. Lights on the airplanes and helicopters are extinguished. And they 'fly under the radar', which, it seems, is actually possible. They take a middle route over water between any solid land, flying as low as possible until the drop point. My pal told me to read the book, *Cocaine Cowboys*. In that, drug-running pilots apparently flew into Florida at an altitude of fifty feet. That is some dangerous flying!"

"It's despicable... the whole damned thing," said Tom.

"It certainly is. Anyway, don't you worry about that. You concentrate on getting well. And for God's sake, never mention what I just told you to anyone, or I'll be out of a job and would probably get locked up, as would you. This kind of high-level operation is covered by the Official Secrets Act, because of the international nature of the thing. People in other countries could be put in jeopardy and might even lose their lives.

"You played a part in an important bust, albeit by a twist of fate.

"What you need to think about is that the second most beautiful woman in your life will be coming to see you later. Although not dressed as a teenybopper, I'd hope. The nurses would think she's your daughter." Scott winked at Mary, who seemed actually to blush at being referred to as 'the first most beautiful,' even if in a roundabout way.

"She'll be talking to you from outside the window, though. The ward sister won't be pushed any further, surgeon or no surgeon. Mhairi will go for mandatory counselling, of course. And that's something for you to look forward to as well. PTSD, and all that shrink stuff. But best to be sure, eh? And, not to spoil your day... *about you, Dempster,*" he put on a stern voice. "The Chief doesn't know whether to reprimand you or give you a medal.

"The rules are clear. You call in a Gold alert, and then you stay put, or if in danger, you get the hell out of the danger zone, right? You don't go blundering into the wolves' den without a weapon to hand and some backup!"

"A... adrenaline got the better of me, boss," said Tom.

"'Wannabe hero' got the better of you, more like. '*Die Hard* Syndrome!'"

Mary was smiling under a hand over her mask. She knew that Scott was just winding her husband up. The boss had already put in a recommendation for Tom and Mhairi to be awarded the Queen's Police Medal for Gallantry. They might not get it; but at the very least, they would get a commendation. Aim high and expect lower, as the saying goes.

"But," Scott said with a half-grin, "you'll be glad to hear that Chief Constable Macfarlane is also coming to visit you later this evening. Now there's a treat, huh?"

"Oh, God!" said Tom. "Shoot me now... or get those doctors to knock me out again... please!"

Tom was going to be okay.

Chapter Seventeen

PAUL WHEELER WAS NOT only in the Greenock area to survey a pub he intended to buy, principally for money laundering; he had also arranged a meeting with Malky Boone, his 'man in Inverclyde', at the Seamill Hydro Hotel where he and Alexandria had booked a luxury suite for a week's stay. No low-budget Travel Lodge for the kingpin of Glasgow's gangland!

Malky had put on his best bib and tucker: a four-hundred quid brown sheepskin flying jacket, a cream-coloured Ralph Lauren polo shirt, tan chinos, and brown Italian-leather loafers, again Ralph Lauren. Malky knew how to dress for an occasion when he had to.

At the reception desk, when he asked for Mr Wheeler's room, the receptionist called on a smartly dressed woman, who was the manageress, and she informed him that Mr Wheeler was expecting him, and then she showed him up to Wheeler's suite.

Do you tip a manageress? Malky thought. Then, thinking it might demean her, he just said thanks and pressed the door buzzer. A hotel room with a buzzer. That was a novelty to him.

Paul Wheeler opened the door and greeted Malky with a firm handshake. "Malky, my man. Good to see you. Come in, come in." Paul was dressed in expensive jogging gear, but he didn't look like he'd been jogging.

"I'm going for a wee run later," he said. "In the gym, on the treadmill, mind you. This weather is damned-well unbelievable. They'll be giving this storm a stupid name next. It's a pity for tourists who haven't seen Scotland at its best. I'm glad you made it. I'm hearing the roads are wild oot there."

"Roads flooded all the way doon," said Malky. "I had to slide past big tree branches at a couple of points on the road. Cars stuck here and there, some just abandoned. And I got a free car wash on that coastal stretch just before Largs... seaweed thrown in. Glad I took my 4x4 instead o' the Merc."

"We'll you got here in one piece. Anyway, you just sit yourself down, and I'll get you a wee dram. What's your poison?"

Coming from a gangster, this phrase took Malky aback for a second. "Eh, I'll hae a wee whisky, thanks, Paul. I'm driving, so make it a wee one... with... erm, you got Irn Bru?" He thought that Paul might think this sacrilege.

"Ah-ha," said Wheeler, "'Scotland's other national drink... Made in Scotland frae girders.' Of course I've got it. They've stocked my bar up here so well, I could stay in this room and go on a bender wi' some pals for a week, and there'd still be booze left."

Paul fluctuated between a posh Edinburgh, Morningside accent and a west coast Doric twang. It reminded Malky of an actor, the late Iain Cuthbertson. Fitting, he thought, as Cuthbertson often played the part of a hardened crime boss. Wheeler had a boyish face, and the deep, throaty voice did not fit. The only blemish he had was a four-inch scar that ran from the edge of his left eye to halfway down his cheek. The gallus hard man that had slashed Paul and left this scar was soon after found to be 'resting in pieces' in six separate bin bags that had been scattered across Glasgow city centre. A warning to all: *you don't mess with the Wheelers.*

Malky had met Paul before, but he hadn't met Alexandria.

She made her entrance from the bedroom, fully made up, and wearing a long, slinky black silk dress that clung to her figure. Neither of the Wheelers were masked. It seemed they didn't worry too much about COVID. Malky wondered if there was any truth to the rumour that the super-rich had access to a secret vaccine.

"Ah," announced Paul, "here's the good woman. Alex, meet my pal, Malcolm Boone. I'm sure you've heard me talk about him."

"Melkim," she pronounced it, "I'm so pleased to meet you." Then she kind of squeaked, "Oh, and I just love your jacket. Paul, you must get jacket like thees." She held out her hand, and Malky, ever at a loss about what to do in such company, lifted it to his lips and kissed the back of it.

"Pleased to meet you, Alexandria. I just love your accent; I hope you don't mind me mentioning it."

Alex squeaked again, "Oh, so gallant. You please call me Alex... we friends already, okie dokie."

"Ahem," Paul gave a polite cough, "Aye, er Malky, take that heavy jaiket off. It's warm enough in here, don't you think? And here's yer drink. I put ice in, okay?"

Malky removed his jacket and Alex took it from him and hung it up, sniffing the sheepskin as she went and making almost sensual noises of approval.

Malky imagined she could purr like a cat if she wanted to. *Hope my jacket isnae minging with sweat,* he thought, his face reddening.

"Ice, aye, that's jist how I like it."

Paul thought a wee anecdote was in order. "When I met Alexandria, I told her she had a good Scottish name. She didn't get it, so I showed her Alexandria in Dumbartonshire on a map, and she was fair delighted. But in our hoose noo, I cannae call her Alex... if I dae, a' the lights switch on and off, the heating switches on full blast, and the oven heats up."

It took Malky a minute to get it. *"Ha-ha,* right. You've got a smart home... with that Alexa gadget. *Ha-ha!* That's a good one, Paul; that's a friggin' bumper."

"The worst of it is, when I shout, 'Alex, come to bed', the waterbed vibrates like fuck."

Malky actually thought it was a lame joke, but he laughed heartily to please his host.

Alex said, "I know Alexandria now. Eez where you buy very good sheepskin coat, no?"

"Aye, you're right. Antartex Village is in the Lomond Industrial Estate. Their sheepskins are famous throughout the world," said Paul.

"Did they no close doon?" asked Malky.

"Shit, I dunno, Malky. You might be right. Mind, every fuckin' thing in Scotland seems to be closing doon. We should hae went independent afore the English stole oor oil!"

"*Freedom,*" yelled Malky in imitation of Mel Gibson in the film *Braveheart.*

"*Freee-dom!*" shouted Paul, getting into the spirit of things. "Here's to us! Wha's like us? Damn few: an' they're all deid!"

He chinked Malky's glass and finished the toast with "*Sláinte! —good health.*"

Alexandria was mystified by this ritual. "Paul," she said, "I go get my nails done in salon. Leave you two... you talk beezness, yes... I come back, no more beezness, okay?"

"It's a deal, my darlin'. And nae flirting at the cocktail bar, okay?"

"Ho... I no flirt, darlink. I married woman. I flirt, you kill the guy. I no flirt."

She put on a white fur bolero over her dress, and blowing kisses, she left.

"You're lucky to have such a gorgeous wife, Paul. I envy you."

"Thanks. She is beautiful. But she's also tough as they come. She was brought up mafia. She'd stick a stiletto, the knife kind... well, the other kind tae... in the back of anyone who crossed her."

"Well, that's just a bonus... wife and bodyguard all wrapped up in a tidy package, huh?"

"True. She's got my back, you could say," said Paul with a chuckle.

"Is this suite clean?" asked Malky.

"Aye, well, there's a nice cleaner comes every morning... new towels, bathrobes, hoovers the carpet... you know, the usual hotel stuff," replied Wheeler.

"Naw, I mean, is it clean... erm, electronically, like?"

"Christ, aye, man. My tech guy sweeps the place every night. He has found absolutely nothing. I put him up in a room. I could do the same for you, if you want to have a bevvy session."

"Naw, I'm okay, but thanks for the offer. With my team, I've always got to think that when the cat's away the mice might play."

"Smart," said Wheeler, sipping his drink.

"So, we can talk aboot the castle?"

"That's why I asked you here, Malky."

Shit, Malky thought, remembering the 'what's your poison?' remark.

"Balls up!" said Malky quickly. "Absolute fuckin' balls up. It should never hae happened. There were nae leaks to the polis; nae opo by the Drug Squad or the customs. Apparently, a couple of polis were on a completely unconnected surveillance job. Something aboot the murders of they wee lassies."

It was obvious that Malky knew nothing about any Drug Squad operation that might have been going on at the time of the bust.

"Oh, you don't need to explain, my man. I got all the details from another source... one that, let's say, is unimpeachable. It was one of they coinky-dinks that maybe happen once in a thousand years. Just bad luck. But we lost the product, and Special Branch have got a hold of our couriers. If all of them, or even one of them, turns grass, it might come back to hit us like a runaway train."

"I dinna think they'll talk. They're used to bullshitting the Met. They're all known to the rozzers. They are IRA... or whatever the hell they call themselves, noo. The Real IRA? The New and Improved IRA? IRA Version 3.1. Who knows?"

"Hah, I know what you mean. Since Blair's deal, everything is fucked up. The old PIRA guys would have kneecapped or offed drug dealers. Noo, drugs are their primary source of income. I'm no worried about the arms. A dozen Kalashnikovs, six probably shitty pistols from Poland, and a dozen hand grenades. The IRA still has caches of arms all over the place. Probably thousands of them. After a tip-off, one was found recently in a crypt under a Catholic church. Now, that's some real militant Christianity, right there! Anyway, the arms were just to be a wee bonus for the Geordies. They were to be off to Newcastle by lorry the next day. Some weird deal between the Geordies and the Aberdonian tosser that got himself beat up by a lassie. No, it's the product is the big loss. It was something special."

"Special?"

"Aye, it was a new line, so to speak. Something 'new and improved,' flown into the Republic from Rotterdam. A... a sampler."

"And my patch was to be the testing ground for this, erm, sampler?" asked Malky.

"From what I heard; you'll be doubling your profit. And you doubling means me doubling. It's big in the States. Cut it with heroin or cocaine... blows the junkies' minds."

"And this magic ingredient is, what exactly?"

"Fentanyl. Cheap as chips."

Malky frowned. "I've heard of fentanyl, Paul. It swept across the States like a hurricane. But..."

"Nae need for 'buts' Malky-boy. The druggies get used to the cut. Maybe a few get it wrang at first. But that's the way it often goes with... let's call them 'early adopters.' You know, like the punters that went for Betamax instead of VHS. It's business, man... just business. I know that it's being used here already. But this batch, and what's coming, is half the price of what we were paying. Some French chemist found a way to make it dirt-cheap.

"The Froggie chemist was found dead. Suicide by hanging was the verdict. But the case stank to high heaven. It looked to have been staged. Anyway, the 'method' was soon spreading to other underground chemists. God bless the free market, eh?"

Going for Betamax didn't kill folk, though. Malky knew that this 'business' would probably mean deaths. Not that that accidental overdoses bothered him too much. These stupid junkies were all YOLO. But he knew this new mix would spread like a virus. And you never wanted to kill off your customer base. To say the least, Paul's new, cheaper product would present problems.

Malky's recent BOGOF had been a new marketing ploy that had become popular with what were known as the 'county lines' of dealers in the UK, so called because they crossed all county boundaries. The county line meant the mobile phone line used to take the orders of drugs. Malky didn't use kids as couriers, but he was following the trend set of 'cut price—high quantity.'

He had a supply line of his own, set up via old comrades from his Afghan war days, some still working there as contractors. Incredibly, his end-run mules were grannies—pensioners supplementing their state pension—who flew into Inverness from Amsterdam. Paul knew about Malky's sideline and, so long as it didn't affect *their* deals, it was approved of. "Business—it's just business," was a favourite saying of Paul's.

Fentanyl cut or mixed with other drugs could be more deadly than cocaine or heroin on their own. Traffickers did this as a way of reducing their costs and boosting their profits. Their unwitting customers end up buying a product that is mixed with a drug that takes only 3 mg to be lethal, as opposed to 30 mg of the uncut drug. Excessive drug overdose deaths would bring unwanted attention... not just from the police, but from those worthies in parliament, always looking for scapegoats to draw attention away from their failures.

'War on drugs: total joke,' Malky used to say. 'You cannae hae a war on substances. And like with the atomic bomb, ye cannae put the genie back in the bottle.' He'd soon reconcile any scruples he had when he was counting the extra cash, though.

"So, there will be more of the cheap stuff coming?" he asked.

"*Ha-ha*, aye, but you can be sure it'll no' be coming up the Clyde to Newark Castle."

"How then?" asked Malky.

"The Container Terminal."

"You got to be kidding, Paul. That place is sewed up tight with private security. Ye couldn't smuggle a packet of Old Holborn baccie through that joint."

"Already have," said Wheeler with a satisfied grin.

"Whit? Smuggled baccie?"

"Nope. A nice sample box full of tins of talcum powder. All with false bottoms; all with fentanyl."

"How the hell...?"

Wheeler cut him off. "Now, you should know better than to ask, Malky. Remember... everybody stays in their ane lane. Operational security. As ex-SAS, you should have that drilled into your skull, man."

"Okay, Paul. I got you. I'm one of they guys that always wants to know how the magic trick is done. Or how Houdini escaped them cuffs, hanging frae a locked safe, frae the Golden Gate Bridge."

"Hah, I'm a bit like that myself. I went through a phase of buying expensive, professional magic gear. I even had some sent over from the States. I gave Alexandria a real fright when I 'cut my wrist, blood spouting everywhere.' You might have seen it done on Penn and Teller. I even had a 'cut the lady in half' setup that I tried on Alexandria. She was fair chuffed when she learned how it was done. And you know what?"

Malky shook his head.

"The fact is, that once you know how a trick is done... well, the magic has gone out of it. Like a kid finding out that their pressies came from their parents, and there's nae Santa Claus. At least you could blame Santa for the shitty ones, you know?"

"Right, I understand. I wanted an electric guitar like Hank Marvin's one Christmas when I was aboot seven or eight, and the bastards in the music shop convinced ma folks that a nylon-string acoustic would be the best thing to start me off on. I was so fucking disappointed. Anyway, I took the back off ma granda's pocket watch, and got three toothpaste tube tops and stuck them all on with glue. Like pretend knobs, you know? Looked like shit, but I thought it was beezer. I never did learn to play the bugger!"

Paul laughed. "You were a born entrepreneur, Malky. And you remember what that shithead George W Bush said? He said... he actually fucking said, 'the problem with the French is that they don't have a word for *entrepreneur!*'"

They both went into fits of laughter.

When they recovered, Malky asked, "How do I get the product frae you, then?"

"Amazon."

"There ye go again, man. Ye cannae resist a wee joke."

"No, I'm serious. You give me the address and the stuff will be delivered in an Amazon box by a legit Amazon delivery guy. He does a lot of work for me. The polis havnae sussed it out yet; probably never will."

Malky clapped his hands, giving a small round of applause. "You're a genius, man. A pure fuckin' genius."

"Another wee dram to celebrate?"

"Nah. I'll toast the deal with just Irn Bru. Ye widnae want me to be breaking the law, and get done for drunk driving, noo, would ye?"

Chapter Eighteen

THE CAR PARK AT THE Free French Memorial on Lyle Hill in Greenock where the first body, that of sixteen-year-old Sylvia Smith, had been dumped, had been cleared of crime scene tape once SOCO decided that they had gathered any evidence pertinent to the case... i.e., none! Nothing that proved to be of evidentiary value, at least.

Now, though, a new crime had taken place. The white marble Cross of Lorraine had been defaced... spray painted with Nazi swastikas. And the tarmac, too, was covered in vile slogans, anti-French, anti-immigrant, and anti-Jewish in nature.

Inverclyde councilman, Reg Blaney, was leading a team made up of volunteers, Boy Scouts, Boys' Brigade, and Army and Navy cadets, to clean the mess off. The thrum of a generator filled the air. Men from the company that did wheely bin cleaning in the area had volunteered and were using their high-pressure hose to help.

Uniformed Inspector, Brian Small, was there with two PCs who were helping with the clean-up. The PCs were wearing coveralls over their uniforms; Inspector Small was not. He was a great believer in the saying 'you don't keep a dog and bark yourself.'

Standing six-feet-three-inches tall, immaculate in his Inspector's uniform, his peaked cap banded with the standard black and white Sillitoe tartan, hi-viz vest outshining those of the bin cleaners, of course, and the two silver pips on his epaulettes denoting his rank, he stood head and shoulders above the councillor as the two did much pointing, shaking of heads, and displayed other visual signs of outrage. After all, the press was here.

There were no mainstream TV crews, but *Inside Inverclyde* blogger, Tam White, was filming the scene with his sophisticated web cam that was mounted on a gimbal for stability and had a small 'dead cat' windshield over the microphone.

A pair of army veterans had showed up, sporting their medals as they and others would do at this spot every Remembrance Sunday. Tam was interviewing them for a *vox populi* piece on the incident. The local *Greenock Telegraph* reporter, and her photographer, and the reporter and photographer from the *Daily Record*, stood beside Tam. The reporters were pointing tape recorders to capture the interview. The problem was that the noise of the pressure hose was drowning out the voices.

It was clear, though, that the two veterans were not mincing their words. Then, suddenly, the power hose stopped, and loud as a foghorn, one vet was shouting, "... And hanging's too good for the Nazi bastards!"

"Erm, sorry," said the veteran. "I get a bit worked up when it comes to fascists. These medals are my father's from World War II," he pointed to two rows of six medals on the right-hand side of his blazer. And these are mine." Two medals on the left.

None of the reporters asked where he had earned his two medals. It was the visual that counted.

The two officers who'd been scrubbing away with brushes took a break and leaned against the fence at the back of the car park.

One whispered to the other, "Some folk say it might have been better if the Nazis had won. We'd nae be in the state we're in noo." That was PC Peter McIntyre to his clean-up partner, Billy Kelly, a new young recruit, just out of Tulliallan training school.

"I've heard it said," replied the lad, deferring to his older partner, and feigning agreement with most of what McIntyre said.

"And you know what else, son," said McIntyre in conspiratorial tones. "Sometimes the Jews dae this kind of thing themselves. To get attention, you know? The Shylocks are aye looking for compensation o' one kind or another."

"Really?" said PC Kelly. It was his alternative stock reply to McIntyre's conspiratorial revelations about the bankers, about the New World Order, about white replacement, about the weakening of the white race through miscegenation. Every racist conspiracy you could think of, and McIntyre had something to say about it.

As was often the case with these types, McIntyre was nothing like the supposed model of Aryan perfection. He was medium height, stockily built, and bordering on overweight. His most noticeable features, though, were his ears. They protruded from his head almost straight out. He had, as a Scot might say, 'sticky-oot jugs.' From schooldays on, he had been teased, called 'Big Ears' or 'Dumbo'. Even when he joined the police (some say to exact revenge on those who had bullied him) his colleagues referred to him as 'Big Ears', and most folk in the area knew who Constable Big Ears was.

"*Ahem!* Er, Tam," called out Councillor Blaney. "This might be a good time for an interview now the machine is off."

"I'm daein an interview noo, cooncillor," shouted back Tam, "A vox potpuri. You know, the voice of the *real* people."

The other reporters laughed, but they headed over to the councillor and Inspector Small, who had indeed been peeved at the lack of attention. Tam followed.

"If I may make a statement." The Inspector cleared his throat. "There is no place in Inverclyde for this kind of racist nonsense. Indeed, there should be no place for it in the world at large. But there always will be outliers, young men and women, knowing nothing about history, and being indoctrinated by so-called leaders who, if truth be told, are only in it for the money."

Tam interrupted, "Noo, where dae ye get that idea from, Inspector Small?" He had a subtle way of emphasising the Inspector's surname, that always rubbed Small up the wrong way.

"I did a study of this in my university days," said the Inspector, with an uplift of his head. "Since the advent of the Ku Klux Klan in America, and probably even before that, monetary donations, sales of lapel pins, paraphernalia, uniforms, printed tracts (now internet site hits) have raised phenomenal amounts of money for the hatemongers."

"A bit like the polis, then, only we pay for it," quipped Tam.

"That is an outrageous thing to say! I will not have that, Mr White... and I demand an apology!" bawled the Inspector.

Tam's face went scarlet, and it was obvious from the looks he got that his attempt at sarcasm had failed badly.

"Oh, er, aye... you are dead right, Inspector. Sometimes my mooth spouts oot rubbish before my brain is engaged. I offer my most sincere apologies."

"Hmm, accepted in good faith. Now, are there any *sensible* questions or comments to be made?"

Councillor Blaney had a wee speech prepared.

"I agree with the Inspector. We will not tolerate this kind of hateful incident in Inverclyde. If anyone has any idea who might have perpetrated this blatant act of racist vandalism, your identity will be kept secret if you phone the police tip line on 101.

"And before the press leave, I would like to recite the words on the plaque, in memoriam:

"This monument is dedicated to the memory of the Free French Naval Forces who sailed from Greenock in the years 1940-1945 and gave their lives in The Battle of the Atlantic for the liberation of France and the success of the Allied Cause."

Inspector Small, who had respectfully removed his hat, replaced it on his head and saluted. The two veterans saluted too, 'long way up, short way down,' their backs ramrod straight.

Out of sight, around the corner, Kelly saw McIntyre spit. Kelly decided to request a new partner first thing in the morning.

Seemingly oblivious to the pathos, when Tam was walking away, he whispered to the *Telegraph* reporter, Rhona Munro, "I screwed that up. I should hae said the Masons instead of the polis." He wasn't sure if Rhona laughed, or not, behind her COVID mask. *More of a grunt than a laugh,* thought Tam. *Ye cannae please everyone.*

————— ◉ —————

IT SURPRISED THE KILLER to find out just how much he enjoyed it. He had killed many times before. But those were mercy killings. There was no mercy to be shown for these little sluts. All he had for them was outright hatred. They were vermin to him. His reputation, and that of his family, was under threat from lice-infested rats; and there was only one solution. *Extermination!*

————— ◉ —————

THE NAZI BOYS' NEXT target was almost predictable. There was a pattern to these kinds of intimidation tactics. The vigilante group that was staking them out had guessed correctly. Tonight would be the defacing and overturning of gravestones in the cemetery. The vigilantes watched from the darkness of a grove of trees. They'd expected to hear the shouting of slogans, the yells of *yahoo*, the battle cries of fascism. But they did not. These little shits went about their work in silence.

"Over here," one would say in a half whisper. "There's one over here." Then the sound of paint spray cans, or the sound of a boot to stone.

The pack left the cemetery by climbing over a wall, then they swaggered down the street, high fiving each other, patting backs, and playfully slapping the backs of shaved heads. But quietly. Any talk was at conversation level.

They didn't realise that they were being followed.

When they got to the first-floor flat in Newton Street where the leader lived, only when they were inside did they let loose.

There were four of them. A cell of four, supposedly to represent the four cardinal directions, and to keep them from implicating others of their type if arrested by the police. Each cell had a leader who could have contact with the leader of another cell. They were, of course, all sworn to secrecy on the penalty of death. Most took this to be merely symbolic; but you never could be sure.

They had been told that there were 'Secret Masters' out there. Powerful men in industry, in the police, in the army, even in the government. And when the time was right, there would be a *coup d'état*; democratic politics would be overthrown, and a far-right-wing, authoritarian Fourth Reich would be established under a new *Führer*. This insurrection would bring them all to positions of power, as they had been promised. How they could *all* be given positions of power wasn't discussed. But then, bullshit doesn't have to make logical sense: it just has to look right and smell right. No doubt, some of them dreamed of being concentration camp guards... or even commandants. That was the mentality of these morons.

The four were: leader, Joseph Brownlee (Bruno); Gavin Ritchie (Mabawza); Stanley Howie (Kaiser); and Mark McManus (Marky-boy).

Brownlee's flat was like a shrine to Nazism. A large portrait of Hitler had pride of place above the fireplace. It was the iconic 1937 official portrait by Heinrich Knirr, with the *Führer* looking stern in his light-brown Bavarian jacket, swastika armband on his left arm, and Iron Cross over his heart. On either side of this painting were two smaller portraits, identical in size to each other. One was the 'Hitler-as-a-Germanic-Knight', the other the 'Hitler's-face-on-black-background' that had been used in political campaigns. On the opposite wall hung a giant swastika. There were posters, all either pro-Aryan or anti-Semitic in nature. As expected, the two types were rigidly segregated.

At each side of the mantle shelf there stood two silver candleholders, embossed with swastikas in oak leaf clusters. They appeared to be genuine silver. A thick candle in each had been part-way burned down to add to the effect of realism. In the centre of the mantelpiece was an old-fashioned wind-up clock that had the Wehrmacht black eagle on its face, its talons clutching a swastika. On each side of the clock, there were two small Perspex boxes. One held a Nazi Party Member's lapel pin; the other, a silver SS death's-head *Totemkopf* tie pin on black velvet. Two ceremonial swords, presumably with some German or Nazi significance, were hanging on the wall-space above the front window, and below the crossed swords, the window had thick red velvet curtains hanging in tidy folds in front of closed Venetian blinds.

On a table was a wind-up gramophone of 'His-Master's-Voice' design. There was a stack of old gramophone records beside it: 'The Speeches of Adolf Hitler' (a set of twelve), '*Deutschland Uber Alles*', 'Lily Marlene', and incongruously, presumably only because they came with the player, 'The Mason's Apron' by Jimmy Shand and his Accordion Band, and 'Sonny Boy' sang by Al Jolson. One had to wonder if these 'Aryans' knew how badly Shand and Jolson would have been treated during Hitler's regime.

There were other memorabilia, including an SS officer's long leather overcoat draped over a chair, and a black, with gold eagle and spike, Kaiser's helmet, sitting in a corner. The latter presumably in memoriam to the *first* time the Germans had *lost* a world war. The lot must have cost a fortune, even if some of it were replicated; and there didn't seem to be any replicas here. Bruno apparently had a trust fund, but no one knew who from, except Bruno.

Being connoisseurs of fascist fashion trends, the four had decided on a retro look. For their inspiration, they looked back to Mosley's Black Shirts. But they had added a modern twist, wearing black leather bomber jackets, and brown chinos with calf-length black Doc Marten boots. It made them look about as intimidating as a fart in a cowshed and had earned them a lot of kickings they would prefer not to admit to. Rather than being the 'alt-right', these guys were the 'alt-wrong'.

Stan was the first to let loose, once in the safety of the flat. "Fucking A, guys, was that a blast or what?" He put on the leather coat, then picked up and donned the Kaiser helmet. That's where he got his nickname of 'Kaiser'. He goose-stepped from one end of the room to the other, arm outstretched in a Nazi salute. Then, he stood in front of the portrait of Hitler, retracted his arm to his chest, then thrust it out again, shouting with a very put-on German accent, "*Die Vernichtung Der Juedischen Rasse In Europa, Mein Führer!*' 'To the destruction of the Jewish race in Europe, My Leader!'"

The other three stood and joined him in a salute. "*Heil Hitler!*"

Kaiser turned and, losing his faux-German accent, asked, "Where's the lager, Bruno? I'm thirsty as hell, man."

"Where it always is, you dickhead," replied Bruno, "in the fucking fridge. And bring us all a bottle. Keep the rest cool in the fridge. There's bugger all in there apart frae lager, anyway. And don't try to see if the light goes oot when ye shut the door, or you'll get yer nose stuck again."

The others cracked up with laughter. Obviously, Kaiser had never really done that, but Bruno had made the story up to explain Kaiser's wonky nose.

Bruno said to Marky-boy. "Wind her up and give us some *Deutschland Uber Alles*. And mind ye don't scratch that record... it's a fucking collectors' item."

To give them their dues, they all could sing the song in German, even if it was the only German they knew, apart from a few racist words, and a few not-so-polite phrases to do with '*fräuleins*' and '*ficken*.'

They'd all just started on their lagers and began singing along when the front door was kicked in!

SMASH!

Six burly lads burst in on them. They all wore nylon stockings over their faces with COVID masks over the stockings. They all were dressed in white coveralls. They each carried a long, heavy-duty Duracell Maglite flashlight.

The attack strategy was simple. Hold the torch, hand up over the shoulder, beam pointing forward, blind your victim with the beam, then bash him in the face, the throat, the head... whichever target presented itself... and then, get stuck right in, using the torch as a baton. Bruno, Marky-boy, and Mabawza were soon on the floor, bleeding, and getting the shit knocked out of them. Kaiser's helmet had saved him from the first blow, but as he scratched at his opponent's face, then tried to hit him with a lager bottle, a knee to the groin doubled him over and the helmet was pulled off his head and thrown aside. That's when he got hit hard on the nose by a Maglite.

"This is the problem wi' skinheads, lads. Ye cannae grab them by the hair, but..."

Kaiser's attacker grabbed him hard by both his ears and delivered a crunching headbutt. His wonky nose would be even more wonky now!

Spitting out blood, Bruno pleaded, "We've had enough. We surrender!"

"Ye cannae surrender, son. This isnae a war, yet!" said the biggest and heaviest of the vigilantes.

"All right! We give in. We tap oot. We cry uncle," Bruno tried.

His answer was a vicious kick to the face that knocked him right out.

"Give in, my arse," said the man. "This isnae a game, you fuckin' pieces of shit. You change your ways... or we'll be back. And next time it'll be sawed-off shotguns, no' jist flashlights!"

Kaiser made a muffled sound, more of a groan.

"You got something to say?" asked the vigilante leader.

"Mmm, naw, n... nothin'," mumbled Kaiser.

"That's good, son. Because if ye did hae something to say, I'd take that fuckin' Hun helmet, and stuff the spike up where the sun don't shine, okay?"

He gave the lad a heavy kick in the stomach to rub the message in, then he said, "Right, lads. Trash the place!"

And trash it they did, including the gramophone and the records. Hitler's portrait was smashed to pieces, the swastika torn down and ripped to shreds with a knife. They tore up the posters and put those and the pieces of flag into the fireplace grate. They'd wait till they were leaving before setting a fire. But there was one more message to be given.

The vigilante leader got a jug of water and threw it over the unconscious Bruno.

He spluttered to consciousness with a start. The big guy was now straddling him, pinning him down.

"Noo, I'm gonna tell ye a wee story that my old man told to me. World War II veteran was my dad... on oor side. Most folk know aboot whit the Nazis did to the Jews. But not so well known is that along with the Jews, there were millions, maybe five million or more, from other groups that were to be exterminated. Gypsies, homosexuals, socialists, Slavs, disabled people... any group that the Nazi bastards had deemed to be impure. *Der Untermensch*... inferior people.

"And there was one group that hardly gets a mention."

He held up a small lapel pin with a blue flower design on it.

"D'ye know what flower this is?"

Bruno shook his head.

"It's a forget-me-not, son. Some Freemasons wear these in memory of the thousands of their brethren that were exterminated by the Nazis. And I don't want you to forget that!"

He pushed the sharp pin hard into Bruno's forehead.

Bruno cried out in pain.

Another lapel pin was pushed in by another of the vigilantes, then another, as they each took a turn. Bruno's forehead was left bloodied and decorated with six forget-me-not lapel pins inserted neatly in the shape of a cross.

"Don't forget, noo...," said the leader. As the group began to leave the flat, he squeezed a bottle of lighter fluid onto the rubbish in the fireplace, struck up a match, and threw it into the grate.

"... The only good Nazi is a deid Nazi!"

Chapter Nineteen

IN SOCIOLOGY THERE is a term, "the paradox of tolerance". The origin of the idea is attributed to the philosopher Karl Popper, who was supposed to have coined it in 1945. It goes like this:

In a tolerant, liberal society, what is to be done when that society is threatened by an intolerant and implacable enemy? Outright pacifism can only lead to the destruction of the liberal society, to be replaced by an intolerant totalitarian State, where absolutely no dissent is allowed. Indeed, dissenters would be exterminated.

DI Scott was hearing rumours about an attack on some neo-Nazis by a group of vigilantes. No official complaints had come in. It was scuttlebutt, as they say in the armed forces... rumours that spread faster than a wildfire.

A much younger Scott had, like Inspector Small and many other students of their generation, studied the rise of fascism in Spain, Italy, and Germany before the outbreak of World War II. It was part of his ultimately successful effort to earn his BA degree in European humanities. Now, as an older and more worldly-wise man, he was witnessing the Overton window, the current socio-political norm, move further to the right, and it was a paradox he was compelled to consider. The rumours had brought the dilemma to the forefront of his mind.

Should an anti-Nazi group of vigilantes, here and now, be pursued and prosecuted if they broke the law by exacting retribution through violence for acts of vandalism?

After all, as a police officer, he was sworn to uphold the law. So, the answer currently was a clear affirmative.

But what if the judicial system was turned on its head, as Hitler's regime had done via the Enabling Act? Would he 'go-along-to-get-along' with an oppressive government? The answer he came up with was intellectually unsatisfactory. If that time ever came, he would decide then, and he hoped that he would stand against evil, no matter the cost.

Scott had left the station early that night for the second time in a week. Many nights he'd be there, or out on a job, until midnight or later, arriving home to catch a wink of sleep, only to be called out on another job later still. There were no 'set hours' for CID.

These unsocial hours were one reason his ex-wife, Maria, had filed for divorce. It was only one of the reasons, though. His being caught having an affair with a social worker that he'd met on the job hammered home the last nail.

He had enjoyed a Skype call with Pauline for half-an-hour after he got home. The talk was all volcano.

"Pepe sneaked me into the exclusion zone, all kitted out in protective gear, of course. I saw the monster face-to-face, Ron. I couldn't help but think of that quote from Nietzsche. You know the one. 'Be careful when you stare into the abyss, for the abyss will stare back at you.'"

Nearly correct, thought Scott. Maybe your university years weren't a total waste. He thought it, but said nothing.

Pauline continued, "The noise is phenomenal. It sounds noisy on the YouTube feeds, but that's nothing compared to when you get close to it. It rumbles and growls. You can feel the vibration under your feet... then *BOOM!* It explodes, louder than a thousand cannons like the one at Edinburgh castle, and throwing massive lava balls into the air. And the colours, the reds, yellows, golden colours in real life... the best artist that ever lived couldn't replicate that palette."

Ron thought about asking her who she thought was the best artist that ever lived. But he couldn't get a word in edgewise. Pauline had always been like this. Quiet as a mouse until she got excited about something, then you couldn't shut her up.

So, Pauline continued with her news, and Pepe and his wife came in on the call, and when it ended, Ron realised he'd hardly said more than a few sentences.

After the Skype, he had made some cheese on toast. Although a challenge to his migraines, it was all he could be bothered making. And he had always carried in his head the romantic image of Sherlock Holmes and Watson deciding to make cheese on toast with a toasting-fork and pan over their cosy fire at midnight, after a long day where 'the chase had been on.' No doubt it was an image dreamed up by scriptwriters, and never mentioned by Conan Doyle, but the notion remained in his mind. Of course, he had resorted to the electric grill, even though he had a real fire lit in the grate of his fireplace.

Any time he had tried to make toast with a toasting fork, it had ended up a black charcoal mess. However, there was something hypnotic about a proper fire, watching the flames, seeing the embers settle, little sparks suddenly cracking and spurting. He always had a fire guard set in front for safety, though. Maybe reverence for fire was a primeval instinct, a remnant imbedded in the human psyche from cave dweller days. As he nodded off, he thought about Prometheus, about Vestal virgins, about the John F Kennedy's eternal flame... to Arthur Brown and his crazy world... then to more romantic thoughts of Suzanna Hoff and the Bangles... he drifted off to sleep, the empty whisky glass falling noiselessly and empty onto the thick rug by the side of his chair.

The dream was very vivid.

A younger Scott, his wife Maria, and their four-year-old daughter, Pauline, were hiking up the long, winding trail to the *Observatorio des La Roque de Los Muchachos,* the astronomical observatory that sat on the top of the 'Rock of the Boys'. A monument at the summit marked the highest point on the Island of La Palma in the Canary Islands, at nearly eight-thousand feet above sea level. The climb was arduous, but it was a fine sunny day, and the three of them were in good spirits. Scott had carried Pauline on his shoulders for most of the climb.

The view on reaching the summit was spectacular. A cloudless cerulean blue sky sat above a solid unbroken layer of white fluffy clouds that looked so substantial that you felt that you could walk out on them and tread your way all the way back to Scotland.

The sun was a massive ball of fire in the blue sky, and Scott felt one of his migraines coming on. He covered his eyes from the glare with his hand. But when he took his hand from his eyes, it was night-time. The sky was pitch black, with the stars shining so brightly that they, too, were almost blinding.

"Look Daddy," said Pauline, pointing to the sky, "there's Orion, the hunter."

"Clever girl," said Maria, "and there is Sirius, the Dog Star, brighter than all the others, and even brighter than the three planets, Jupiter, Saturn, and Venus, all in a row pointing down to the horizon."

Scott was holding Pauline's hand when she suddenly became excited, jumping with joy.

"There, Daddy... did you see it? Did you see?"

He had seen it... a bright streak flashing for a second, straight down toward the earth... a meteorite burning up in the atmosphere.

"That was a falling star, Daddy. Your falling star. And one day, Ronnie, you will be a falling star, a falling star, a falling..."

Like Jenny Docherty in the video he had watched, his wee girl's voice had turned into a demonic, low-pitched male voice.

"A falling star, Detective Inspector Scott... there will be more murders... and I'll be keeping an eye on you... and on your daughter... eyeless in Inverclyde... a falling star... falling... falling..."

Each word echoed like he was in a cave. Yes, thought Scott... Plato's cave. A shadow moved from his side to behind him. As he turned, he was horrified to see the grinning face of Jenny Docherty, made up like the witch from *The Wizard of Oz*. Her hands reached out and pushed him and Pauline off the rock. They hurtled toward the ground, him holding tight to... not Pauline, but to Danny Docherty, with his yellow top boots. The boy was laughing and shouting *'wheee!'*

As they broke through the clouds, Scott could see where they were going to land... into the fiery maw of the erupting volcano. When you glance at the abyss, he thought.

Beep, beep, beep.

Still falling... getting hotter.

Beep, beep, beep.

"Can't breathe."

He was half awake. His head was pounding, and he could hardly pull himself fully awake.

Beep, beep, beep.

He began to come round, but those fluffy clouds... they were still in his head, causing confusion.

Beep, beep, beep.

"Smoke alarm?" He was coming awake. "No fire, though! No!"

Beep, beep, beep.

"If only that damned carbon monoxide monitor would stop bleeping.

"Carbon monoxide!"

His instincts made him push himself out of the chair. He stumbled to the bay window and opened the left panel wide, then the right, gulping in the cold, fresh air. And then he staggered to his back door and threw it open. Outside, he sat on his doorstep. It must have taken at least fifteen minutes for his head to clear. But the headache was worse than any migraine he'd ever suffered.

He threw his head back and laughed. "You stupid, stupid bastard," he said out loud, "You nearly offed yourself with CO gas." And then he vowed never to have cheese on toast at bedtime, never, ever, again.

Chapter Twenty

PC ALEX ALEXANDER, Double Alex, seemed to be in a good mood this overcast, drizzly, cold winter's morning.

He's usually a grumpy bastard in the morning, thought his new partner, the young PC, Billy Kelly, who was standing in for Alexander's usual partner, Tom Dempster. Tom was still off on sick leave, after having been shot in the arm, and in all honesty, Alex thought that Tom was milking it a bit.

"Guid morning, sunshine," said Alex as he tapped the roof of the patrol car and got in the driver's seat of the Peugeot 308. The car had been newly washed that morning and looked good with its half-Battenburg style livery—white body, with high-visibility yellow and blue rectangles along the sides and rear. The word POLICE, and the crest of the division in light blue, adorned the white bonnet.

"Doesn't look like a good morning to me," said Billy.

"I wisnae talking to you, son. I was saying good morning to the car."

"What the heck have ye done to yer face?" asked Billy, noticing the scratches on Alex's face.

"Well, son, I was oot drinking last night, and I had a wee bit too much of the whisky to be able to fully master the walking hame bit. I had a fight with a hedge. The hedge won."

"Ye didnae hedge yer bets then," said Billy with a laugh.

"Ooo! What have we got here? A wee joke frae the bold Billy. I might split ma sides laughing,"

"It's that smirry rain that soaks you through to the skin," said Billy, looking out the window at the puddles in the car park.

"Wet, wet, wet. Just the usual fir this time o year. You'll be too young to know of the band, *Wet, Wet, Wet*... wae the singer Marty Pellow. They came frae Clydebank and said they named the band efter the weather there. Clever, eh?"

"Lack of imagination, I'd say."

"Anyway, we'll be snug as two bugs in a rug in the car here, unless some inconsiderate bastards decide to start a crime wave. You'll need to get wet, mind you, at oor tea break. You'll need to go into the café to get ma bacon roll, and the one with the runny fried egg."

"Why dae I have to go every time?"

"Privilege of seniority, son. You're like my apprentice, see, and apprentices dae all the running. That's the way it's been since time immemorial, and that's the way it'll always be."

"Ahh, good. The heat's coming through now," said Billy, rubbing his hands together. "We'll be off then?"

"Oh shit, afore we go, I've got something to show ye. It's in the back."

"Dae a really need to get oot? I'm just warming up."

"It'll no take a minute; come on."

Double Alex opened the hatchback's rear door and pointed.

"Ye ever seen one of them? I put it in here earlier for safe keeping. I had it in a bag in my locker. It might be worth a bob or two at the pawnshop. I recovered it from a skip. Maybe a piece of costume wear?" Alex lied.

What he was pointing at was a German Kaiser-style military helmet with a big spike on the top.

At around eleven that day, the two officers were now engaged in one of the most important rituals of policing country-wide... the morning tea break. The smirry rain had turned into a downpour.

Constable Alex Alexander sat in the warm, dry police car, while his junior ran into the café at Dubbs Road in Port Glasgow. Alexander had shouted to him when he was crossing the road, pointing to his own face, and mouthing "mask". The lad gave a thumbs up and pulled his FFP2 mask over his mouth.

It was absolutely chucking it down, and PC Kelly had to make two trips to the café and back, one with the teas, and a second with the food, since the café was not McDonalds and didn't use multi-purpose trays for carry outs.

"It couldn't get any heavier," said Kelly, as he flopped into the passenger seat for the second time, soaked to the skin.

"A bag with two rolls isn't heavy, son," said Alexander, deliberately misunderstanding the comment.

"Nah, man. The rain. It couldn't get any heavier."

"You think so? Do ye no remember the flooding? Roads closed all along the A8, torrents running doon the Clune Brae, burns overflowing, trees doon, branches everywhere?"

"Aye, that's what I mean. It'll be the same here in nae time. It couldn't get any heavier."

Alexander moaned, "The bag my rolls are in is wet through. Could ye no hae put it under yer coat, or something?"

"Ah, well, if you'd gone to McDonalds' drive thru like I asked, your grub would've been handed right to you... and we could've scoffed it nice and hot in the car park."

"I dinna like McDonalds. Number one, they only dae them shit breakfasts at this time of the day. Number two, ye canna beat a nice greasy Morton's roll with bacon, and one with a runny egg. What you got?"

"A ham and cheese toasted sandwich."

"That sounds a bit tasty, son. Gie us a wee bite to try it," said Alex.

"No way. You take a 'wee bite'," Billy made air quotes with his fingers, "and there goes half my sarnie."

"I'll remember that the next time you want something from me."

"When would I ever want something from you?"

"Ye never know, son," said Alex, making a start on his greasy bacon roll with a weird tearing sound, like someone pulling Velcro apart.

"Yummy. You canna get these many places, noo."

"Get what?"

"Morton's rolls. There's nae other rolls like them. Every other roll is soft and squishy... nae bite to them. A Morton's roll is bound to pull oot any loose teeth you've got. In fact, I think the dentist on Bruce Street is in cahoots with the Pa... pa... pak... uhm... The wee shop run by that dark-skinned fella. Vikram, aye, Vikram, likeable lad that. So, he sells the Morton's rolls, and the dentist fixes up the damaged teeth."

"Were you about to utter a racist remark, there, old-timer?"

"Me? Who? Me? Mind you, it takes a bit of re-learning when you've been brought up calling our racial minorities by nicknames, ye know?"

"Maybe try just treating human beings like human beings?" ventured Kelly.

"Uh-huh. Aye. You are right there, lad." He was getting to grips with the runny egg roll. "Noo, this is an art, so you don't get egg yolk all doon yer front. When you bite into the yoke, you have to suck like fuck... like this..."

Splurge.

"Dammit! Shite!"

The yoke exploded and ran down his chin and onto his hi-viz vest.

"Shite, shite, shite!"

"That's a great technique you got there. Do you think anybody will spot the yellow egg yolk on your yellow vest?"

Suddenly, from behind, there was the sound of a car skidding to a sudden stop, horn blaring, along with the loud boom, booming of a car stereo turned up to eleven.

The two cops, who were parked in a parking bay at right angles to the main road, looked over their shoulders to see a lime-green Ford Fiesta that had its windows down despite the rain. Out of the passenger-side window hung a couple of boys, waving and giving the middle finger. With the blond-haired boy in the back seat, it was two middle fingers... a kind of emphatic 'fuck you!' Over the boom, boom, there was yahoo-style screaming of "Fuck the polis!" and "Fuck the filth!" and, well, true-to-form, some "Yahooos!"

"The wee bastards," said Alex through gritted teeth. "Two of them in the passenger seat. One must be on the other one's lap. Crazy-dangerous, that. And nae seatbelts! Is the one in the back seat a lassie? Right, Billy... secure the teas... the chase is on!"

As he went to pull out, a van had just double-parked in front of the café, thus blocking the police car's exit route. It was a Morton's roll van.

Alex put on the lights and siren and pumped the car horn. Leaning out of the car window, he shouted, "Get oot the way, ya daft gowk. Shift! This is a police emergency!"

The van driver, who had just begun to exit the vehicle, eyed the two coppers and then the yahoo car. He shrugged, got back in the van, and shaking his head and laughing, he pulled the van forward... slowly.

"And ye cannae double-park here!" shouted Alexander as he pulled out of the parking bay.

Another shrug from the driver.

There was a screeching of tires as the Fiesta took off, followed by a doppler fading of the boom boom.

PC Kelly held on tight to the hand grip above his door.

"Call it in," ordered Alex as he spun out on to Dubbs Road proper.

"We're not supposed to give chase if it might endanger the public. The roads are becoming hazardous."

"Bloody-well call it in!" shouted Alexander, flooring the accelerator. "Pound-to-a-penny, that's a stolen motor. I will use due caution... noo, *call it in.*"

Kelly called it in. But he discerned something different in Alex's demeanour. He'd never seen him like this before. It was as if something dark, something sinister had come over his partner... and he didn't like it.

By the time Alexander had reached the Boglestone roundabout, the yahoo car was speeding down the Clune Brae. Another car was on the roundabout, and Alex nearly side-swiped it as he skidded round the outside lane. Well, there wasn't exactly an outside lane, just space enough to squeeze past. The driver of the other car blasted his horn and held a fist in the air.

"Due caution?" said Kelly. "You call that due caution?"

"I'm a trained pursuit driver, son. So, shut it, and call oot the directions if I lose the buggers. Okay?"

Kelly didn't answer, but clung tighter to the grab handle above the passenger door and braced his feet against the front of the footwell.

A hump in the steep, downhill Clune Brae nearly sent the police car into flight. It bounced back onto the road with a thump. Kelly's stomach was in his mouth.

"Jeeesus Christ!" Kelly cried out.

"Jesus is no gonna help us here, son," said Alexander, gripping the steering wheel tighter. "They're heading for the Newark roundabout at the bottom of the brae. First through the Lidl roundabout. Noo, watch which way they go. Into the toon, or oot toward the motorway."

The windscreen wipers on the police Peugeot were on high speed, and even at that, barely keeping the window clear of rain.

"Heading right... third exit carrying on to the A8 toward the M8," Kelly reported over the radio.

"That's the way, Billy. Keep calling it in. Keep the control room informed," said Alexander. Kelly radioed in the make and colour of the car being pursued and kept the control room up to date with direction and speed... when he could catch his breath.

Despite the blues and twos, a car had entered the roundabout from the direction of the motorway. Alexander blasted the car horn, and just... just brushed past the front of the wayward vehicle. He skidded around the roundabout, applying full acceleration as he exited onto the A8, eastbound. The police car fish-tailed, but Alexander quickly compensated and sped on.

A call came over the radio. Kelly answered, giving the direction of the pursuit.

Control replied, "Traffic car stationary on surveillance, your direction... stationed at ramp quarter mile before Junction 30, Erskine Bridge. Will join pursuit there."

The traffic division often had marked cars on raised purpose-built slipways at the side of the motorway, checking for speeders. An assigned tactical-phase-trained driver would take over the pursuit commander roll from the driver who had initiated the pursuit, that is, PC Alexander.

"Copy that," said Kelly. Then to Alex, "Watch out at the Langbank roundabout: it's a deceptive chicane."

"Here we come now, Billy, hold on to your hat." Billy was holding on, alright, but not to his hat, as Alex negotiated the roundabout.

"We're on the M8 now," said Alex.

"Continuing pursuit, now on M8 eastbound. 70 mph. Will end pursuit if they reach 80," Kelly reported to the control room.

The control room operator said in a calm voice, "You can fall back a bit, but keep on track as Traffic take over. Be aware. Report of intermittent flooding on M8."

They could just make out the taillights of the yahoo car. Alexander looked at his speedometer. He was doing 75 mph and climbing.

"If they get up to 80, I say we call it off," said Kelly, holding on like grim death to the grab handle, also known, quite seriously, as the 'Oh shit' or 'Jesus fucking Christ' handle.

"A shitty wee Fiesta. I don't believe this. The bloody engine will blow if they daft bastards push it any more," said Alexander. They could just make out the flashing lights of the traffic car up ahead, ready to join the pursuit."

They were flying past cars, vans, and lorries that, thankfully, had all slowed down and were keeping to the inside lane; but the spray that was being thrown up didn't help visibility.

They saw an almost imperceptible wiggle of the taillights of the Fiesta.

And then it happened!

The small car aquaplaned, did one complete three-sixty, then ploughed forward with the momentum, crashing down onto its bonnet, then rolling... once... twice... three times. Sparks flew from its contact with the road, as it finally skidded to a smoking halt upside down. It had just passed the traffic car when the accident happened, and the police car rolled off its perch and made its way to the wreck. Immediately, the traffic guys lit red flares and threw them well back across the two lanes behind them.

There was no fire at the wrecked Fiesta... yet.

"For God's sake, Alex," said Billy, his tone angry, "was it worth that?"

Alex didn't reply as he drew closer to the wreck. He was watching as, out of the driver's side window of the wreck, slithered a young boy. Seemingly unhurt, the boy pulled up his hoodie and legged it up the grassy left bank of the motorway.

The radio blared, "RTA, reported, M8 just before Erskine bridge exit. Ambulance and Fire Brigade en route. Assist occupants if safe to do so. Additional patrol cars are on way from Paisley. Block both lanes."

The police on scene didn't even try to catch the driver. The priority now was to try to help the other occupants. Approaching the Fiesta, on foot now, Alex and Billy couldn't figure out how the driver got out of the tiny space that had been a side window but was now squished by the impact. Billy had snatched a fire extinguisher from the Peugeot.

"Keep that fire extinguisher ready," said Alexander to Kelly, who was watching for the least spark. He could smell petrol.

There was only one sound coming from the twisted wreck... low moaning from what used to be the rear seat.

"Don't try to move," said Alexander, wiping the rain from his eyes. "The fire brigade and ambulance are on their way. If you are hurt, moving might make things worse. Try to stay still and keep calm."

The groaning increased in volume. It was coming from only one person in the wreck. Then the moan took on words, "For God's sake... help... me... mister. I cannae feel my legs." It was a young girl's voice, although Alexander had mistaken her short blonde hair to be that of a boy when at Dubbs Road.

"Who else is in the car?" asked Alexander.

"I dunno," came the weak reply. Then a pause, then a scream.

"Bonzo! Bonzo is in the front seat." The voice got higher and more frantic. "he's... he's... oh fuck! He's no got any heid, mister!" Screaming, "Oh, Christ, his heid is in here beside me. Get me out! Get the heid away from me!"

Alexander was lying down, shining his torch in. Sure enough, the body in the front had been decapitated, and the severed head was next to the girl.

"What's your name?" he asked.

"Aargh! Don't shine your torch on the heid!"

"Okay," Alexander pointed the torch away. "Noo, what's your name?"

"Caitlin... my name's Caitlin."

"And what's your second name, Caitlin?"

"I'm no supposed to tell ye that... no to tell the polis, like."

"That's okay, Caitlin, we'll no worry aboot that the noo. Listen! You hear that? That's the fire brigade and the ambulance getting close now. They'll get you out of there in nae time at all," Alexander tried to console the terrified girl, who was squashed down in a tiny space by the car's battered roof.

"Get them to get Bonzo's heid oot first. He's staring at me!" said Caitlin in an ever-increasing panicky voice.

"I'll tell them, hen. But don't worry. He's no gonna dae ye any harm. It's you we've got to think about. Try not to look at... Bonzo is it?"

"Aye, Bonzo. It was him that got the car. 'Joyride', he said. Some fucking joyride!" She spat out a mouthful of blood.

"That's the way, Caitlin. Keep your mouth clear. Try to stay still in case you make things worse."

"Worse? How can it get any worse? I'm stuck in here, I cannae feel ma legs, blood's pouring oot ma head, and Bonzo's eyes are staring at me."

Alexander sensed a slight change in Caitlin's demeanour and tried the black humour approach, "Well, it could hae been worse. You might have messed up your nice hairdo. What's that, a pixie cut?" Through the blood, he could just make out that she was blonde with very short hair, so he guessed at the pixie cut.

"Aye, I suppose," said Caitlin, coughing up more blood. "Feeling numb, mister. I cannae... cannae... be looking ma best. I need... I need ma beauty sleep..." Her voice faded, and she closed her eyes.

"No!" shouted Alexander. "No! No! No! You can't go to sleep. Caitlin! Keep your eyes open, darling! Don't go to sleep on me, okay? Here are the firefighters now." She didn't open her eyes. "Caitlin... dammit! Open your eyes!" No response. Alexander beat the wet tarmac with his right fist, over, and over, and over, until it was bloodied.

"Constable," said the chief fireman, putting a hand on Alexander's back. "Constable... we'll take over now... we're going to use the jaws of life. You need to stand back."

"Damn it to hell!" bawled Alexander into the rainy, cloud-filled sky, with the loudest voice he was capable of. He got up, and looked the fireman in the eye, rain and tears running down his cheeks. In a moment of complete confusion, unaware of the stupidity of his request, he pleaded, "If you can, get the head out first. It's frightening the lassie. Her name is Caitlin."

PC Billy Kelly came over and helped his shaking, slouching partner into their car.

"You drive, Billy," said a devastated Alex, his hands shaking, his body quivering, his head stooped. To Billy, it looked like Alex had shrunk into his uniform. The bluff, confident officer who was known to be a bit of a joker had disappeared, like a half-deflated Michelin man outside a car dealership.

"When we get to the station, I'll turn myself in," said Alexander.

"What do you mean 'turn yourself in.' For what?"

"Failure to end a pursuit in adverse conditions. Disregard for human life. Reckless endangerment. Dangerous driving... there's probably more."

"Christ, Alex. You did what you thought was right. Those youngsters could have killed an innocent person or persons driving like that... like bloody maniacs."

Billy didn't realise how relevant this comment was.

"Aye, son. But that doesn't justify my actions. I was driven by... oh god... never mind. It was the god-damned red mist, the thing they warn you about in training. I was wrong, and I'll take what's coming to me. And you... you stick to your story that you asked me to call off the chase."

"I cannae dae that, boss."

"You'll do it, Billy. You wouldn't be telling a word of a lie. I'm no' having your ruining your career on my conscience as well as..." his voice trailed off. "So, just dae what I tell you, Billy, for both our sakes. Got it?"

Billy didn't reply.

When they arrived back at the station, the Peugeot was impounded so that its computer logs could be analysed.

In the heat of the moment, Alex had forgotten something. The Hun helmet in the boot. Not that anything like that mattered now.

———— ◉ ————

IT WAS ONLY AT THE debriefing that Billy learned about Alexander's tragic history. His fourteen-year-old daughter had been killed in a hit and run. The car responsible was being driven by teenage joyriders. The car was later found burnt out on a piece of waste ground. No one was ever apprehended. But Alex's daughter ended up on a ventilator with severe brain damage. It was Alex who had to give permission for the machines to be turned off. The event led to the breakup of his marriage. The normally ebullient Double-Alex had developed a black side that he kept well-hidden from his colleagues. His daughter had been called Katy Lynn.

Alex was inconsolable when he learned that Caitlin was the same age as his daughter, Katy, when she had been killed. Caitlin didn't make it. She was already dead when she was freed from the mangled wreckage. One other boy had been killed, other than Bonzo, that is. When the other lad's torso was pulled out, the bottom half of his body remained in the wreckage until it, too, was extricated. He'd been completely cut in half by the passenger side of the Fiesta's bonnet that had been ripped in half and pushed back like a guillotine blade into the front seat section during the impact.

None of the teens had been wearing seatbelts.

The driver was eventually apprehended. He had suffered only a sprained wrist and cuts and bruises. He was thirteen years of age.

———— ◉ ————

NO MATTER THE TRUTH coming out about the accidental nature of Danny's death, the Docherty family were still being hounded by ghouls who were convinced that there was witchcraft, or a paedophile ring, or some other crazy theory involved with his death.

The family's hatred of wee Matt was palpable. And Hilda and Jenny never reconciled. Jenny was convinced that had Danny been sleeping beside Hilda, none of this would have happened. But Danny had been a bed-wetter, and Hilda insisted that 'he loved his ane wee room.'

Thomas and Jenny ended up moving to Yorkshire.

Granny Hilda, however, didn't give a damn about the harassment. Her home was in Beggie Road, and in Beggie Road she would stay, come hell or high water. And some of her harassers got more than they bargained for; that is, if they got close enough.

For Hilda had to wear an ankle monitor, an electronic tag, and she was restricted in her movements. She was out on bail after being charged with child endangerment and for obstructing the police in the course of their enquiries by lying to them. But court cases were backed up because of COVID and there was no set date for her trial to begin.

Danny's red sou'wester was never found.

Chapter Twenty-One

THIS ONE WOULD BE EASY, thought the man. This one was justified. The first two were simply a distraction to draw the police, as was the taunting letter he'd sent. 'Serial killer in Inverclyde.' They'd love that. People were fascinated by serial killers. He'd heard that some crazy women wrote letters to them in prison; even wanted to marry them, and sometimes, did actually marry them. What's up with that? Sickos, the lot of them. But that wouldn't happen to him, because he would not get caught.

Had there ever been a serial killer who was a respectable professional man? You'd have to go back to 10 Rillington Place, and serial killer John Christie. Was Christie respectable? A secret abortionist? Christie probably thought he was respectable.

Bible John? We don't know because he was never caught. He got his nickname because he had quoted Bible verses to the ones that got away. Picked up his victims at the Barrowland Ballroom in Glasgow. Well-dressed and well-spoken from the descriptions of survivors, short neatly styled brown hair at a time when most young men had long 'hippie' hair. So semi-respectable, at least. Hmm, he thought. Ah, yes... Dr Harold Shipman. Now there was a 'respectable' professional turned killer.

His cellphone rang. No caller ID, but he knew who it would be. She was the only one who had the number of this... what do criminals call them? This burner phone.

"Yes, I've got your money. Where are you? At the corner at the Star Hotel in Port Glasgow? No, that's no good. Walk down to the Health

Centre car park. Round the back... where the high flats are... what? Do you want this money or not? Right, be there! About half an hour."

He'd take a chance. There might be CCTV there, or there might not. He should have checked that. Anyway, a thick fog had descended, as often happened at this time of the year, rolling in from the Clyde. It seemed like Mother Nature was on his side. He'd muddy up the number plates of his car and wear a disguise. Little chance of being stopped by the police. They were most active when the pubs and clubs let out; the establishments that hadn't been shut down because of infringements of the COVID regulations, that is.

His experience of playing a woman in pantomimes and farces run by the local players' club at The Arts Guild Theatre would stand him in good stead. But not a parody, obviously. He'd make up, and dress up, as a middle-aged woman. He had a selection of wigs for his acting roles. The brunette one, he thought. That was the most convincing looking.

She was there. Of course she was there. She thought she was getting a payoff of ten-thousand pounds. She was leaning against a lamppost, the fog giving the lamplight a kind of halo. If she hadn't been an ugly wee bitch, thought the killer, he would be reminded of Lily Marlene, 'Underneath the lamplight...'

He buzzed down the passenger side window. "Get in!"

"You've got to be fucking kidding me!" The girl bent down and poked her head in. "You're a cross dresser? If no', yer disguise is shite. And no way I'm getting in this motor with you. Hand oot the dough, and then bugger off."

"The money is in the boot in a briefcase. You can keep the briefcase as a bonus."

"Aye, that's me alright! If the cops see me walking aboot with a briefcase, they'd lift me for sure. I've got a couple of empty Tesco bags. The money goes in them."

"Then you will need to get in to transfer the money. Look, I'll open the trunk. You get the briefcase, and I'll give you my car keys until you put the money in your bags."

"O... Okay," she was looking all around, getting suspicious. Nobody in sight as far as the fog would let her see. She was wary, but the thought of all that money drove her on.

He pressed a button, and she heard the boot click open.

"Noo... the keys!"

He stretched over and gave her his car keys.

She got the briefcase, and reluctantly entered the car. She sat the briefcase on her lap, the first bag opened in the footwell ready for the transfer. When she opened the case, she gave a little gasp of excitement. It *looked* like ten grand. Should she count it? Instead, she made do with rifling through each of the bundles to make sure there wasn't paper in the middle.

"When I count this, if it's short, even by a twenty, the deal's off and I go to the polis and report that your boy raped me. I've still got the nickers I was wearing and the skirt. Squirty wee bastard, that boy of yours. But no' quite fast enough with the pull-out routine. Plenty of DNA, right? Like Monica Lewinsky. Us lassies have the upper hand, noo. The 'Me Too' thing. Gave us a wee trump card. *Ha-ha*, Trump... the Donald, get it? What a fucking tit that guy is! That fucking hair."

While she was blethering excitedly and bending forward, stuffing the money in her Tesco bags, the man surreptitiously pushed the protective cap off the syringe he had been concealing and in one quick movement, he stuck the needle into the side of her neck and pressed the plunger.

"Wha...?"

"She didn't make a sound after that but looked at him for maybe a second, wide-eyed, surprised. Then her head dropped forward onto her chest.

There was a thump at the back of the car, and his heart skipped a beat.

A drunk guy staggered by the passenger side, using the car for support. That's when the killer noticed that the window on that side was still open.

"Sorry, missus," the drunk drawled, speech thick with the drink. "I'm a wee bit sozzled, ye know? Celebrating round at Sudgies. I hope them bloody lifts are working," he said, pointing to the high flats, the lights indistinct in the murk. "I'm on the top floor. *Ha-ha*, one guid thing aboot that... if yer drunk, ye don't notice the building swaying in the wind. If the lifts are oot, I'm buggered. I'll need to sleep in beside the bins. And no' for the first time. When you're pissed, the smell isnae sae bad."

The drunk was swaying. He looked like he was trying to bring his eyes into focus.

"Yer wee lassie isnae looking so well," said the man, swaying, staggering backward, then forward. The killer leaned toward the drugged girl and mimed a drinking motion.

"Aha, she's pissed too. You take her hame missus. Wan of they Relieve drinks... make her drink it before she goes to bed. And get her to down a pint of water. Works for me, every time. Every time, missus. Noo, where's the flats gone?" He was looking gawkily through the fog. "Aye, right, got it! That-a-way..." and he staggered off.

If nothing else, it showed the killer that his disguise had worked... at least on a drunk, in the fog. He'd called him 'missus'. That was the important thing. Going by the state of him, he'd probably wake up tomorrow with no memory of the night before.

Ketamine was a very useful drug, thought the killer, as he fumbled to find his car keys. She'd dropped them in at the handbrake-well, and it was a task to fish them out.

Ketamine... It had worked before, and it worked again. The further, erm, details, he would see to later. Ligature, eyes, breasts, and a bonus for the pathologist... because he really wanted to find out if the little bitch had actually been pregnant.

Chapter Twenty-Two

DI SCOTT GOT THE CALLOUT at 9 a.m.

His home was an upstairs flat on Ashton Road in Gourock. The front bay window normally gave him a splendid view across the Clyde. But the view was not so splendid this morning.

He could just about see the yachts moored in the bay; he could hear the tinkle of the occasional cowbell that came from one or two of them as they rolled on the rise and fall of the tide. It wasn't excessively windy, but dense cloud shrouded the hills opposite, and they obscured his normally mood-uplifting view of the entrances to the three lochs on the opposite bank of the river: The Holy Loch, Loch Long, and the Gareloch... plus the majestic hills of Argyle. There had been fog overnight that had only partially lifted.

The roads looked wet, although any overnight smirr had ceased for now. It had been foggy when he'd got home; he remembered that he'd needed his fog lamps on, it was so bad. He grabbed his ready bag, which contained all the 'detectivey' things he'd need, skipped down the stairs to his parking bay, jumped into his BMW, and started the engine. The BMW Alpina D5 in racing green had been bought with 38,000 miles on the clock, but it had never let him down.

Ashton Road, Cloch Road, past McInroy's Point, where the car ferry to Hunter's Quay in Dunoon was docked, and then speed restrictions ended and he opened up on the winding A770, zooming past the Cloch lighthouse, to pass the Cardwell Garden Centre on the left. Then, when oncoming traffic was clear, he made a sharp turn to the right, and he was there. Lunderston Bay.

A marked patrol car with its light bar flashing was parked at the far end of the car park, at the toilet block. Two PCs were footering about with crime scene tape, as if they were wondering if the whole bay needed to be taped off. He could see the SOCO van that had driven on the grass to the furthest accessible spot. Over a stream, he could just make out the blue forensics tent that was half hidden by trees at the top of a rise, next to the coastal footpath. The view of the Cowal Peninsula was still obscured by low clouds, and it looked like the gloom was gobbling up the river by the second, heading toward the bay. He predicted that the bay would soon be engulfed by drizzly rain. He pulled forward, intending to drive past the picnic tables that lined the edge of the car park, and park beside the SOCO van.

One of the PCs held his hand up in a stop signal.

Scott rolled down his window and flashed his warrant card.

"New, are you?" He didn't wait for an answer. "Well, son, it would behoove you to get to recognise your superior officers."

The fresh-faced PC tried to salute and dropped the roll of crime scene tape that immediately started to unwind into a tangled mess and roll along the ground.

"Jeesus", Scott whispered to himself.

He manoeuvred past the picnic tables, and spludged across the wide waterlogged grassy area to arrive at a little wooden bridge that crossed the fast-running Lunderston burn. Here was where the Scenes of Crime van was parked, its sides splattered with mud. The van was empty. The team was already at work, the tent illuminated.

One thing Scott had learned from working in Inverclyde was to keep wellingtons in his car boot.

The downside to wearing those was that it was a bugger to fit the extra-large size light-blue forensic booties over his size tens. He managed, but it was clear as he crossed the bridge and trudged to the tent that the covers would not stay blue for long.

"Ahoy! SOCO," he hailed as he approached the tent.

A head popped out of the tent flap. Covered by an all-in-one forensic suit, with the hood up, string pulled tight around the face, there was a slightly comedic Teletubby look to the wearer.

"Be out in a sec, Ron," said Nisha Chandara, and she immediately pulled her head back into the tent, pulling the flap shut.

Scott could see the flashes from a camera taking photos inside the tent.

In fact, it was the forensic pathologist, Professor Hamish McLeod, who exited the tent first. With him was DS Cameron.

"How did you get here so fast?" Scott asked her.

"Got a lift from Hamish."

"Christ! You two ganging up on me, now?"

"No. We got married at Gretna Green last night. This is our honeymoon," said Pamela.

"You're kidding, right?"

"Aye, boss. But you should have seen your face there for a second."

Hamish said, "I should be so lucky! Now... Pronouncing life extinct, at..." he looked at his watch, "at... 9.32 a.m." He wrote a note on the form on his clipboard. "There you go... especially for you, Inspector."

"It would help if you told me what life is extinct, and in what circumstances," said Scott. "I already know about the dodo."

"Silly me. Of course. You can go in, Ron; they've finished with the photos and video. Nothing to do with the dodo unless that's the dead girl's name, which, given the modern propensity for parents to name their children from 'The Book of Stupid and Misspelled Names' wouldn't surprise me one bit."

"Can ye not just tell me?" Scott had an understandable phobia of dead bodies.

"Best you see for yourself."

"Really?"

"Really," said the prof.

As Scott ducked through the tent flap, a voice shouted, "Whoah, stop right there!"

Nisha Chandara was holding out an arm, palm forward.

"You're not going to throw up on my crime scene again, are you?"

"That was a one off," said Scott. "A bad prawn curry madras with an extra helping of botulism or salmonella or something."

Nisha, who was second generation Indian, said angrily, "If it had been any of those, you would have been hospitalised. And any Indian restaurant or carry-out I've been to was as spotless as..."

"It was a joke, Nisha," Scott interrupted.

"Well, jokes like that get Indian food a bad name. I admit that chilli peppers and curry blends in Indian food can give one the trots, due to a chemical called capsaicin that gives chilli peppers their heat. Capsaicin is also a potent irritant that can irritate the stomach lining during digestion. Now, if you just go easy on the..."

"It was a flipping joke, Nisha. And I'll not be sick in here if I can stand near the flap... just in case."

The body was on a put-up examination trolley.

Nisha began, "White female, age around fourteen to sixteen, short bleached-blonde hair with brown roots. Deep ligature marks around her neck. Breasts mutilated by a sharp instrument, abdomen cut open, resembling a caesarean gone wrong. The absence of blood on the body shows that the wounds were carried out after she had been dead for some time... possibly even refrigerated... but the post-mortem will tell us more."

Scott still hadn't looked directly at the corpse.

"What about her eye colour? You missed that out, and I can guess why."

"Hmm... you can tell me... if you ever find them," said Nisha with a frown that was clear from the lines on her brow

"Dammit," said Scott. *"Number three."*

"Looks like number three," said Nisha. "If it's the same perp... he's escalating. If I were a detective, I'd predict that next we may find an eyeless severed head, with body parts and the torso being found later in plastic bags dumped God knows where."

"You could be right... but I'm glad you are not a detective. Well. I mean, I hope you are wrong."

After telling Pamela that she could damned-well get a lift to the station with her new husband, Hamish, since he'd brought her here, Scott trudged back to his BMW, then negotiated the picnic tables until he was back on the tarmac at the toilet block. Contemplating what he'd just witnessed, he almost failed to notice that the two constables were still unrolling crime-scene tape. They'd started at the entrance to the car park and were three-quarters of the way to the toilets. But they had not blocked the entrance. They were trying to tape off a line about five-hundred flipping feet in length, the silly buggers, thought Scott. As he passed them, he rolled down his window.

"Hold up! No, no, don't try to salute, okay? I hate to tell you this, lads, but you can start to rewind all that tape. They're nearly done with the crime scene. They'll certainly be done before you could finish. So, no need for that amount of tape. But, good job, lads. If you'd kept going, you could have tied off at the Cloch lighthouse. If ye didn't run out of tape, that is."

The lighthouse was a good mile up the road. "And if you'd use the noddle, you only need to tape off the entrance."

Do we really need to initiate a training course in how-to put-up crime scene tape? The answer appeared to be yes.

They looked like they were ready to chuck the job in, right there and then.

As he headed to the police station, he mulled this fresh case over in his mind: Same MO, but one mutilation step further. Same MO, but a ripped-open abdomen. A crude abortion gone wrong? An unwanted pregnancy? No. There was no mention of her actually having been pregnant. Nisha would definitely have mentioned that. But maybe not, until an autopsy was done. Still with the missing eyes, though. He was beginning to form a germ of an idea. But then it was gone.

"Back to basics," he said aloud to himself. "Back to bloody basics, Ron, old chap."

Chapter Twenty-Three

———◉———

"JENNIFER TATE," SAID Karen Hamilton, the civilian analyst on the murder cases. "Fifteen years of age, runaway from a care home, no known address, drug addict, prostitute, mugger, shoplifter, and general pillock of the community. She has, erm, she had form and her mugshot is on file."

"Are you sure it's her... I mean ... without the eyes?" asked DS Sandra Hamilton.

"Aye, well, lookee here. That better?"

Karen had photoshopped a pair of eyes from the 'before' picture she had up on the computer screen and she overlaid them over the 'after' picture, making the eyes lie accurately over the empty eye sockets.

"Yep. It's her alright," said Sandra.

"And if we were in any doubt, here's a photo of her rear, taken at the autopsy."

Just above the girl's buttocks, in the small of her back, was a tattooed sign. "Please Use Rear Entrance" with a big red arrow pointing down.

"Confirmed by the care home that she showed this off all the time. She had it done when she was thirteen."

"Damn it," said Scott. "No worthwhile forensic evidence at the scene. Any tire tracks were obliterated by our Hurricane bloody Esmerelda, as the twats at the Met Office are now calling it, after the fact. Shades of 'Michael Fish's Big Mistake,' methinks! There were signs of a bonfire, some empty cider cans, empty bottles of vodka, and some disgusting wet roaches and cigarette butts. I think when archaeologists in a hundred years time dig up that site, they'll still find soggy cigarette butts. But that beach party, if that's what you want to call it, seems to have been weeks, maybe months ago. The volunteer 'Clean-Up-Lunderston' folk operate in the spring and summer and autumn... and a worthy job they do. And, I mean, this weather isn't conducive to open-air partying, is it? The lab will test the debris for DNA, and fingerprints; but there's little hope of them coming up with a match to anyone on file. It's all old stuff. It's a dirty job, but somebody must do it, right?"

Karen said, "The community wardens tell me that these parties at Lunderston were pretty common in the summertime. They were illegal gatherings, anyway—but double-banned this year because of COVID. They'd try to break them up, but it was a hopeless task. The kids would shout, 'Call the polis. They cannae arrest us all!' So many were underage, too. They knew they could do anything they dammed well liked. And, unbelievably, many of them had been dropped off by their parents.

"The boss had been talking about a task force to deal with these 'flash-parties' that happen at other isolated places too; all arranged on social media. But what with the cutbacks, staff shortages, and the COVID thing, I guess the boss has put it on the back burner."

"Kids gone wild," said Scott. "It's a wonder there aren't YouTube videos with that title."

"Erm... there are, boss," said Karen. "I'm scouring any local ones I can find, looking for faces. The last one was at Hallowe'en. There's not so much door-to-door guising, nowadays, and what there is, with younger kids, they usually have an adult with them. That is a good thing. But some older teens had come up with the idea of a 'Furries Flash Fancy Fuck Fest' to be held at Lunderston. Inventive name, at least, boss."

"Inventive? It was goddam criminal. And, in case you are wondering, I do know what Furries are."

"Oh, I can just see you in a Furries costume!" said Karen.

Scott thought for a moment. "Okay, do tell. What costume for me?"

"It's obvious, boss. Deputy Dog, of course."

———— ◉ ————

LATE THAT SAME NIGHT, Scott was in the murder incident room, looking at exhibits, sticking pins in the velvety section of the Big Board, and attaching different coloured string, connecting the pins, undoing the lot, then starting over again. It was an old-fashioned method. But sometimes it worked for him. Back to basics.

His phone rang, and he answered it.

"I'm sorry to call you so late... it's me, Sinead, from HQ." It was the unmistakable Irish accent of the senior lab technician at Tulliallan, Sinead O'Reilly.

"Late?" said Scott, "it's only just gone eleven."

"That's late for me, Inspector; at least it used to be," came the reply.

"Now, less of the Inspector stuff, Sinead. You know you can call me 'sir'!"

She laughed, although that wee joke was used just about every time, by every bloody annoying CID officer of rank.

"Aye, okay, R... r... Ronald," she said, as if Ronald was a funny name. "Thing is, I've come up with a find that's probably important."

"Go on, don't keep me in suspenders," quipped Scott.

"During the evidence analysis for the third victim, they bagged two very short chestnut-coloured hairs that were entangled in the girl's dark pubic hair. Curtains didn't match the pelmet, as they say... or is it the other way round? Anyway, they were so short, it's a wonder they were found. Combed out, I presume, and put in an evidence bag and then overlooked until I was doing my review of everything. But we are very short on staff here with the..."

"COVID crisis." Scott interrupted.

"Exactly. We have lots of staff under mandatory isolation due to contact with people they have met socially. Yet, we have not had one confirmed case among the lab staff. But it slows things down, you know?"

"Same here, and most places. Just pray you don't need an emergency visit to a dentist. Anyway, short, brown hairs, and the new victim is dyed blonde with...?" He waited.

"With short brown roots... but they're still much longer than these. Her natural hair doesn't match with these chestnut hairs," said Sinead. "Chestnut, you know? As in 'a chestnut mare'"

"A horse? Hairs from a goddam horse? Well, there's a turn up for the books. From her history, I don't think Jennifer Tate was into bareback riding... well, not the horsey kind. Then, you never know. Some folks will pay a lot to satisfy their sexual peccadilloes."

"Peccadilloes, *ha-ha*. That word always makes me laugh; I don't know why. Anyway, I thought you'd like to know right away. Oh, and another thing... despite the abdominal incision, she was not pregnant.

"And, shit, I nearly forgot. There were traces of the drug ketamine in her bloodstream, and a puncture mark on her neck. I'll send the report by email, in case I've forgotten something else."

"Bloody hell. The rate you're going at, I wouldn't be surprised if you forgot to tell me you have DNA and have found a match," said Scott sarcastically.

"What? For the horse? Seriously, though, this info is brand new. Just discovered. I've been working round-the-clock trying to make up for the absentees. But there are only twenty-four hours in a day, and I've been working twenty-five!"

Scott said, "I understand. Send off that email ASAP. Then, it sounds to me like you could do with some sleep."

"Red Bull gives you wiiings," said Sinead in a sing-song voice.

"And a bloody heart attack," warned Scott.

"Aye, well, there is that. Okay. Sorry about the delay. Seriously. I'm off... email on its way. Good luck! See you sometime, *Sir* Ronald."

He made to answer, but she had hung up.

Scott left the station and drove straight home. That is, what would be home if his wife and daughter were still living with him. Now, it was just 'the hoose.'

It was too big a house for one man. He'd been looking for a small flat but had found nothing suitable. In the meantime, he had all but abandoned the upstairs floors, and that left him with the living room, bedroom, bathroom, and kitchen.

The bottom flat was now vacant. The old lady who had lived there had died three months ago. She had no relatives to pass the property on to. There was a 'For Sale' sign, and he was sick and tired of prospective buyers ringing the front doorbell, thinking it was his flat that was up for sale. He didn't use the front door; he went in and out through the kitchen door at the rear.

Young house buyers didn't just rely on a survey, as he and Maria had. They did their research on the internet. Due diligence. And invariably they found out that, if global sea levels continued to rise, Ashton Road would be inundated. That didn't worry Scott. It wouldn't happen in his lifetime, barring some catastrophic event of the kind that the conspiracy nuts talked about. But he reckoned that the 'For Sale' sign would be there for some time to come.

Scott turned up the living room radiator. He couldn't be bothered setting the coal-burning fire that was the centrepiece of the room. Besides, he remembered that he had almost poisoned himself with carbon monoxide the last time he'd lit it. It turned out that a flue was blocked, and the chimney was backing up while he slept. That meant a chimney sweep. The only one he could find came from blooming Ullapool, way up north, and the price for the job was exorbitant. Not as expensive as the quote he got to replace some roof tiles with the same, *ancient*, they said, slate as was on his roof. Five-thousand quid!

Twenty-five thousand to do the whole roof. A couple of buckets for the drips would have to do.

Local thieves that used to go for lead were recently targeting slate. Now he knew why.

Local thieves, sheesh. What a bunch! He thought about last Christmas when the refrigerated van, that a butcher in Port Glasgow was using to store turkeys for the extra seasonal demand, was broken in to and all the turkeys stolen. The perpetrators were never caught; but Scott consoled himself with a silly fantasy that a reformed Ebenezer Scrooge had bestowed a turkey on every Tiny Tim in Inverclyde.

He poured himself a generous two fingers of Bells and sat in his comfy chair in front of the dead fire. He'd have to get one of those false flame things that never really looked like actual flames.

If a brain could itch, his was itching. Something... something was pulsing through his synapses. Nearly... then... *whoosh*... the idea was gone. He was missing something. Something that should be obvious but was eluding his thought processes. *Maybe the carbon monoxide had destroyed some of my brain cells,* he thought. There was something very strange about the horsehair find though. There had been no sexual element to the first two murders. In fact, they had been fully clothed, albeit the clothes were punctured. That the perp had contact at all with Jennifer Tate's naked body was perplexing. Why this mutilation? He'd have to find out. That was the key—Scott knew that therein lay the answer.

Listening to the waves lapping on the shore, the tinkle of the bells on the moored yachts, and the swish of cars passing on the wet road, he had only half finished his whisky when he nodded off, some instinct making him put the glass on the coffee table beside him before he fell into a dream about Dickens' *A Christmas Carol*, mixed up with Santa dropping turkeys down chimneys where they instantly burned to a crisp, leaving Tiny Tims in tears and starving.

Scott's dreams were nothing if not inventive!

Unusual for the DI, he overslept the next morning. He had a crick in his neck and rolled his head until he heard a crack.

He phoned in to say he'd been held up and would be at the station in about half an hour. Of course, they'll all be thinking it was a hangover... which it wasn't. Not from about a quarter of a gill of whisky.

He showered, aiming the flow at his sore neck until the pain eased off. He dressed, sprinted out to his BMW, and, keeping to the speed limit, he was at the station at ten o'clock on the dot.

In the Incident Room, things were buzzing. The email from Sinead O'Reilly had been sent to the collective in-box, and everyone was trying to relate the new information to the case as it stood.

Michelle Chen began with, "They were all petite, blonde, or dyed blonde; they were all drug users; they were all known to prostitute themselves for drug money. And they were all 'no known fixed address.'

"In some parts of the world, nobody would even investigate such cases. In Mexico..."

"We're not in bloody Mexico," snorted Scott. "We're in Scotland, and here everybody counts."

"There was a time when..." began Michelle.

"Right. I know there was a time when, let's say, fewer resources were put in when it came to street walkers. But those days are long gone. The Bible John case instigated the biggest manhunt in Scottish Police history."

"And he was never caught," Michelle was trying to save face.

"Thanks for the vote of confidence, Detective Constable Chen," said Scott with a scowl. "You've been listening to too much crap from the oldies. You've no idea what you're talking about."

Michelle knew that when the DI resorted to full titles when talking to junior officers, it was time to shut up.

"About Bible John," said Sandra, trying to reverse the trend of negativity. "He was reputed to have said that dance halls were 'dens of iniquity.' He didn't target prostitutes in particular, but there have been serial killers who said that they were doing 'God's work' by eliminating 'sinners." Could there be a religious motivation?"

"Christ, I hope not," said Scott. "If that's the case, we can expect a lot more murders. There's no end of sinners out there if you believe that kind of nonsense. No, my mind is honing in on the Jennifer Tate murder: especially the abortion element. Somebody got her knocked up and didn't want to pay for an abortion. A bit extreme... an overreaction... but it could be."

Sandra said, "But it was not an abortion, boss. It was more akin to a case I read about where a childless, mentally I'll woman drugged a pregnant teen and cut out her baby to have as her own. In that case, the baby actually survived, although the mother, sadly, did not. What if our killer wanted to see *if Jennifer was pregnant?* I can't think of any other reason to open her up."

A new voice chimed in. It was that of DC Richard Toomey who, after the closing of the Danny Docherty case, was free until he'd have to testify in court: so, he had been re-assigned to the prostitute murder inquiry. "That kind of thing has happened before. A celebrity or politician being blackmailed... decides to take matters into his, or her, own hands. Not everyone can face the consequences of 'print and be damned' like the Duke of Wellington did."

"Bit of a historian, Toomey?" asked Scott, with a raised eyebrow.

"BA in History from Glasgow Uni. First class honours, boss."

Scott, who hadn't expected that reply, said, "Aye, then. Good for you, son. A degree in history will serve you well in Greenock police. I'd bet there are tons of academics for you to banter with in the staff canteen. You know... things like: 'Was Bonnie Prince Charlie a poofter?' Or maybe 'the Darien misadventure'. Or 'Bought and sold for English gold'... or maybe even 'Who was responsible for the First World War?' That's a good one to chew over with a mug of tea and a bacon butty." Scott had a degree himself, but never boasted.

Toomey didn't know if the Inspector was being serious or sarcastic. So, he did what he did best and brown-nosed, just saying, "Thanks, boss," with a glaikit look on his face.

"What Sandra said seems to make the most sense," said Scott. "This was to all intents and purposes an exploration. Why? God only knows!"

DS Pamela Cameron spoke out: "We've got ketamine. We've got horse hairs. We've got surgical procedures being carried out. Put the three together and what profession comes to mind?"

"Bingo!" shouted Scott. "A veterinarian. Now, why does that make my brain itch? What was the profession of the man who discovered the Tower Hill body?"

"He said he was a vet," said Sandra.

"Aye, but not a military vet. A goddamned veterinarian. That's to say he'd have access to drugs, the kind that are used to anaesthetise horses for medical procedures, or to 'put down' untreatable sick animals. He'd have protective clothing. He'd have access to an incinerator to burn evidence. He'd have surgical tools, like a scalpel, for instance. It's been staring us in the face. Damn, damn it!" shouted Scott.

"Sir," said Michelle, "I think you'd better look at this. His name is Arthur Watt, isn't it?"

"Aye, so...?" said Scott.

"Look at the duty roster for today. Item Three."

"Oh my God," Scott said, then read aloud: "Item Three: PC William Kelly and PC Janice Refford. Routine shotgun license and safe storage inspection... oh my lord ... at the residence of Mr Arthur Watt, RCVS, veterinary surgeon. Good God Almighty! These kinds of coincidences don't happen in real life. They only happen in crappy crime novels, or in the movies, or on the TV."

"Well, this one is happening to us, right now, sir," said DC Chen.

Chapter Twenty-Four

———— ❦ ————

SCOTT SHOUTED, "SANDRA, urgent... get the balloon up! I want everyone to be involved... the Chief Constable, the Chief Super, uniform Inspector Small. We'll need tactical firearms, a trained negotiator, K9, and enough bodies to set up a cordon. A pin on the shared Google map where this bastard stays. And one to pinpoint his surgery.

"Silent approach... that means everybody. Make that crystal-clear! No lights, no sirens, K9 to hold back unless called for. And for Christ's sake, get dispatch to contact the two PCs... discretely. You monitor that personally, Sandra.

"They are to use codes only. Got that... ACPO 10 codes only. No direct approach until Refford and Kelly are clear of the building.

"You all know your jobs, so get to it. Pamela, you're with me."

"Sir?" said DC Chen with an anticipatory look.

"Aye, okay, Michelle. Backseat. You'll be riding shotgun... erm... sorry... terrible choice of words.

Let's go!"

———— ❦ ————

THE VET'S SURGERY WAS on Greenock's Wellington Street. It had to be covered, even though Scott knew that the gun license check would take place at the registered domicile where the gun and gun locker were. He'd have to check...

However, he didn't have to. His staff were already on it. The hands-free phone in the BMW rang, and he answered.

A breathless Sandra Hamilton said, "Arthur Watt has a house on Union Street. But get this. That's not where the shotgun is registered and kept. He has kennels up the back of Wemyss Bay. He breeds beagles. And not for folk wanting cute puppies. He breeds them for 'medical research.' I think that's a euphemism for pharmaceuticals, and cosmetics, and maybe even germ warfare agents. I've seen that kind of testing on YouTube. It's cruel to the extreme. He has been targeted by the animal rights folk, in the past. They unlocked the kennel doors and let the dogs out. Apparently, the next morning, the beagles were all back in the yard. It was the only home they knew."

Scott asked, "Where are these kennels?"

"Position pinned on communal map, boss. Everyone informed of the locus. Bad news is that PCs Kelly and Refford are already there. We did a 10-27–*what is your position?* And Refford replied 10-23–*arrived at scene.*"

"Damn it," shouted Scott. "Sorry, Sandra... I didn't mean that for you. What's the situation report from the responders?"

"They are all en route. Helicopter will probably be there first."

"What? Who ordered the chopper? It'll be a dead giveaway if our perp is at all suspicious. What stupid bastard ordered..."

"Chief Constable Macfarlane," said Sandra.

"Can it be recalled? Or at least kept at a distance?"

"The Chief would have to order that, boss. She requested it for tactical oversight. You want me to contact her?"

"Dead right, I do. Stupid bloody bit..."

Sandra cut in. "Will do, sir. Right away." And she rang off.

DC Chen looked at the map on her iPad. This emergency map overlay was password protected and was only accessible to the police, fire, and ambulance services. A pin was marked 'Suspect Watt's Kennels'.

"When you get to Wemyss Bay, the kennels are up past the new housing estate. I'm afraid, after the houses, there's only a single-track farm road to get to them."

"Okay Michelle," said Scott, "get on the phone and ask them to liaise through me. Otherwise, we'll all be tripping over each other."

———————————

THE BEAGLES WERE GOING mental.

PC Kelly whispered to his partner, "I'd bet that Mr Watt doesn't sleep here at night. It would only take an owl hooting, or a rabbit chancing its luck for that lot to start up."

"I guess you don't sleep here at night?" asked Kelly, raising his voice to be heard.

They were in the hallway of a substantial one storey brick building that was set aside from the kennels. Even in the hallway, there was the smell of disinfectant, chloroform, and formaldehyde.

"Look," said Arthur Watt, with a peremptory tone, "I am a very busy man. Here is my license, and the shotgun is in the secure locker, here." He pointed to a sturdy-looking grey metal gun locker that was mounted on the wall next to where he was standing. "Do you really need to inspect the weapon?"

"Yes, sir. Just open the locker and let us see that your shotgun is secure, and we'll be on our way," said PC Kelly.

The vet fumbled in the pocket of what looked like a tan-coloured grocer's overall that reached down to the top of his Hunters rubber wellington boots. Kelly noticed the boots. He'd wanted to buy a pair to go fishing up at Killin. There is a trout steam there, a particular favourite of his. But the price was way too much of a luxury for his PC's salary. Over a hundred quid. Ach, that's just for the bloody name, he had thought. Hunter, *Balmoral*, no less. Noo, what wee lady with grey hair, and corgi dugs might that refer to? He'd settled on wellies at a third of the price.

The vet was very tall, at least six-three. His scalp was bald and freckled, but he had sides of thick, white hair. Clean shaven, he had a very ruddy complexion, and he displayed a snooty attitude.

These damned cops were just a nuisance. If only they knew his secret. He wore a self-satisfied grin as the thought crossed his mind while he opened the gun locker.

"It's not loaded, is it?" asked Janice.

"Of course not! What do you take me for... an imbecile?"

Janice was standing just a foot or so behind Kelly, and slightly to his left. She just shrugged a 'sorry-I-asked' shrug.

"You see that it is also chained and padlocked," said the vet, unlocking the padlock.

"Um, I think we've seen enough for our purposes," said Janice.

Her Airwaves personal radio crackled to life. Reception wasn't very good up here.

"We have... an urgent call ... for you to attend. Proceed immediately to... location 10-30; report of a disturbance, 10-42. Repeat 10-42, over."

"Wilco," said Janice. "Over and out!"

She kept smiling. Either she was hearing things or the two of them were in imminent danger. Code 10-30 meant 'Danger' and code 10-42 meant 'End Shift'.

"Okay, Mr Watt. We have an urgent call to attend. Everything here seems hunky-dory." The two PCs had devised a personal code between them. 'Hunky-dory' meant... 'get the hell out of here.'

It wasn't by any means overhead, but they could hear it in the distance... the sound of a helicopter.

"That'll be Prince Charles," said Kelly, thinking on his feet, "I heard he was flying up to Balmoral for the holiday season."

"Prince Charles? I think not," said the vet. "You know, don't you? Is this some kind of sting operation? When you lot resort to codes instead of plain language... something is going on. And that beeping you can hear is my trespass alarm. I had it installed and set to ignore only small creatures. Animal rights nutters and police are not exempt. It caught you two as you arrived. But it resets after two minutes if there are no more disturbances. But it is still beeping!"

He was pointing the shotgun directly at PC Kelly's chest.

"We're not here for anything but the license check..."

Kelly lunged forward, hoping at least to deflect the long double barrels. Was the gun really unloaded? As he reached out...

Boom!

It was loud enough to split an eardrum in this enclosed hallway. Kelly's chest took the blast, and it threw him backwards. PC Refford caught him under the arms, a look of shock and horror on her face, as she saw that the vet had swiftly auto-ejected two smoking cartridges and replaced them with two live ones.

"You said it wasn't loaded!" said Janice, as she and Kelly sank to the floor. She was trapped underneath her partner as she cradled him in her arms. He was moaning and clutching his chest.

"I lied!" said the vet.

That is when the place lit up. Blue flashing light bars turned the hallway into a disco for just a moment then powerful spotlights shone in through the window at the back of the hall, and a shaft of bright light came from an open door further up the hall and off to their right.

Outside, the building was lit up from all sides. The kennel dogs were really howling now.

"This is the police!" a voice came over a loudhailer. "You are surrounded by a team of armed officers. I repeat... armed officers who have been authorised to shoot to kill if necessary. If someone is hurt, you must let them be recovered for medical attention. Put down your weapon and come to the front door with your hands up where we can clearly see them. If you follow my orders, you will not be harmed."

Watt pointed the gun at Janice's head.

"Armed police!" came a shout from behind him. Instinctively, he turned, swinging the shotgun around. That's when his head exploded from the impact of a full-metal-jacket round fired by an officer who had entered through a window in the lab, out of sight of Watt. Two more shots in rapid succession hit him in the chest. His autonomic reactions suppressed by the severing of his spinal column; the vet didn't pull the triggers on the shotgun. He stood for maybe a second... then he fell straight down.

Janice was cradling PC Kelly. There was blood seeping out from his chest. His stab vest had helped, but the myriad pellets from the shotgun shells had all but shredded it. The bastard had fired both barrels.

Doors crashed open. Windows were smashed in.

"Get an ambulance," shouted Janice, tears running down her face. "For God's sake, get an ambulance."

"Already outside," said the officer with the Sillitoe-banded baseball cap, worn back-to-front. "I had to take the shot. I was sure he was going to blow your head off."

At that, Janice looked down at her arm, and saw blood spatter, and what she thought were bits of brain matter. They had come from the vet's head, but she didn't know that.

She fell into a dead faint.

Kelly groaned, clutching his bloodied chest.

"See to her first," he said with a croaky voice. "Her name is Janice Refford... and she's a fucking hero!"

The place looked like pandemonium, but it was organised chaos. The two officers were stretchered out to the ambulance where Kelly's wound was staunched, and a plasma IV had been inserted in his arm.

When she came round, Janice protested about being taken to the hospital.

"I just conked out. There's nothing wrong with me."

But the ambulance doors slammed shut, and lights on, and sirens blaring, it bolted away. At least she could reach over and hold her partner's hand.

"He's going to be fine," said the paramedic. "Lost a bit of blood. We've stopped the bleeding with CELOX pads and given him a sedative. They'll fix him up good at Inverclyde. He is unconscious, now, but keep holding his hand, in case he comes round."

"What did you inject him with?" Janice asked.

"The usual... a wee shot of ketamine," replied the paramedic. "That stuff can knock oot a horse!"

———— ◉ ————

THE SINGLE-TRACK FARM road had been blocked off by a police car. The police helicopter had returned to base. Inverclyde Royal Hospital was close enough for the ambulance to do the job.

DI Scott, DS Cameron, and DC Chen were standing beside Scott's BMW.

Chief Constable Macfarlane came up to them looking very pleased with herself.

"Excellent result, Ron," she said with a thin-lipped grin. "Our sharpshooter saved the taxpayer a fortune that would have been spent if this had gone to court."

Always about the money, thought Scott, before saying, "Aye, boss, good result... one PC shot and the other traumatised. We could have done without the..." he was going to say, 'blasted helicopter', but checked himself, "... without the drama. 'Softly, softly catchee monkey' as the saying goes."

"This opo was as 'softly, softly' as you could get, DI Scott. What is it you are trying to say?"

"Oh, nothing, ma'am. You're right," Scott bit his lip. "You pulled out all the stops. Even down to the chopper."

The chopper comment went right over the Chief"'s head.

"The response times were amazing," she said, "one for the books, huh?"

"One for the books," said Scott. But in his mind, he was thinking 'the botched-operation books' along with the Boyle case.

"You will be tasked with interviewing the family. A wife and a son, I believe?"

"Yes, ma'am. We just about have the *how* and the *where*... still to find out the *why*." Scott had already formed a theory about the *why*, but he didn't want to share it just yet.

"SOCO doing their stuff," said the Chief, pointing to the suited-up figures who were laying down metal stepping-plates in the hallway. "There might be some enlightenment from that angle."

"They will be looking for three sets of eyes. That is, if Watt didn't just discard them," said Scott.

"Trophies," said DS Cameron. "Serial killers often keep trophies."

"Correct," said the Chief. But how would he keep... erm... organs?"

"He's a veterinarian, ma'am. Has access to formaldehyde," said DC Chen.

"Of course. What a gruesome find for SOCO, if that's the case," said the Chief. "But I suppose no more gruesome than what they're used to."

"Francis Tumblety," said Michelle.

"Who?" asked the Chief Constable.

In order to burst Chen's bubble, Scott said, "Francis Tumblety, ma'am. He was a quack American doctor who became a suspect in the Jack the Ripper case. Friends said that he would invite folk to dinner, then show off his collection of human uteruses, preserved in jars of formaldehyde. He was homosexual, and a virulent misogynist. It's a criminology case well worth looking up."

"Hmm, you're a Ripperologist, sir?" asked Chen, who'd had her thunder stolen.

"No. Just a curious bastard with an eye for the gruesome," said Scott.

"Well, this is all very interesting," said Macfarlane, "but Jack the Ripper was never caught. We, on the other hand, got our man."

"True, ma'am. If only Inspector Abberline of Scotland Yard back then would have had access to the resources we have today... helicopters and all... Jack would most likely have been caught," said Scott.

Not knowing if this was a flippant remark, or not, the Chief just said, "Precisely!" and she turned and walked away, seemingly oblivious to the not-so-subtle criticism that Scott had aimed at her.

Hamish, who had overheard the mention of Jack the Ripper, approached and said, "You two will have to have a talk with me about Jack, sometime. Because I know for certain who he was. And it wasn't any of the suspects mentioned in all of those Ripper books."

"I'll look forward to that," said Scott. "Maybe some time I'm steaming drunk!"

Chapter Twenty-Five

—◦—

"I DIDN'T THINK HE WOULD go so far... resort to murder, you know?" said the teenager, who was trembling. He looked pale and drawn, and he had tears in his eyes. "I mean, when we found the body on Tower Hill, it seemed like it was by pure chance. I was haunted by that find. Still am to this day."

"Aye, I can see that, son," said DI Scott.

Scott and DS Pamela Cameron were in the living room of Watt's residence on Union Street. The boy's mother was in Inverclyde's Ardgowan hospice, dying from oesophageal cancer. No doubt a further trauma that had added to the father's worries and concerns.

A man driven mad by grief, thought Scott. And with a reputation about to be destroyed, blackmailed, and his son's freedom under threat. Of course, that could drive a person to madness. But that was no excuse. Under the McNaughton rule, an insanity defence was judged by the ability to tell right from wrong. It would never have applied in the Arthur Watt case, had the man been tried.

The house was tidy and clean. The detectives assumed that the son had dutifully taken on the household chores. That was commendable, thought Scott.

"Would you like me to make you a wee cup of tea, James?" asked Pamela.

Arthur may have named his son James after James Watt, a name of monumental fame in Greenock... the man who reputedly had invented the steam engine after watching the lid of his kettle shake with steam from the boiling water. That was probably apocryphal, but the legend persisted.

"No thanks," said James politely. Then he reconsidered. "There's an Irn Bru in the fridge."

"I'll get it," said Pamela. "In a glass, or out of the can?"

"Just the can, please."

Sandra went through to the kitchen. As she went to open the fridge door, she paused for a moment. *Were there glass jars with eyeballs in there? Don't be daft,* she thought, and she retrieved the ice-cold can of Irn Bru.

James thanked her for the drink and pulled the tab... *pwfishh.*

"I'm sorry. My manners," he said. "If you'd like tea..."

"We're fine, James," said Scott, turning on a compact Olympus digital recorder that he had sat on the coffee table in front of him. "I'd like you to begin at the beginning. We have your permission to record this interview?" Scott added.

James, being seventeen, he was no longer classed as a minor, but Scott had to get the boy's permission on tape.

"Sure," said James.

"I was at a Hallowe'en barbecue party at Lunderston Bay. Dad didn't know about it. I got a taxi down. I told him I was going to a mate's house in Bishopton."

Scott glanced at Pamela for just a second at the mention of Lunderston Bay.

"There was a bonfire... not really a barbecue. But some folks were trying to roast marshmallows or cook sausages. Most ended up in the fire. The food, I mean not the folk.

"There was a Bose sound bar playing mp3s, volume up full bung. Most of the lassies were dancing with each other. The boys were lying about drinking cans of cider or beer, and necking vodka... I think it was vodka... out of bottles.

"I had met my mate, Sammy Deans, from Bishopton, as we had arranged when the word went out on Facebook, TikTok, and Instagram. But I met him at the flash party, not at Bishopton.

"He was sozzled already. He'd brought a tarp, and we were sitting on it. I just had a can of Strongbow. I'd bought six on the way down.

"Then this skinny wee lassie came over to us. 'Room for one more?' she asked. 'My arse is all wet frae sitting on that wet grass.' She didn't wait for a reply, and just plonked herself down on the tarp. We couldn't help but notice that, although she had on a kind of pink furry jacket, with a hood that had teddy-bear ears, or maybe it was supposed to be the Pink Panther... Anyway, it only came down to her waist, and below that she was wearing a wee pink miniskirt that had hiked up to her panties. Her legs were skelpin' with the cold. Almost everyone else was dressed up in Furries costumes. Me and Sammy hadn't had the time or inclination to get costumes, so we probably stood out. Sorry, maybe I shouldn't have mentioned the miniskirt part." He looked at Pamela, his face flushing with embarrassment.

"I'm not a fan of that fashion. Too old, really. But if I were a teenager, I'd probably go with the flow, James, and be wearing skirts up to my arse when off-duty. I've seen girls waiting in line outside clubs in the middle of winter, shivering, with hardly anything on. It's like high heels. They suffer for fashion. So, don't be embarrassed. Tell us everything. Exactly as it happened," said Pamela.

James smiled at the way Pamela described the miniskirts. He flushed even more, but continued, "She had a bottle of vodka. She offered a drink 'to heat us up.' Sammy took a swig. 'It's bloody straight vodka,' he said, coughing.

"'Whit? Ye think this is the Tontine Hotel? Ye want fresh orange or Coke? Maybe ice and lemon? And a wee jar o' caviar?' she said, giggling.

"I declined the vodka and offered her a can of cider. She took it and swallowed down the lot... in one go. 'I always win the yard of ale competitions,' she said, 'something to dae wi' my gullet.' Then she... erm, I don't know how to put this ... she did that gobbling motion with her hand to her mouth."

"Okay," said Scott. "We know what you mean... like mimicking a blowjob, right?"

"Aye. We thought it was funny, her doing that, and looking like she's twelve or something.

"Then, after a while, she comes out with, 'See that bush over there? I'm going behind it for a pish. If the two of you want a shag, gie's a minute and follow me over. I'm feeling randy as fuck. Don't worry, I'm over sixteen, and have nae diseases. Well, you'll have to take my word for the diseases bit. Any of you two got a Johnny?'

"Sammy said he had a couple of condoms in his wallet. 'Right, you bring them. And bring the wallet. If you perform well, it'll be a freebie. If not, it'll cost you a tenner... each.'

"She'd a bit of a job getting up, showing off her panties in the process. They were see-through, and we could see her..." He stopped, looking at Scott, and avoiding eye contact with Pamela. His face had now gone crimson.

"Understood, James," said Scott. "Don't hold anything back. We're all men... and women of the world, son. Nothing we haven't heard before."

Pamela gave Scott a wee dunt with her elbow.

"Well," said James, "we did it. I didn't want to. But Sammy egged me on. He went first, then he gave me the second condom. It was my first time, and I had a massive hard on. Sorry, Detective Cameron."

Pamela waved her hand in a 'no problem' motion.

"I was kind of awkward at first. Then, it was only about a minute in when I felt I was going to come. I withdrew... but the damned condom burst. I couldn't believe it. Sammy told me later that he'd had those condoms in his wallet for years."

"Hopeful schoolboy syndrome," said Scott, giving James a knowing look.

James continued, "Sammy thought it was funny, and I could have thumped him. Anyway, I had sprayed her with spunk. She'd kept her panties on, only pulling them to the side, you know?

"She laughed and said 'Good job, sonny Jim. That'll cost you a twenty spot, you wee wanker. He gets a freebie. At least he knows how to shag.'

"I gave her two ten-pound notes. And that was it, basically. Or so I thought."

"She'd got your DNA. So, she decided to blackmail you," said Scott.

"Right. Well, not me... my dad. She'd asked around, I take it, and somebody must have recognised me, and told her who I was."

"Jesus, son. How could you have been so stup...er... naïve?" said Scott, not expecting an answer.

James buried his head in his hands and wept. Pamela passed him a box of tissues, and when he recovered, he went on with the sordid story.

"Dad gave me a right rollicking. He went on about a respectable reputation in ruins; your life will never be the same; this will kill your mother if she finds out.

"Dad told me she'd approached him and told him the story. The way she told it, she'd been raped, was pregnant, and if the baby was born, a DNA test would prove that I was the father. And she'd kept the soiled clothes, she told him. Dad didn't tell me how much she'd asked for 'to pay for an abortion, with added compensation.' I found out later that she wanted ten-thousand pounds. That seemed like a lot, even considering my dad is fairly well-off. I told him I'd pay him back when I got a job. He just said, 'Never mind. I'll fix it.' I didn't for a second think that..."

"That he'd resort to murder?" said Scott.

"Three murders, for God's sake! Why the other two? They lassies had nothing to do with it," said James, anger in his voice.

"We think they were meant to put us off the trail. Red herrings suggesting a serial killer whose signature was removing eyeballs," said Scott.

James finished his can and squashed it in anger.

"It's my fault," he shouted. "It's all my fault!"

"James," said DS Cameron, "I think your dad was a tormented man. What with the animal rights protests, your mother's illness, and... well, I think the blackmail was the straw that broke the camel's back."

"Do you have any questions for us?" asked Scott, hoping to quell the boy's anger.

"Will my mum get to hear of this?"

"The nurses and carers have been instructed to keep any news of this tragic incident away from her."

"But she'll be wondering why dad isn't visiting."

Scott thought for a minute, then he said, "The lesser of two evils, James, would be to tell your mum that your dad had to attend an important conference... let's say in Switzerland... and he'd be away for a while."

"I'll try. But she could always tell when I was fibbing."

"That's a chance you'll have to take. Anything else?" asked Scott.

"The dogs," he said, "will they go to suitable homes?"

The boy obviously didn't know why the dogs were being bred. The beagles had been claimed by the Hawthorn-Wallace research facility in Glenrothes, Fife, that had a standing contract with Arthur Watt. Scott realised that James was very, very naïve for his age.

At this stage, Scott didn't want to pile on the misery.

"I'm sure they will be well taken care of," he lied.

Tragically, or some might think, mercifully, as things were to turn out, James wouldn't have to lie to his mother. She passed away at around 11pm that night.

Chapter Twenty-Six

THERE HAD BEEN A SLEW of drug overdose deaths on Scott's patch, ironically because the fentanyl cut cocaine and heroin were too pure. Crystal meth was in abundance, too... and the poor body-ravaged buggers who got hooked on that would probably be better off dead.

Scott suspected that Big Malky and the seemingly untouchable Mr Wheeler were behind this influx of drugs.

Scott had run into Wheeler two years ago when a dealer called 'the ferret' had been gunned down while sitting in his car in Tesco's car park in Port Glasgow. The crime boss was questioned, but the assassination couldn't be pinned on 'this upstanding, philanthropic businessman', as Wheeler's expensive brief had put it.

Wheeler actually *was* philanthropic... spreading a bit of cash about was good for business, as Al Capone, John Gotti (the Teflon don) and the Kray twins had learned. You want the 'little people', *hoi polloi*, behind you.

Scott knew Wheeler's history. You don't go from running ice cream vans, (albeit selling drugs in the city's housing estates) to becoming Glasgow's premier crime lord by being a nice guy.

Scott remembered an anecdote about a lady visitor to the city, a social worker unfamiliar with the territory, pulling up behind a parked 'Mr Happy' ice-cream van that was playing 'Greensleeves' over its tannoy.

Since it was a hot day, she was not surprised to see a rag-tag bunch of kids buying what looked, to all intents and purposes, like ice cream cones.

When the queue had been served, she jumped out of her car and caught the driver/salesman before he drove away.

"I'll have an ice cream cone... one with a chocolate flake in it, please," she said.

The reply from the man left her completely baffled.

"We don't sell ice cream, missus. Just the cones," he said with a wink. Then he moved to the front seat and drove off, a tinny 'Greensleeves' dopplering down the road.

"No mean city!" thought Scott.

His team might not be able to bust Paul Wheeler; but they could have a go at Big Malky if they could pin down what abandoned flat, what 'bando', he was currently using as his gaff. The Drug Squad, he had heard, was working on that, and Scott hoped he could be 'in on the kill', figuratively speaking.

———————◈———————

SOMEONE HAD FOUND OUT where Malky was based; somebody who had contacts at the lower levels of the drug trade.

Ensconced in his new gaff, a bottom floor flat in Petrie Street, a street that seemed to have the most boarded up flats in Greenock, Malky and his lieutenants were busy cutting the white powders and apportioning them into twenty quid baggies. The Russian girls had done a runner, and Malky had put out the word that he needed new 'packers.' But until they were supplied, they'd need to make do.

The 'made men' were all there:

Duggie Fyfe, Tiny Wang, Raymie Smythe, Gordo Bryce, and Mack MacIntosh were hard at work. The usual temporary CCTV was monitoring the street leading up to the flat. It was a dead-end street, ending with a high brick wall, above which ran the Glasgow-to-Gourock-and-Wemyss Bay railway line. So, they were looking for the approach of vans or cars that might be Drug Squad. There was an iPad Air sitting on a stand on a spare table that was dedicated to showing the cam feed. The cam was so small that anyone passing would be hard pushed to spot it. The fact was that nobody had any reason to be on *zombie* street. Malky didn't deal to punters from here, of course. This was the hub, and his lieutenants went from here to contact their dealers at prearranged meets.

Malky and his men had a quick escape route already planned: out the door of the flat into the close, then down the stairs at the back that led down to a couple of cellars. Hopping over the wrought-iron railings on a landing there, they'd be dropping around ten feet into a wooded and overgrown area that used to be a public park but had long since been abandoned to nature by the council.

The entire street of sandstone tenements was scheduled to be demolished. A sheltered housing complex was to be built on the site. Until then, these run-down tenements were deemed 'zombie' buildings, just like an infamous array of abandoned streets around the old Glasgow Road area in Port Glasgow. That almost deserted area had been used by a film company as a set for a zombie apocalypse movie, and by a group of YouTube adventurers who had posted a video of them exploring the empty lower flats. That went viral under the title 'Zombie Town, Scotland.'

It was sad to think that generations of Portonians had lived on these streets. Once there had been a hairdressers, a fish-and-chip shop, and a shop that sold electrical goods. There was also Clune Park primary school where thousands of kids had once learned their ten-times tables, etc. Now it lay abandoned, the insides gutted by vandals and fireraisers.

"Senga still no' talking to ye?" asked Gordo.

"Nah," replied Malky. "My bitch sister still blames me for Kevin's death. Says I was a bad influence on him, making him think he was a tough guy."

Kevin MacArthur was a seventeen-year-old cousin who had been stabbed to death outside a Greenock night club after an altercation with a Polish sailor about the older guy eyeing up young girls.

"Backward Agnes isn't a bad-looking bit of stuff," said Gordo, misinterpreting Malky's 'bitch' remark.

"Aye, she's known to be a bit of a 'come on,'" said Duggie.

"I heard she likes to get 'cum on' her face, the mair the better. Like that Japanese... whit's it called... kabuki?" said Gordo.

Malky jumped up, knocking his chair over, and ran at Gordo. Grabbing him by the collar, he pulled the man out of his chair and punched him twice in the face hard.

Gordo, unaware of his transgression, bent over, blood pouring from his nose.

"What the fuck? What was that for?"

"Nobody, but nobody, talks aboot ma family like that."

"But you called her..." began Gordo, snivelling and holding his T-shirt up to his face.

"I can call her whatever I like. She's my fucking sister. But you... don't you ever cross that line again. And that goes for the rest of you."

As Malky crossed the rubbish-strewn floor to pick up his chair, Tiny, who was monitoring the CCTV, said, "Christ Almighty, would you look at the state of that?"

They crowded round the iPad to see what he was referring to.

A dishevelled old tramp with long, dirty-grey, straggly hair was staggering up the road toward the flat. The man had his head down, occasionally swaying, occasionally stopping, as if trying to miss the cracks in the pavement. He wore a long, dirty, tan-coloured, and stained raincoat that had seen better days, and a rope was tied twice around his waist, knotted to keep the coat closed, the ends hanging down to his knees.

"Fuck me," said Tiny, "it's fucking Aqualung, *ha-ha*."

In unison, they all sang, "Dah da dada dah dum," imitating the opening riff of the *Jethro Tull* song by that name.

"Want me to go oot an' punt him?" asked Tiny.

"Nah," replied Malky. "I think that might be Gordo's faither come looking for him."

They all laughed, including Gordo, who didn't want to provoke Malky further.

Malky continued, "Anyhow, when he gets to the railway wall... pished as he is, he's probably no' noticed that yet... he'll turn around and realise he's on the wrong street. That's if the old sod even knows he's in Greenock.

"This yin looks kosher. But you usually only see that kind of professional 'man-of-the-road' type garb in Glesga. I've heard folk say that they've seen these bastards taking cash frae well-meaning punters. When night comes, are those tramps sleeping on the streets? Are they fuck! They head back to their Mercs and Beamers and drive off to some posh hoose in Bearsden or Milngavie."

"Right enough," said Tiny. "Gordo's old man looks harmless enough."

Another round of laughter.

"Let's get on with business," said Malky, "Tiny... you keep watch on that iPad and make sure Aqualung passes, goin' back doon the street."

The tramp staggered past the entrance to the close, then ducked down below the camera, and quietly made his way to the front door of the flat. Working quickly, he undid the rope from around his waist, and tied one end to the doorknob of the flat opposite the bando. Then, pulling the rope as tight as possible, he tied the other end to the bando's doorknob.

It was an old trick that him and his pals used to pull on folk living in flats with opposite doors. 'Door knocking.' You tied the doors like this, then knocked both doors and ran away. Of course, neither resident could get their door open until they phoned somebody to untie or cut the rope. The tramp had improved on the method by super-gluing the knots at the doorknobs.

From behind the door of Malky's flat, he could hear the song Aqualung playing loudly on somebody's iPad. He got the joke right away. They'd seen him and his disguise had worked.

He opened the letterbox, carefully, quietly, and peered into a long hallway. Nobody to be seen. The music and chatter was coming from a room at the far end of the hallway. He used masking tape to hold the letterbox open. He then pushed rolled-up newspapers and rags that he'd had stuffed inside his coat through the gap. Then, for his pièce de résistance, he sat and fumbled at the back of his coat.

It was a conjurer's method for concealing things that would be produced to the astonishment of the audience.

He wore a strong leather belt inside the raincoat. Attached to it, at his back and hidden from the front view, he had hung four plastic containers, each containing nearly a thousand millilitres of petrol. They were pee bottles with handles: the kind used by incontinent folk or kept in cars for 'emergencies.' You couldn't store petrol in them for a long time. But for this job; they were perfect. That was the real reason that he had been walking half bent over and stopping now and then to fix the load.

He undid the caps of the petrol containers, pulled a funnel out of his pocket, and carefully poured the petrol onto the newspapers and rags.

No time to waste, the tramp produced a Zippo lighter, wiped it clean, held it in his gloved hand, flicked the wheel, and watched the Zippo flame ignite. And then he dropped it onto the petrol-soaked paper behind the door.

Whoosh!

He stood back from the door and tested the rope. If something went wrong, he'd try to keep the rope taught by sheer physical strength.

Malky and his cohorts smelled the petrol before they saw the smoke. Running out to the hallway, Mack was first to shout "Fire!"

As the acrid smoke spread, it was already becoming difficult to breathe. They didn't know that if they had tried to get out by the front door, battling through the flames, they'd never have got the door open. But none of them even tried. Already the flames, helped by the rubbish strewn floors were too fierce to allow any of the occupants to get to the door. The 'door-knocker' ploy was a bit of overkill on the part of the fire raiser, but he wasn't sure how fast the fire would take hold, and he was taking no chances. He need not have worried. As it happened, the petrol caused an instant inferno.

"Try the windows," Malky shouted. Already, he couldn't see any of his mates through the suffocating smoke, but just heard panicked shouting, coughing, and scraping and banging.

The windows, however, were boarded up on the inside as well as the outside. The boards were butted up to the inside frame and nailed tight. Without a crowbar you couldn't get purchase to even try to rip them off.

"Somebody... call the fuckin'... fire brigade," croaked Malky, coughing and spluttering, a cloth held up to his face. There was no water supply to the building, so they'd been using bottled water. It was futile to try to use that to put out the fire, but he did manage to soak the cloth.

"Whit...aboot... the ...gear?" asked Gordo, coughing from somewhere in the smoke.

"Never... mind... the fucking gear... we're gonna fuckin' die here!" replied Malky, hardly able to get the words out.

And they did die there... horrible deaths.

⸻ ◉ ⸻

THE FIRE HAD ENGULFED the flat at an uncanny rate. Wooden floorboards, and wall insulation that had not been fireproofed, went up like the proverbial matchsticks. The smoke and fumes were poisonous, and if there was one saving grace in this situation, it was that they'd probably all have been dead before the flames consumed their bodies.

When the tramp used their escape route at the back of the building to flee, having to hitch up his raincoat to get over the fence, and remembering to roll like a parachutist to avoid injury when he landed on the ground below, he heard the distant sirens. Somebody had called it in. Maybe one of Malky's lot. Probably someone on a passing train. But the firefighters would be too late. He was almost certain of that.

Wee Terry man, man, still dressed as a tramp, was savouring his revenge. His plan had worked perfectly!

Chapter Twenty-Seven

———————◉———————

FIRE MASTER BERT NUGENT knew right away that an accelerant had been used, and that the source had been at the back of the front door below the letterbox. His experience and intuition told him that petrol was the most likely flammable liquid to have been used. The presence of residues in the soot left by petroleum-based accelerants can be a dead giveaway that arson has been committed. However, a complete forensics examination would be needed to confirm his suspicions.

The brigade had managed to extinguish the blaze only after it had spread to the flat above. The whole building and all its neighbours were due to be demolished at some unspecified time in the future; but this was deemed a crime scene... in fact... a murder scene once the charred bodies had been discovered.

After the deaths of two adults and a child in an arson attack on a house in Helensburgh in July 2011, a CSI-style squad had been set up to investigate all suspicious fires in Scotland.

Police Scotland and the Scottish Fire and Rescue Services would work in tandem to ensure that as much of the crime scene as possible would be preserved for analysis and for evidence.

Detective Inspector Ron Scott and his team would be representing the police; Chief Nugent, Strathclyde Fire and Rescue; and Professor Hamish McLeod led the forensics team including SOCOs who had been specially trained at the fire brigade training centre in Cambuslang, on the south-eastern outskirts of Glasgow.

Scott, as SIO, would run the investigation from the Serious Incident Room at Greenock police station.

At nine o'clock the next morning, Scott met there with Chief Nugent and Professor McLeod. Scott's team had set up the big board, as they called it, and had pasted up six photos, mug shots of the suspected victims as they had been when they were alive. Below three of them were three gruesome photos of three burnt bodies. Three victim photos had nothing below them, and three burned-corpse shots were lined up beside them under a '?' sticky note.

Nugent asked Scott, "Are you sure these three are the victims?"

"As sure as I can be until the professor finishes his investigations and does the post-mortems," answered Scott. "Karen here," he pointed to Karen Hamilton, who swung her wheelchair round to acknowledge, "Karen has been receiving intelligence from phone calls, and from various anonymous social media posts, that the flat was being used by Malky Boone and his five compadres.

"Inverclyde drug dealers and their customers are royally pissed off. Malky was their supplier. Until another 'big man' takes over, they'll be stymied. Visits to methadone treatment centres will increase substantially. Since eight o'clock this morning, Inverclyde Royal Hospital, local GPs, social services, and pharmacists have already been warned. Desperate addicts can soon turn violent."

"So, the drug community knew where these guys were located, but the police didn't?" said Nugent.

"The Drug Squad were closing in on Mr Boone. But you have to understand that these abandoned flats are everywhere in Gourock, Greenock, and Port Glasgow. The supply operation moves frequently. Even vacant shops can house these bastards. You must remember the vacant shop on the high street where the Drug Squad busted an Albanian gang growing cannabis and cooking crystal meth. Quite a change from its previous use as a Pound Shop! And I'm disappointed to have to say that we suspect that there are informants within our own ranks."

"You suspect?"

"Well, we know of one case that is under investigation at the moment, of an officer, who must remain nameless at this time. He was arrested for another serious matter, and once he had been nicked and was safely out of the way, dealers who had used his services called in to expose him. That required a search of his home for evidence. After bundles of cash were found hidden around his house, investigators brought in a search dog. They found a 'secret' entrance at the bottom of a hall cupboard. They had to use a suction cup to lift it, it was so tight and well-disguised to look just like the floorboard. It led to the crawl space under the house. There, they found a large quantity of marijuana, cocaine, and heroin, alongside lock boxes with thousands of pounds of cash. It looked like he didn't mind how he got paid."

"And you think there are more like him?" asked Nugent.

"I'm not at liberty to say any more, I'm afraid; investigations are ongoing." said Scott with a shrug of his shoulders.

Nugent had heard the rumour that the former chief constable was under investigation for colluding with major crime figures. But for now, everything was still hush-hush.

"They all succumbed to the toxic gasses, and were unconscious before being consumed by the flames," said the professor, sensing that the conversation between Scott and the fire chief was entering dodgy ground.

"Yes... the pugilist position of the arms. Every one of them has his arms and hands up in a boxer-like stance, fists clenched," said Nugent.

DS Pamela Cameron, who was Scott's second-in-command on this case, said, "I've heard of this. What causes it?"

Before Nugent could show off, the professor was happy to provide an explanation:

"In the case of an arson fire or, let's say, of a car accident and fire, the body is generally badly decomposed, but the skeletal structure remains largely intact. So, the burned body will assume a pugilistic posture. This term arises from the similarity of the posture to that of a boxer in the ring; the arms are raised up in a defensive position and the hands are tightened into fists. The legs may be bent into a defensive stance as well. As a body burns, the muscles contract and the flexor muscles, being stronger, overpower the extensor muscles, thus giving rise to the pugilistic position of the body."

"That was a wonderfully concise explanation, Professor McLeod... I congratulate you on your brevity," said Chief Nugent, with a look like... well... with a look like someone had stolen his thunder... or his fire.

Nugent was an officious type. He had come up through the ranks and was proud of his position. He was one of those men who looked better with his uniform hat on rather than off. The sides of his hair were curly and ginger. His scalp was freckled. His nose always seemed to be red, like he had a severe cold, and his diction was nasal. He had what others described as 'beady eyes', with small black pupils that never seemed to move. Instead, he moved his head a lot, and his detractors had nick-named him 'Noddy Nugent'.

"So, you have identified each individual?" asked Nugent, as if he hadn't been paying full attention.

"Three definite, their photos right above the relevant corpse photo. We need the professor's autopsies for the other three," said Scott, "although common sense tells us they were all Big Malky's lieutenants."

"Common sense, it is said, is not so common," said Nugent with a sneer. Everyone ignored him.

"Autopsies will be carried out at the mortuary at Inverclyde Royal. They are scheduled for..." the professor looked at his watch, then at the wall clock, "eleven this morning. So, I'll have to leave you. I hope I'll be able to ID the other three for you. Although it is likely that they are the rest of Boone's top men, there's always the possibility that one or more of the three are not who we think they are."

"Thank you, Hamish," said Scott. "We'll be anxiously awaiting your results. Thanks for joining us this morning."

The professor turned and left.

"Sir?" Karen spoke up. "From all the intel I've gathered so far, I get the impression that nobody was allowed to visit Malky's centre of operations, other than his five lieutenants and female packers. So, I'd say we can be certain..."

Scott interrupted, "Thanks, Karen. Your input is always welcome. And I tend to agree with you. But it's better to be safe than sorry. We don't want to have anything wrong when this case is sent to the procurator fiscal."

"How did you ID the three 'positives'?" asked Chief Nugent, using finger quotes.

"Malky wore an SAS signet ring. On the inside was inscribed, 'HDAW - MDB - TREG.' As you may, or may not, be aware, the Special Air Service, refer to themselves as 'the Regiment.' I phoned an ex-SAS friend of mine late last night, and he said the rubric meant, 'He Dared And Won - Initials - The Regiment.'" explained Scott. "Malky's full name was Malcolm David Boone, MDB.

"The second ID was that of Mack McIntosh, nicknamed 'Mack the Knife' because his favourite weapon was an eight-inch chef's knife. He had left the knife impaled on an inside window board that had been hacked and scratched. He was found directly below.

"The third was Tiny Wang. He had been the tallest and heaviest of the group. He was found in the hallway. He must have been trying to get to the front door. His corpse was clearly the bulkiest of the victims."

"Hmm, I think I'll wait on the forensic results before I give you the three 'positives'" said Nugent. "You know, but for my professional ethics, I'd be tempted to say, 'Good riddance to bad rubbish.'"

"You more or less just have," said Scott with a scowl. "I take it that the brigade would have extinguished the fire even if they knew who was inside that flat?"

"Of course, of course, Detective Inspector," said Nugent.

But from those beady eyes, Scott thought he saw that the phrase, "although the response might have been slower" had been left unsaid.

Scott did not like hypocrites and dissemblers: he did not like Noddy Nugent one bit.

Chapter Twenty-Eight

PAUL WHEELER WAS STAYING at his mansion in Rothesay on the Isle of Bute.

"I sorry about nice man Malky. What a terrible way to die," said Wheeler's wife Alexandria.

"I don't think many people would call Boone 'a nice man,'" said Wheeler. "And I won't get any return on my quite heavy investment."

"Ah, Ah! You say to me no talk beezness. You say, what I don't know, I can't tell, yes?" said Alexandria, wagging a finger.

"Yes, of course. I'm not myself today. I need to unwind. I think I will go and soak in the hot tub. You want to join me?"

"Maybe later, darling. I have a few things to sort out with our hopeless maid, Tanya. Anymore incompetence, I fire her, okay?"

"You are the mistress of the house. That's your business, Alex."

Alexandria suspected that the eighteen-year-old Tanya had been doing more for her husband than just organising his suits, shirts, and ties. She had smelled her cheap perfume on him, more than once.

Paul went out to a purpose-built outhouse that had been converted into a jacuzzi and steam room. He felt the water. Just perfect. Scotland's weather was not conducive to outdoor spas. But inside this garden chalet, it only needed a small electric fan heater to keep the atmosphere hot, the spa being on all the time. The super-rich Wheelers didn't have to worry about high electricity bills.

He took off his dressing robe, climbed the three steps at the rim, and slid into the hot water in only his shorts. He used the remote control to turn on the thirty-three hydrotherapy jets. Then he picked an ambient LED light setting and some mood music, and put his head back to relax, the water bubbling and the jets acting like a gentle massage.

He was facing away from the entrance door, and he had opened the radio-controlled blinds of the picture window he was facing. A dull, grey, rainy day outside made him close the blinds again so as not to spoil the ambience. Rothesay could be beautiful in the summer, but at this time of the year, it was bleak. He had really only come to the area to do the deal with Malky. He was looking forward to a planned trip to Nassau in the Bahamas... 'to visit his money', as he put it

"Hmm," he thought, "it would be seventy degrees there, and, to top it all, Tanya was to accompany them." Just thinking about her lithe, youthful body gave him a hard-on.

He heard the door open behind him and felt a rush of cold air.

"Oh, God, Alexandria, I'm glad you've come to join me; but shut that bloody door. You're letting the cold air in."

The door clicked shut.

"The water is just perfect, Alex. Jump in."

No reply.

Paul had to turn on his side and crick his neck to see behind him. His final view of anything in this world, was of a figure, dressed all in black, ninja style, face covered by a mask, and wearing dark glasses. The figure was holding the still-running fan heater. There was nothing the crime boss, the gangster, the hard man, could do as the live heater was thrown into the water beside him.

Chapter Twenty-Nine

"BLOODY HELL," SAID DI Scott to his two Detective Sergeants, Pamela Cameron, and Sandra Hamilton, "they're dropping like flies."

"And definitely not from natural causes," said Pamela.

"It's like that bastard Nugent was implying. Like someone is exterminating the rats that we've been after for years," said Scott.

"Karma," said Pam.

"Kismet," said Sandra.

They were in the Serious Incident Room in Greenock police station. The photos of the before and after Malky squad had been fully lined up. Between skeletal measurements, DNA samples, and relatives and friends reporting them missing, Malky Boone, Duggie Fyfe, Tiny Wang, Raymond Smythe, Gordo Bryce, and Mack MacIntosh would no longer be a blight on Inverclyde.

There had been incidences of break-ins to chemist shops. And, more seriously, a staff nurse had been held with a Stanley blade to her throat, after a botched attempt by a desperate junkie to force her to get him opioid drugs. Fortunately, that situation had been resolved without harm... discounting psychological harm... to the nurse.

Backed up by an armed response team, a hostage negotiator had talked the man down, promising immediate treatment with methadone, and entry into a drug rehab centre. The drug rehab centre turned out to be HM Prisons, Greenock. But the promise had not been a lie. The emaciated, twitching man was brought out of his enforced cold turkey and received the rehab treatment he had been promised.

"So, what happens now?" asked DS Cameron. "Who takes over from Malky?"

"Better the devil you know?" asked Sandra.

"Aye, well, you may be right there. Glasgow is now facing a turf war, and it won't be pretty. It was suspected, but never proven, that Wheeler was financed by the Russian mafia. They are not just the invention of some paranoid schizophrenics. They do exist; and it will be they who will ultimately decide who the new kingpin will be," said Scott.

"But Inverclyde won't be drug free in the interim," said Sandra.

"Good Lord, no," said Scott. "Gear will flow in from all over the country. Nature, as they say, abhors a vacuum."

"So, we'd be as well banging our heads against a brick wall?" said Pamela.

"Sure way to cure a headache," said Scott.

"Or get put in a padded cell," said Sandra, circling her finger round her temple.

"Maybe we are all mad," said Pamela.

"Well, I don't deny that I am mad. 'I'm mad as hell, and I'm not gonna take it anymore!'" he quoted from the movie *Network*. "So, let's get out there and do what we do best... catch criminals!"

———— ◉ ————

WHEN THERE HAD BEEN a temporary relaxation of the COVID travel bans, Terry had hopped on a plane and escaped to his uncle's Scottish pub on the 'Costa del Crime' in Malaga, Spain.

He had been given an attic apartment on the third floor of the busy pub and was to pay for his keep by bar tending.

Two weeks after Terry arrived, at four in the morning, the pub was firebombed by a succession of Molotov cocktails. Six people, all resident staff members, died from smoke inhalation, among them wee Terry man, man. Whether it had anything to do with the arson attack on Malky's gang, nobody knew. Terry had left no clues at the crime scene to lead the police to him. But some of those 'in-the-know' were aware of Terry's torture by Raymond Smythe, ordered by Malky.

However, it could have been nothing to do with Terry. Gang-related crime was rife on the Costa del Sol.

'In 2018, the Spanish government figures showed a six-year high of 113 organised crime gangs operating in Malaga province, which includes the Costa del Sol.

'There were fourteen UK-led crime firms... the fourth most prevalent after Spanish, Moroccan, and Colombian mobs. The UK figure for 2018 was almost double that of 2016, when it stood at eight.' reported the *Sun* newspaper.

And now, after the relaxation of the COVID travel restrictions, more criminals than just Terry had arrived in Malaga. And they were much more dangerous than wee Terry had ever been.

Chapter Thirty

DETECTIVE INSPECTOR SCOTT settled down in his comfy armchair in front of his... well he hadn't lit his real fire since he nearly killed himself with CO poisoning... so he sat in front of a faux-flame heater that was shite compared to the real thing.

His choice of music tonight was Samuel Barber's *Adagio for Strings*. And, as usual, he had poured a generous nightcap of Bells Scotch Whisky.

Scott was lonely. He had to admit that. Since the breakup of his marriage, and his daughter leaving home to make a career for herself, this house didn't feel like a home. He'd closed off much of it supposedly to make it feel less empty, although his cleaning lady had been instructed to air out Pauline's room and keep it just as she'd left it. Now, his reduced space seemed claustrophobic at times.

He looked forward to tomorrow night when he had arranged a Skype call with his daughter Pauline who was doing voluntary work in volcano ravaged La Palma. She had told him on their last call that she was very busy helping those who had given her lodgings, Guarda Civil officer, Pepe Cuevas, and his wife. They were old friends of his that he had met while staying at his now destroyed holiday villa on the west coast of the island.

Scott thought that his daughter had seemed rather strange on her last call, but he couldn't put his finger on it, so he put it down to stress.

The news was not good. Any time someone predicted a 'slowing down' of the volcano on Cumbre Vieja, it hit back with a vengeance, lava cutting off more roads, destroying more plantations, and engulfing more homes and businesses.

Scott pondered on how similar to this a crime wave could be. A period of relative calm, followed by an intense eruption. The difference was that the La Palma volcano would stop erupting at some point and stay calm for maybe fifty years or more.

With the recent spate of murders on his patch, he hoped things might return to simmering instead of boiling; to venting rather than erupting.

How many nights, thought Scott, had he fallen asleep on this chair? When was the last time he had enjoyed an uninterrupted sleep in his bed? The unpredictability of the job was part of the excitement of being a detective. He knew his phone could ring at any time, day or night... anytime a serious crime needed to be investigated.

He took a gulp of the whisky. Maybe tonight he'd make the effort and drag himself to bed. The *Adagio* was lulling him to sleep, though.

Ding dong.

His doorbell. His bloody front doorbell. None of his team would ring the front doorbell, at... he looked at his watch... at 11 p.m. They all knew that he used his back door, because the front door was down a steep flight of stairs. At least the back stairs were staggered with three landings. He was tempted to ignore it.

Ding dong.

Damn. Scott got up from his chair and headed down the stairs. He had a good idea who it would be: either a Chinese or Indian meal delivery to the wrong bloody address. It had happened before. In fact, one night, in frustration, he had just taken in an already-paid-for Indian meal that wasn't for him. It was one of the best Indians he'd ever enjoyed. What was that? Theft by finding?

Ding Dong.

"Okay, I'm coming," shouted Scott.

He opened the door and gasped. He got such a shock that he spluttered, "Oh my God, I thought it was an Indian!"

"My tan that good then?"

He was amazed to see a beaming Pauline, her suitcases at her feet.

"Hi, Dad," she said. "I thought I'd surprise you. I didn't mean to be so late. Flight was delayed. Home for the holidays, just like the old days, huh?"

Dad! thought Scott. *She called me Dad.* He gave her a big hug, tears welling up in his eyes.

"Welcome home, love. Just like the old days."

THE END

EPILOGUE

Double Alex was never brought before a tribunal regarding the incident on the M8. Alex had taken temporary sick leave. A week to the day after the deaths of the joyriders, he had sealed off the doors and windows of his living room with tape. He had then consumed what was revealed to be an overdose of Co-Codamaol tablets, washed down by whisky, after he'd lit four Bar-Be-Quick Disposable Barbecues to produce carbon monoxide. Obviously, Double Alex had wanted to take no chances that his suicide might fail. He had left a sign on his front door to inform anyone who called, or the emergency services, of the dangerous toxic fumes. Nobody had noticed the sign until Chief Superintendent Sam Miller had come to check on how his old friend was coping. Alexander had been dead for three days by then.

———— ◉ ————

PC BILLY KELLY RECOVERED from the shotgun blast, but was still haunted by the suicide of his old partner Double Alex. Nevertheless, Billy stayed on in the Greenock force, and six months later he married Janice Refford who had quit the force and was now running a shelter for abused animals.

———— ◉ ————

JUST AS MALKY BOONE had predicted, after an 'exhaustive' inquiry, no charges had been brought against former chief constable Stanley McBride. He had been allowed to retire from the force on full pension. Sally Macfarlane was installed as fully fledged Chief Constable, no longer 'acting.'

———— ◉ ————

THERE HAD BEEN NO ARRESTS made, so far, for the murder of Paul Wheeler. There was not a lack of potential subjects. Given his lifestyle, there were *too many* suspects. Investigations were still ongoing, led by the Serious Crime Squad. Although her involvement couldn't be proven, it had been noted that his wife, Alexandria, had taken over Paul's legitimate businesses. She was also, however, suspected of being the Russian mafia's new crime boss in Glasgow and the west of Scotland. Her maid, Tanya, had disappeared as if from the face of the earth.

———— ◉ ————

PAULINE HAD DECIDED to stay in her old bedroom in the Ashton Road 'home', as it now felt. The volcano experience, although exciting and salutary at one and the same time, had made her wary of any more foreign travel. She and her dad kept in touch with Pepe and Marianna by Skype and were glad to hear that the volcano had gone quiet just as quickly as it had erupted, and it would be unlikely to blow again, if ever, for many years to come. On the eve of December 14, the volcano fell silent after flaring for 85 days and 8 hours, making it La Palma's longest eruption on record. Spanish Prime Minister Pedro Sánchez called the eruption's end "the best Christmas present ever."

———— ◉ ————

PAULINE WAS HAPPY WITH her new job as a staff nurse at Inverclyde Royal Infirmary, and her father, Detective Inspector Ron Scott, whom she still called 'Dad', didn't feel just so lonely anymore.

End of Epilogue

About the Author

Callum Dalziel is a new author in the genre often referred to as "Tartan Noir". He has lived in Inverclyde all his life, and felt that the area deserved to be featured in a Scottish crime novel. The themes in the SCOTT'S LAW series are hard-hitting and certainly not for readers under-18.

Author's Note:

Under "poetic license" I have taken some liberties with the geography and some urban features of Inverclyde. Some places are altered, re-named, or invented to suit the narrative. "My" Police Scotland is not intended to represent the procedures or personnel of the actual entity; nor are the characters herein in anyway representative of the good people of Inverclyde.

************ *ERRATUM* ************

On page 51, para. 3, page line 16, the phrase should read '... he missed the orderly regime ...' instead of 'regimen.'